Game of Truth
The Athronian Chronicles, Book 1

Game of Truth

The Athronian Chronicles, Book 1

C. A. Casey

SilverDragonBooks
a Division of
Renaissance Alliance Publishing, Inc.
Nederland, Texas

ISBN 1-930928-62-9

First Printing 2001

9 8 7 6 5 4 3 2 1

Cover art and design by LJ Maas

Published by:
Renaissance Alliance Publishing, Inc.
PMB 238, 8691 9th Avenue
Port Arthur, Texas 77642

Find us on the World Wide Web at
http://www.rapbooks.com

Printed in the United States of America

To my parents who always wanted me to write fiction. To Bary "The Muse" Johnson—thanks for the labyrinth.

I would also like to thank my editor, Elaine Roberts, for doing a superb job of nit picking. Thanks Laney for your hard work.

The Land Out of Time
O n b e r s a n

Chapter One

Unlikely Heroes

Kaston's pounding heart prevented him from hearing sounds from the surrounding forest. He felt that he had been running far too long to not be closer to Baniston than he was. Not daring to stop to listen, he grimaced through the gripping aches in his lungs and legs as he pushed past the tangled underbrush of the ancient forest.

The serpent vines seemed to reach for him, teasing him in his attempt to do a heroic deed. A noise. Too close. Footfalls easily crunching through the traitorous undergrowth. He was never going to outrun them, much less warn the others. The dismal thought was enough to push him forward. He had to warn the others.

Detouring from the direct path he loped through the dense trees and he crashed his way to the fields in the rolling hills above Baniston. His exhausted mind wondered whether the Ghouls were chasing him or if he was simply in their way as they lumbered at a nonstop pace to the nearest inhabited place. It didn't matter. The Ghouls would find Baniston soon enough. The unfortunate mistake was that the Ghouls had spotted him before he saw them, preventing him from making this maniacal tear to the village undetected.

He made quick back glances without slowing or tripping or

falling down and long heartbeats passed before he saw a half dozen Ghouls thumping towards him. Their large unwholesome faces were blotched with yellow fur surrounding glaring black eyes. That alone was enough to inject fear into every muscle in his body. Taller and thicker than any man he had ever seen, they were clothed in blood red and clutched massive weapons forged for bashing rather than impaling. Each weapon was the creation of the Ghoul who wielded it, twisted gruesome parodies of common apparatus of war. Finally stumbling into the first neatly furrowed field above the village, Kaston ran faster than he ever imagined possible. Even if it killed him he had to get to Baniston before the Ghouls.

Kaston glanced back and gasped. They were too close. For all their bulk and burdensome weaponry, they moved with a determined speed. Not able to catch his breath Kaston willed his legs to keep moving. He had to keep moving.

Afer managing to scramble up and over the next hill he was relieved to see the meandering road bobbing through the late morning fog rising off the Kittle River. Not far now. He ran the words through his mind in a desperate litany.

The scratching of wheels against the worn road stones echoed from around the hill away from the village. Kaston clenched his eyes shut in a quick prayer that it was headed for Baniston. Another field still had to be crossed before he touched the large smooth stones of the road, and the Ghouls were so close he could hear their deep grunts. Relief seeped through his constricted thoughts as the wagon rambled into view. Farmer Tragador was going into town for supplies.

The shaggy haired farmer absently shook his reins against the pair of stocky horses. He thought he heard his name coming out of the fog. The farmer frowned as he looked up the hill and puzzled over the unusual disturbance in the thin layer of mist. Something seemed to be cutting through it. His eyes widened at the flash of red emerging over the hill.

"Wait," came a frantic, almost inhuman cry right as he was ready to set his horses running. Kaston burst out of the fog and threw himself into the back of the wagon. He was tossed against the thick end panel as the vehicle jolted down the road at a perilous pace.

Kaston curled against the back of the wagon trying to settle his body down. Sweat rolled into his eyes and the stinging forced him to hold his neck cloth against them for several long heartbeats. Tragador cast frightened glances over his shoulder every safe moment he could. The Ghouls were on the road, following without slowing.

Kaston wrapped the neck cloth around his forehead and damp strands of flaxen hair, fought the unrelenting bounce of the wagon and pulled himself up to look out the back. As he squinted into the fog, he thought they had lost the Ghouls until the mist swirled a bit and reflected an unnatural pink hue. The pink faded further and further back as the wagon clattered down the road. Kaston took deep calming breaths knowing that they would make it in time to warn the people of Baniston.

"Those are bloody Ghouls," Tragador rasped as he pushed his team far beyond their accustomed pace.

Kaston glared at him. Some comments just didn't deserve a response. "We've got to get to Baniston before they do." His voice sounded unnaturally strained.

"And then what?" The farmer arched a shaggy eyebrow and glanced back at the young man.

Kaston leaned back against the rough timbers. The mixture of fog and sweat soaked his light cotton shirt, prickling his skin with chills. Everyone had to be warned, but that wasn't enough to stop Ghouls. At least that's how the frightening fireside tales went. As far as he knew, Ghouls hadn't been seen in that district for centuries. His mind froze on the thought that he would warn Baniston and it wouldn't matter.

The change in the sound of the horses' hooves against the road jarred him out of his chilled reverie and alerted him that they had made it to the cobblestone road of the village. He crawled to the rough seat and pulled himself up to stand behind Tragador.

"Ghouls are coming! Here! Now!" he shouted as hard and loud as his emotion-strained voice allowed.

Curious heads popped out of second floor windows of the tidy stone buildings that lined the major street of Baniston. Shopkeepers sweeping their tiny front stoops before opening for business looked at him with mild surprise. No one showed panic. This kind of alarm was so foreign to them that they assumed it was a youthful prank. Tragador swept his fury-filled eyes around him and yelled, "Get to the Banish Hall Grounds! Ghouls are on top of us!"

That did it. Tragador was a respected farmer. All at once panicked villagers flowed into the streets. Brooms, breakfast and

all things that were important only heartbeats before were forgotten. Not accustomed to panic, the people of Baniston moved
in dazed, quiet shock. Only later did fear overtake them when
they were behind the one high stone wall in the village. The wall
that protected the Banish Hall.

Startled away from her book, Janin looked up as half the
village rushed towards her favorite reading spot. The most
peaceful and quiet place in the village, the Banish Hall Grounds
with neatly trimmed greens and great ancient trees was Janin's
paradise. Even with the unrelenting clashes from the sword and
staff practice of the Banish Hall Guards echoing around the warren of buildings from the dusty practice yards on the backside of
the Hall, Janin felt only peace.

Her large blue eyes widened as she realized her neighbors
weren't stopping at the double wagon-width iron gate. She
pushed long flaxen strands of hair from her face as she tried to
puzzle out this strange activity. She finally slipped the book into
her belt pouch and stood up to get a better look.

Janin gaped at the terrified expressions on the familiar faces
as the people crushed onto the green. Her first impulse was to go
to her family clustered close to the Banish Hall. But curiosity
overcame sense and she sprinted to one of the small openings in
the imposing stone wall.

Remnants of mist from the river swirled around the rushing
people. She frowned, unable to see the cause for this sudden exo-
dus from the village proper to the Banish Hall Grounds. Then her
mind and body froze. Six of the largest creatures, clothed in
menacing red and black, that she had ever seen emerged from
around the corner. Wielding terrible ugly weapons. Ghouls! The
frightening word popped into her mind even though she had
never seen one, except in her mind's eye as she listened to the
ancient stories by the fireside.

Cries of dismay came from behind her, and she turned to see
the Guards, clad only in their light brown cotton shirts and black
leather leggings, crunching through the grass. Not having had
time to pull on their tunics and armor, the Guards, only fourteen
strong, rushed to defend the village with their sparring weapons
and shields. Captain Janvil, voice braced with steel, barked commands as they ran. The villagers, taking confidence in the elu-

sive safety of the green, parted to let the determined Guards through.

The villagers appeared heartened by the Guards' arrival, but Janin could see that they would be cut down as easily as if they were children. The thought was shocking and frightening. Along with everyone else, she had grown up believing without question in the ability of the Banish Hall Guards to protect them from any and all dangers. At that moment, she knew in her heart that these brave souls, lined up across the cobbled road, were about to defend their village to the death.

Shaking from fear and helplessness, Janin squeezed her eyes shut, desperately shouting in her head for the Ghouls to stop. Tears fell down her cheeks as she covered her face with trembling hands. The idea of the Ghouls stopping their rampage was so clear in her mind that it was almost a tangible entity. Her ache to stop them was so intense that a throb of pain pushed against her temples, and then faded just as quickly.

The cacophony of terror died out around her. Feeling lightheaded, Janin lowered her hands and opened her eyes. A gasp escaped her throat as she focused on the road outside the wall. The stunned Guards slowly lowered their weapons. The Ghouls had collapsed and were a lifeless clump before the Banish Hall gates.

At the far end of the Banish Hall Green, Gretna Alcot, Head Elder of the Village of Baniston, stared tensely from her office balcony in the Elders Hall. The other three members of the Elders Council clustered around her, gaping at the citizens they were sworn to protect surging through the streets and pushing onto the Grounds in a panic the serene village had never before witnessed. From their second floor vantage, they saw the Ghouls lumbering at an appalling pace for all their size and heavy implements.

Gretna knew that she was the only one in the village with the ability to stop the Ghouls. The problem was she had no time to prepare, and this action required a great deal of preparation. She had studied and developed many techniques for controlling airflow when she was the Overseer of Weather in Athros. Having little call to exercise these skills during her twelve years retirement in Baniston, she was rusty, to say the least.

Not even hiding their apprehension, the other three Elders exchanged glances. For all their skills as former Overseers, their usefulness to the people of Baniston would only come into play after the Ghouls had completed their destruction. Elder Lanler Xim, Retired Overseer of the Mind, empathized with the terror and panic rising up to her on the spring breeze. The survivors would need her skills to recover their shattered lives. As the Retired Overseer of the Body, Elder Trudlin Cordan grimly envisioned the task of trying to heal too many villagers at once, knowing that some would be lost. She would not be able to save them all. Elder Enle Dunderlin, the Retired Overseer of Truth, knew that she would be accosted by unsolicited confessions of minor consequence due to the guilt that usually came with the aftermath of facing death and being one of the few survivors.

Of course their services would be unnecessary if Elder Gretna could perform a miracle and remember how to mold the air into a solid but invisible wall. The other Elders kept their bodies and minds still as the Head Elder muttered words that did not sound like they had anything to do with air flows. Her labored breathing was as much from frustration as concentration on her task. She was too old and out of practice for this. She was retired, after all. But she had accepted this responsibility when she became an Elder and had to face it now with all the skill she could pull together and then some. Sharp anguish pushed away both frustration and concentration as the Banish Hall Guards positioned themselves in front of the wrought iron gate.

Gretna gasped as fear and panic seized her. She lost, actually lost, the flow of air. She had had it in her control. Never in her long life had it just vanished like that. The Ghouls were too close now, and all Gretna could do was helplessly watch the Guards became the first casualties.

The four women eyed the misty cobbled street with unblinking disbelief. When reality pulled back the blanket of silence from the stunned villagers, Elder Dunderlin leaned over the balcony and peered hard at the street in front of the Banish Hall Guards.

"You did it," Enle said in a husky voice.

"I didn't do anything." Gretna's voice strained against the words, going over her actions in her head just to be sure she did not perform this miracle without realizing it.

Enle raised stunned eyes to her. "Surely, you did."

The other Elders caught their breaths as they watched the

two lieutenants of the Guard gingerly poke their staffs at the lifeless black and red heaps, quickly backing away after each prod. The Ghouls did not stir. The pair of Guards slowly approached the Ghouls once more and jabbed the remaining creatures. Satisfied that they were indeed dead, the lieutenants signaled their Captain. Relief shuddered through the silently watching villagers.

"They're going to think that you stopped them," Lanler said softly. "Telling them that we don't know how they were stopped could be as frightening as the sudden appearance of the Ghouls themselves. Too many unanswered questions lead to fear and mistrust, and these people are not accustomed to such feelings."

Gretna tapped the top of the balcony railing with her fingertips. She wasn't so out of practice that she could just let go of her control on the flow of air. Air control was the simplest skill to learn and was second nature to even a novice Apprentice to the Overseer of Weather.

"Just before it happened I lost the flow of air." The horror of the helpless void she had felt flickered across Gretna's haunted eyes.

"Lost?" Lanler frowned.

"Like it was pulled away from me." The thought came to Gretna as she said it. She clenched her eyes shut, trying to recall the airflow force and direction right before it disappeared. She opened her eyes and scanned the milling groups of villagers. They had recovered from their shock and were clustered in noisy huddles of relief. A small delegation of village leaders gathered and gestured in the direction of the Elders Hall. The Elders exchanged worried glances. They did not have much time to put together an explanation.

Gretna's gaze rested on a solitary figure standing at one of the barred openings in the stone wall. The villagers, when they surged onto the grounds, pressed as close to the Banish Hall as possible so no one else was near the girl.

"What do you know about the presence of Athronian blood in the Outlander population?" Gretna asked thoughtfully as she turned to Trudlin.

"It exists." Trudlin scratched her head. "There have been stories about how Athronian blood can surface in special talents. Gunter, Retired Overseer of Genealogy, made a study of it centuries ago."

Gretna nodded. "I know the study. He suspected that Out-

landers who develop unusual skills are actually Athronians without ever knowing it."

Trudlin shrugged. "It happens all the time with the inhabitants of the Outland. Since these Outlanders are descended from
them, it should be the same here."

Gretna gazed out at the people of Baniston. The Land Out of
Time was so far removed from her beloved Athros and the Outland the Overseers protected that she had trouble remembering
that the ancestors of the native people here were pulled into this
parallel land at a time when the worlds pressed too close
together. The Athronians called this place, where they sent their
retired Overseers, The Land Out of Time because it didn't seem
to follow the time continuums of either Athros or the Outland.

Concurrent with her mindful search for an explanation as to
how she lost control of the air current, Gretna considered her
knowledge of the people. The Land had relatively few Athronians and even fewer capable of having children, being of
advanced age when they finally retired. Banished Athronians
were also sent to the Land Out of Time since their crimes were
usually ethical rather than violent. But there hadn't been a banishment since the ancient Banish Hall was built.

"I think an Outlander did that." Gretna pointed her finger at
the lifeless Ghouls.

Enle frowned. "Then we'd better find this Outlander as soon
as possible."

Eyeing a determined group of village leaders tramping
across the green to the Elders Hall, Lanler took in a sharp breath.
"It doesn't matter who did it. We don't have time to look into it
now. We need something to say to the Village Council."

"Take credit." Enle spat out the distasteful words. The others turned to her with a mixture of disbelief and horror. For an
Overseer of Truth to encourage a falsehood of any kind was
beyond shocking. "Take credit," the Elder simply repeated as if
defeated by her own convictions. Sometimes a lie was better
than the truth, especially when the truth could do greater harm.
"We will find your talented Outlander before anyone is the wiser.
Do you have some idea who it is?"

"Yes." Gretna nodded as her gaze fell on the solitary figure
near the Banish Hall wall. Enle did not attempt to hide her relief.

Chapter
Two

The Unexpected Always Happens When You
Least Expect It

The wind wouldn't be so bad if he had enough sense to stay out of it. Devor's chuckling at the silly logic of this thought turned into an uncomfortably dry cough. Recovering his breath, he allowed a rueful grin as he re-wrapped the long soft leather cloak around his upper body, shifting the heavy pack to give his back more protection. It looked so easy when his guide did it, but the cloak kept falling from his shoulders. As the wind pulled at the brush leather that encased his legs, Devor was thankful he had enough sense to wear a layer of wool underneath.

A wicked splash of frigid air stung his cheeks as he twisted around to observe the effects of the wind on his companion. The leathery skinned Lugarian guide acted as if it was a breezeless day in summer. Devor sighed as his cloak slid away from his shoulders.

Patiently re-wrapping the contrary cloak, Devor repeated to himself the reason he was there. It certainly wasn't to climb the famous Lugar Mountains with the most treacherous scaling conditions in the world. His colleagues back at the Institute always accused him of having a deeply submerged sense of adventure just because he mentioned on occasion that it might be fun to visit the places described in the Tanabran Archives or to try something daring like climbing the Lugar mountains.

Devor blinked to force the tears stinging his eyes to flow down his cheeks. Wiping away the moisture before it froze on his skin, he wondered if his colleagues were right. Despite all the discomfort, he was enjoying this miserable trek. It ignited the same essence that burned within him when faced with an impossible mental challenge.

Terre, his guide, stopped. Devor nearly trampled him before realizing that the walls of the narrow river hollow they were in opened onto a high meadow patched with yellowed stiff grasses and snow. The short, stocky Lugarian eyed Devor as he often had since agreeing to take him to Windfound Mount. This stranger from the other side of the world looked every inch the adventurer he was accustomed to guiding. But he was seeking something rather than wanting to climb the three high peaks. Silver was silver, and Terre had no complaint about the generous fee they agreed upon, but the Lugarian couldn't imagine what was on Windfound Mount that was worth all the trouble this stranger had gone through to get there.

"This is the Valley of Lost Souls," Terre announced as his hard soled boots crunched against the frozen grass. "A battle was fought here. Back when the Overseers walked the earth." Devor gave the sturdy packhorse a tug, and followed. He had forgotten that these people still believed in the existence of Overseers. "Researcher." Terre repeated the foreign word that described what Devor did for a living. "There is silver in that kind of work?"

"A lot of silver," Devor answered as he got into the rhythm of walking on the long strands of frozen grass. "Our Institute is dedicated to solving mysteries."

"If you did that, there would not be any mysteries left." Terre's face creased in a puzzled frown. "We enjoy our mysteries. You would never make enough silver to live on here." The guide nodded decisively. "You still look like an adventurer to me."

Even without knowing, Terre was right in thinking that Devor didn't look like a Researcher. At least he didn't look like the Researchers from Devor's part of the world. Visitors to the Institute of Uncommon Phenomenon were always surprised to discover that their amiable young guide was also a member of the scholarly staff. Many of Devor's colleagues suffered from the rigors of their occupation and wore thick spectacles or were hunched over from years bent in study. Devor, with his neatly trimmed dark beard and hair and his plain light leather tunic and leggings, was so normal, in comparison, that he was referred to as the good looking one when visitors discussed their tour of the Institute. His polite intelligence and soft blue eyes caused many young women to look twice. The combination of being good looking and intelligent was too much for them to resist. He worked on keeping fit and was fortunate enough to have inherited a strong body to go with a strong mind.

"That is Windfound Mount." Terre pointed to a rocky ridge that thrust through the far edge of the Valley of Lost Souls. "It's not really a mountain, like the Three Mountains that the other adventurers seek." Terre glanced back at his companion, still unconvinced that the famous peaks were not really his destination.

"I'm not here to climb but to find," Devor returned patiently. Terre shrugged and led the windblown Researcher across the icy field.

A good sand mark passed before they stood on the rocky skirts of the rounded bare topped ridge. If the wind had been gauged severe as it whipped through the river hollow, it was unforgiving at this strange meeting of the deep valleys that led to the Three Mountains. The large glistening boulders, many times the size of a person, amplified its howling intensity.

"Now I know why they call it Windfound Mount," Devor muttered as he tried to puzzle out why the boulders intensified the wind instead of shielded them from it. Another phenomenon to explore.

Turning his back to the Mount, he used his body to shelter a small leather notebook that he pulled from his belt pouch. He carefully turned the pages until he stopped at a rough drawing. "This is what I'm looking for." He raised his voice so Terre could hear him over the boisterous wind. Terre pressed forward against the wind until he looked over Devor's arm at the drawing.

"Trizwounds." Raising an eyebrow that questioned Devor's sanity, Terre faced the Mount and spread out his arms. Puzzled, Devor turned and looked. When Terre did not offer any more direction, the Researcher clambered over a flow of smaller boulders to where the Mount thrust upward. Leaning against a tall boulder to support himself from the wind, he focused on the jagged stone before him. His next intake of breath strangled in his throat.

"You found what you were looking for?" Terre came up behind him, negotiating the rocks with the sureness of the shaggy goats that thrived in those mountains. He thought Devor mad or, more likely, those who paid him to make this journey.

Devor struggled to take in long deep breaths of as much of the thin air as possible. How could he have made such a stupid error? This would go down in the Institute's store of legendary mistakes. Right up there with Old Thoridin's hunt for the Great Underbeast of Enceland. Now he was sorry he laughed at how someone could be so intelligent and make such a silly mistake. He had just joined those noble ranks.

"Yes, I found what I was looking for," he replied steadily.

The slopes before him were splattered with thousands of impressions of the image in the rough drawing. The problem was, he was looking for a particular trizwound, as Terre called it. He had gotten the impression from his research that there was only one such image etched on the face of Windfound Mount and beneath it was the true purpose of his journey: the legendary Purple Ore. The ore had been legendary until Rascam, a fellow Researcher, found a few slivers of it encased in a wedge of glass in the Tanabran Archives. The legend was that it came from only one place and that the veins were the width of a thread. Devor had spent two years tracking the ore to Windfound Mount. Now he had the choice of defacing the entire Mount until he found the purple veins or returning to the Institute and trying to find further clues that pinpointed the exact location of the ore.

As long as he was there it didn't hurt to look around and perhaps get some ideas from what he saw. If nothing else, he needed to prepare a complete map of all the trizwounds.

"We will make camp here," Devor announced.

Terre nodded. "There is a cave over there. The adventurers use it." He turned back to fetch the packhorse that was contentedly burrowing into the icy grass to find warm blades underneath.

The cave had a low overhang that shielded the wind so completely that the relief from the relentless pounding of air was startling. Terre knelt before one of the walls and carefully pulled out a large stone revealing a depression that had been hollowed by man rather than nature. The Lugarian gave a small sigh of relief that the light colored stones that were definitely not indigenous to these mountains were still there. Devor squinted in the gray light. The stones looked like replicas of the glowstones used by the Overseers. They were maybe a hand-length high and two thirds of that in thickness. Long lengthwise lines were etched into them, and a block script ran across the tops and bottoms.

Terre followed the wall of the cavern, placing a stone in head high niches every several paces. It could have been Devor's imagination, but the cavern appeared to brighten as Terre continued his task. The Researcher, knowing that glowstones existed only in legend, was sure it was just his eyes adjusting to the weak natural lighting. The cave was much larger and deeper than Devor's first impression of it, reaching far into Windfound Mount.

A sharp gasp came from Terre as he turned after placing another stone at the farthest end of the cavern. The Lugarian stiffened and backed across the middle of the floor toward the entrance of the cave.

"What...?" Devor's question was silenced by a frantic wave of a hand from Terre, who did not remove his eyes from the pounded dirt floor. Devor stepped forward next to the terrified Lugarian.

A figure wrapped in blankets was sprawled out with its back to them. Before either man moved or even thought of what to do next, the figure rolled over and cast a calm gray gaze on them. He sat up and stretched as if this was the most normal situation in the world.

"Visitors," he cried amiably. "How nice." The slender-built man, about the same height as Devor and clad in black leather, nimbly climbed to his feet and grinned at them. His skin was a fair contrast to his dark clothing and straight black hair hanging around his ears and in bangs almost into his sharp gray eyes. The overall effect gave an impression of youth but there was nothing youthful in the glint of those eyes or the mature tone of his voice.

Instead of being reassured by the unthreatening nature of the man, Terre's eyes widened and he dropped the remaining glowstones.

"Careful with those," the black-clad man teased. "I might not be able to filch any more for you."

Terre trembled even harder, if that was possible, and fell to his knees. "Please," he stammered. "Please find forgiveness for me."

The young man was taken aback by this demonstration. "He

seems to have the wrong idea about me." His eyes held a strange mix of concern and amusement. "Get up. What are you doing? You'd think I was my cousin or something." At that, Terre's groveling disintegrated into tears, and he ground his forehead into the compacted dirt. Realizing his mistake, the young man dropped to his knees in front of the wretched Lugarian. "I didn't mean to scare you. Please get up. You're embarrassing me." Terre raised his head, realizing that the stranger was on the ground in front of him. He sniffed back tears and pulled himself together enough to sit up.

"I'm sorry," he said, still shaken. "It's just such a shock."

"I admit it's been a long time since I've been this way," the stranger mused climbing to his feet. "Come, stand and tell me your name."

With Devor's help, Terre got to his feet. He still hung his head as if he didn't want to look directly at the stranger. "I am Terre of the Sixth House of Lugar, son of Tomra." He managed to straighten and hold his head up but kept his eyes on the ground in front of him.

"My name is Devor Locke of the Institute of Uncommon Phenomenon," Devor said as he held out the hand that was not keeping Terre from sliding back onto his knees.

"*The* Devor Locke?" The young man eagerly shook Devor's hand. "You wrote a treatise on coincidences."

"Yes." Devor blinked. Talk about coincidences. His preliminary research had been published in an obscure esoteric journal read by only a handful of scholars.

"My cousin is very interested in your work," the man went on with enthusiasm. "I'm Jac Riverson. I wish my cousin were here. She'd be so pleased to meet you."

His words caused Terre's knees to buckle, and both Devor and Jac absently grabbed him and lifted him back up.

"Your cousin..."

"Is a scholar in her own small way," Jac said smoothly. "Your treatise has inspired her to compile her own list of coincidences."

"Really?" Devor could not hold back his growing intrigue. "And she is..."

"A very clever person." Jac grinned as Terre choked on nothing. "Would you like to meet her?"

Terre's face paled and his eyes grew wide. In a blink, he was all alone.

Dorian frowned at the unorganized heap of books, manuscripts, and bits and pieces of parchment that cluttered a good third of the mammoth chamber, twice the size of a playing field. The heaps were piled as high to the ceiling as possible without causing more avalanches than those that had already occurred.

In the ancient Overseer Stories told by the Outlanders, the cavernous chamber was glorified as a white marble monument to knowledge. In truth, it was an airy warehouse-like structure, open to the courtyards of the legendary Palmathon University, the center of learning in Athros. The moderate breeze carrying spring fragrances and the vocalizations of birds imported from the Outland enveloped the place with a sense of tranquility.

"This is it for today?" she asked no one in particular. The twenty-odd purple robed Apprentices, sorting the mess into smaller neater piles, looked up at her. The unconnected expression in their eyes showed that they were trying not to be distracted from their task. They were not just sorting but memorizing the contents of each piece they touched. Dorian smiled. None had yet learned to approach the art of memorization and retention as a natural process that flowed in and out without effort.

Kwen, the most eager of the Apprentices, shook long strands of red hair out of his light blue eyes and straightened his stiff frame. He had been an Apprentice for fifteen years when Dorian joined them as a likable but uninterested twelve-year-old. She took the Apprentice exam on a bet with her cousin and got a score so high that it had never been disclosed. Orvid, the Overseer of Knowledge at the time, feared that it would prejudice the other Apprentices against her. The intervening nineteen years mellowed the differences in their ages and experience, and although Kwen desperately wanted to be Overseer of Knowledge, Dorian, in the end possessed the greater skill and passed the Overseer's exam.

None of the other Apprentices could understand how their wayward colleague who never showed up for work, slept through the lectures and spent her youth trying to acquire knowledge through wildly pursued experience, turned in the highest score ever achieved on the exam. It didn't help that she looked enough like her cousin Jac, Apprentice to the Overseer of Mischief, to be his twin. It also didn't help that she demonstrated an aptitude for mischief as great, or even greater, than his.

Instead of resenting Dorian's effortless talent, Kwen set out to find the secret to her abilities. He tried to emulate Dorian's casual manner. So it appeared, on the surface at least, that the development of the skills required to gain the position of the Overseer of Knowledge was easier for him than the others. Of course he had to work twice as hard on his time off to make up for pretending to be more proficient than he really was.

"We have been assured that this is all there is for today," Kwen answered.

"Oh, well. You deserve a little rest on occasion." Dorian shrugged, not letting on the concern that tugged at the edge of her consciousness. "Anyone find anything interesting or strange today?"

"They're having a problem electing a new leader in Amitta," Toyn spoke up.

Dorian turned to the bright-eyed young woman who had an endless curiosity about the Outlanders and their world. "What kind of problem? I thought their system of leadership was working rather well for something so unique."

"It seems that the two candidates tied," Toyn responded.

"Tied?" Dorian crinkled her forehead. "Amitta has over four million people. How could they be so evenly split to tie that vote?"

Toyn shrugged her answer. "Now they are recounting the votes to make sure the first count was correct."

"Ah, and I'll bet that any recount will be so close that the losing side will demand another recount. And it will go on until they come up with a new way of electing a leader." Dorian grinned at her Apprentices.

The others laughed knowingly at the way Outlanders have been known to handle these kinds of conflicts.

"Shall we place bets on how they're going to solve this little problem?" Nanders asked, wiggling his gray eyebrows.

"You owe each other so much money from all your little bets that it takes the Overseer of Mathematics to keep it all straight," Dorian commented and then laughed at the mock indignation on the faces of the Apprentices.

Still smiling, she sat at the long work-table at the end of the chamber. She opened a small cloth bag and peered into it. Jac had packed her midday meal that morning so she wasn't expecting any surprises. A midday meal packed by her father, on the other hand, had been known to be quite a creative meal. Nodding her approval, she pulled out a thick slice of brown bread and hunks of grilled goat cheese, along with the usual assortment of fruits and vegetable slices.

While munching her food, she settled into the daily paperwork required by the High Overseers. Dorian wondered if the High Overseers ever looked at the crate load of documents that they received everyday from the sorting chamber. Documentation. It didn't matter what anyone did in Athros as long as it had the proper documentation. Each piece of knowledge had to be described and summarized in detail before being carefully shelved in the Athros Archive, where it was rarely looked at. The initial memorization and documentation of knowledge was the job of the Apprentices. At the end of each day they channeled what they memorized into an oddly shaped knowledge stone, otherwise used as a paperweight. Dorian absorbed the knowledge by simply placing her fingers on the stone. Her trained mind distinguished between the knowledge just added and the knowledge already in the stone. She then made the trip to the Archives and channelled the new knowledge into the Great Knowledge Stone which only the Overseer of Knowledge was allowed to touch.

After she poured a cup of steaming tea and wrapped the bread around the cheese hunks, Dorian dipped her pen into an ink stained earthen jar and scribbled her name at the bottom of the parchment sheets already piled on the table. The work was boring but comforting. She actually enjoyed the peaceful atmosphere inside the cavernous chamber with the dusty sunrays slicing across the floor. The muted echoes of shuffling paper and the smell of the leather bindings and parchment always conjured a feeling of nostalgia in her. Nostalgia for something she was convinced existed only in her imagination.

Thoughtfully chewing her bread and cheese, she paused from her work and watched her diligent Apprentices. A strange thought took over her absent musings. Of all the places in Athros, this was where she felt most at home. No matter what the High Overseers insinuated when they found it necessary to remind her that she had never showed up for work as an Apprentice. No matter how much they dismissed her aptitude because she and Jac spent their younger years adding their presence to the Overseer Stories, she knew that in her own way she was suited to this work. Not all Overseers of Knowledge had to be bent, studious, boring creatures who could barely remember to say "hello" but could give you every last detail of the war in South Lazlin or how rice managed to grow in flooded fields. But none of the former Overseers of Knowledge had been as facile as she was in the art of soaking up and retaining knowledge.

Lunch and the paperwork done for now, Dorian decided to visit her office. The High Overseers frowned extra hard when they found out she was not spending enough of her time where people could have easy access to her. Each Overseer was expected to be at the disposal of the other citizens of Athros for a specified portion of the day. Office hours. Dorian flinched at the thought. Fitting oneself into an exact pattern of time was unnatural. To encourage people to think twice about how much they really needed her services, Dorian put her office at the top of the highest tower in the Archives, accessible only by a dizzying ascent of tightly curved stairs. Of course, that also discouraged Dorian from wanting to visit there often.

Before Devor had a chance to respond to Jac's question, he was tumbling down a grassy hill drenched in bright sunlight.

"Whoops. I missed." He heard Jac's voice. "Hold on." The next heartbeat he was seated at a side table in a crowded tidy teashop, open to a narrow sun soaked street, which bustled with oddly dressed people. He wasn't even going to think about how he went from tumbling to sitting without hurting something important.

"Could we have a pot of the special blend?" Jac sat across from the Researcher, signaling to a young man in a brown-striped apron. The young man did not seem surprised by the sudden appearance of patrons at one of his tables and disappeared through a small swinging door at the back of the shop.

Devor carefully removed his cloak and bundle, amazingly unfazed by the abrupt shift in locale. As he looked around, he pulled out his notebook and pencil, calmly thinking that just because this sort of thing never happened to him before didn't mean that it was an unusual occurrence.

"People have reacted in many ways to my little trick but never like that," Jac commented, wrinkling a thoughtful forehead at the Researcher.

"What did you say your name was?" Devor asked, not looking up from his scribbling.

"Jac Riverson," Jac enunciated.

"Why should I be surprised then? Isn't this the kind of trick that Jac Riverson would pull?" Devor met his eyes. The young man in the apron hovered with a tea tray filled with finger sandwiches, a finely engraved silver teapot, and delicate cups.

"Thank you, Gehler." Jac poured out tea and milk for each of them. "And you believe that I am Jac Riverson?"

"My belief is not necessary for me to experience whatever it is I'm experiencing," Devor replied, as he placed the pencil in the little book and turned his attention to the warm cup of tea. Whatever else was real or not, he was chilled from being out in the cold wind.

Jac gazed on him with a thoughtful yet puzzled expression. For a change, he was the one faced with something strange. "You know. You remind me of my cousin."

"The one who's 'a scholar in her own small way'?" Devor's voice held a hint of sarcasm in it.

Jac smiled. "All right. If I'm Jac Riverson, then my cousin must be Dorian Riverson, Overseer of Knowledge."

"This is your story, not mine," Devor commented as he took a sip of tea. "Special blend, you say."

"Very special," Jac replied. "Very costly, but my cousin pays my bills at this shop."

"Your cousin is very generous," Devor murmured.

Jac grinned at him then laughed. "I like you. You believe in coincidences. I believe in fate. I think we are going to become fast friends."

"I hate to bring it up, but we don't exactly move in the same circles." Devor glanced around them. "Much less the same dimension."

"It's not really a different dimension." Jac rubbed his chin. "I know. That's what they teach you in school. It's more like a parallel world."

"Parallel world," Devor repeated. He picked up his notebook and scribbled the phrase. "I take it this is Athros."

"One of the quainter back streets," Jac cheerily clarified. "My family's home is not far from here. Dorian's family lives next door. We both still live at home. I've never had a domestic inclination, and Dorian is too busy to bother with a place of her own."

"That is the first thing you've said that I can completely believe," Devor mumbled as he munched a sandwich with a delicate flavor he could not place. Then he remembered that Athronians did not consume anything that came from animals except milk and those things made from milk. According to legend they had a fabled cuisine unlike anything found in his world.

"Some of those stories have been drastically altered through the ages." Jac rather sheepishly took a sip of tea.

Devor arched an eyebrow. "The one about the dragon?"

Jac almost sputtered his tea. "It was Dorian's fault for us being there in the first place. Anyway, I didn't have anything to do with burning the Overseer of Beauty's wig. At least not on purpose."

A throaty chuckle sounded from the table behind him. "Still can't live that one down, eh, Jac?" Jac turned to a massive man with a jovial face.

"And that is..." Devor looked at the man with pencil poised.

"Gradlink, Overseer of Animals," Jac mumbled as he faced Devor. "Anyway, that's one of the few stories that might have a semblance of truth to it." Another rumble of chuckling reverberated against his back. "Now that we've warmed up, I think we should go look for my cousin."

The tower sitting room always had citizens lounging in the comfortable chairs waiting to explain to Zore Lefke, Dorian's amazingly patient Apprentice, exactly what they needed from the facile mind of the Overseer of Knowledge. Zore was adept at getting Dorian to respond within a reasonable time so there was little complaint about the efficiency of the Office of Knowledge. The only reminder that the service could be more efficient was when Dorian was there. So quick were her responses to even the most obscure questions or confounding problems that she could empty the sitting room as she crossed to her own tiny chamber. Oddly enough, the people did not feel nearly as much satisfaction for the effort of having trudged up the winding stairs as when they went through Zore and received the needed information later by messenger. Sometimes efficiency could be too much of a good thing.

As it was time for the midday meal, Dorian had to face only a handful of people in the sitting room before she slumped into the stiff backed wooden chair next to Zore's plain stone desk.

Zore was a plumpish woman with a few streaks of gray in

her short, light brown hair. Her open face invited others to talk to her. She enjoyed people and, given the chance, would do just about anything to help just for the asking. More importantly, she saw through Dorian's unique outlook on the world and recognized not only her effortless brilliance but also her seriousness about her job in her own way.

"It's been a slow morning," Zore reported, sorting through the papers she kept for each person she talked to. More papers for Dorian to sign.

"Not much knowledge came in either," Dorian mused, absently twirling her pen. It could happen. Knowledge could go in cycles like anything else.

As Zore read through the requests for knowledge and Dorian gave the responses, it was obvious to the Apprentice that her Overseer was preoccupied.

Something flitted around the edges of Dorian's consciousness that was more than a little distracting to her, causing an uncharacteristic frown on the otherwise amiable face.

Zore glanced at her with concern, startled to realize that Dorian looked vulnerable, even frail. Despite her short height, frail and vulnerable were not words that described Dorian Riverson. Her body was sculpted with tight well-developed muscles that, when tensed, bulged through her leather leggings and tunic. These muscles were visible reminders that she was no ordinary Overseer of Knowledge. Dorian spent long sand marks keeping her body as strong and agile as her mind. But that day the muscles seemed to emphasize how thin she was, and the hint of sadness in her deep gray eyes spoke of a vulnerability that Zore had never seen before. It pained her to see the old mischievous Dorian turn into a responsible, serious Overseer.

"You seem to be preoccupied," Zore commented after the business of the day was completed.

"I am," Dorian replied. "And I don't know what I'm preoccupied about. I feel like something's going to happen. Something different."

"It's not unusual to sense these things," Zore mused.

"I've never been as tuned into that sort of thing as Jac."

Zore grinned. "Then it must be something really different."

Dorian sighed. "What could be more different than anything that I've already experienced in my life."

Zore raised an eyebrow. "Different doesn't necessarily mean outrageous."

"I don't know." Dorian shook her head in defeat, then looked up at the sound of footfalls on the outside steps.

A beaming Jac strolled through the door followed by a curious Devor. The amiable woman seated behind the desk smiled welcoming at the newcomer.

In the next heartbeat, Devor froze. More specifically, his insides turned into a surprisingly pleasant mush and he could not move. Everything around him was forgotten except the person sitting in the chair next to Zore.

"Dorian, Zore, I'd like you to meet Devor Locke." Jac turned to Devor and blinked in puzzlement before he whipped around to look at his cousin. Zore was already trembling with laughter as she waved a hand in front of Dorian's eyes. The young Overseer was as spellbound as Devor.

Zore grinned. "She was just saying that she felt something really different was going to happen to her."

Jac laughed. "This is certainly different. Who would have thought?"

"Granwin will be here soon," Zore commented. Granwin, the Overseer of Attractions, was able to sense when an Attraction took place. "This isn't supposed to happen to an Overseer of Knowledge."

"He's a smart one. Researcher at the Institute of Uncommon Phenomenon," Jac explained.

"Really?" Zore studied the pleasant looking young man. "He doesn't look like a Researcher. He must be extraordinarily intelligent to be compatible with Dorian."

"You're right." Jac rubbed his chin. "Imagine someone—an Outlander at that—whose mind is equal to Dorian's. I bet it'll take some getting used to for both of them."

"That will be the least of it."

The metallic click of heels echoed up the curved staircase.

"I came as soon as I could." A scattered looking woman with a shapeless heap of blonde hair and watery blue eyes stepped into the chamber fumbling with the spectacles hanging on a thick chain around her neck. "Dorian's the one?" The spectacles dropped as the woman cast an astonished look at Jac, then Zore. The idea of a practical joke flashed through her mind. "Most unusual," she murmured. "Who's...?" She turned to the young man beside her. "An Outlander?"

"Yes. This is Devor Locke, a Researcher at the Institute of Uncommon Phenomenon in Landersdown," Jac explained.

"Leave it to Dorian to get bonded to the only good looking Researcher out there," Granwin commented as she rummaged through her patched cloth bag. "First, we've got to neutralize the initial attraction." Looking around, she spotted the small round table in a windowed alcove. "Perfect. Please seat our pair at the table. Don't let them even brush up against each other."

"Remember the last time that happened?" Jac chuckled as he led a dazed Devor to the table. "Half the glowstones in the city crumbled." Zore was trying her best to keep from laughing as she gently pushed Dorian to the table.

When the hapless pair were seated facing each other, Granwin walked around the table so her back was to the windows. After dumping the contents of her bag on the table, she sorted through a strange mixture of tools of the trade and personal items. Finally, she extracted a pair of small silver medallions on slender chains and two vials of a brown liquid before shoving the rest of the jumble back into her bag.

She eased the cork stopper off one of the vials, tipped Dorian's head back, and poured the liquid into her mouth. The Overseer's reaction was slow as if waking from a heavy sleep. Granwin poured the contents of the other vial into Devor's mouth, then stood back and waited.

Jac and Zore watched in fascination as Dorian and Devor worked through the haze caused by the Attraction and become acutely aware of each other. Dorian actually blushed when she realized that she was completely smitten with this nice looking stranger with gentle intelligent eyes staring back at her. Devor could hardly catch his breath as he tried to sort through the intense emotions he was feeling for this feminine Jac look-alike with the deep gray eyes.

"Dorian, meet Devor Locke. Devor, this is Dorian Riverson," Granwin introduced softly.

"Devor Locke?" Dorian stammered. "Devor Locke?" She struggled to focus her thoughts. "Coincidences?"

"Yes," Devor managed to say.

"Now, Dorian knows what has happened here," Granwin began, "but you, Devor, have only heard of Attractions in stories."

"Attractions?" Devor tried to pry his eyes from Dorian to look at Granwin.

"Right now, you're feeling confused, as you no doubt recognize, and that other much stronger feeling is love," Granwin explained. "Unlike Outlander love, the love that results from an Attraction never fades; it remains as strong as it is now. The only thing that changes is your ability to cope with it. Since the Attraction is not felt until we are fully mature, many Athronians grow up together and know each other quite well before they are hit with it. Sometimes, as in your case, strangers meet for the first time as adults. Since you are perfectly matched, you will feel like you've known each other all your lives." Granwin picked up one of the medallions. "These medallions control the Attraction, gradually allowing more and more tolerance of being in physical proximity to each other until the bond medallion is replaced by the joining ring."

"That means we won't be able to hold hands for a few days," Dorian said wryly.

"It'll be a novelty for you." Jac gave her a wicked grin. Dorian flashed him a sharp look. Overseer Stories depicting her dalliances were all too common, but she felt uncharacteristically ashamed of them under the present circumstances.

Granwin slipped the medallions over their heads and pronounced, "You are now bonded. May you two have a long and happy life together. Ah, one last thing." She opened her bag and pulled out a small piece of parchment with the words "Bonding Certificate" printed across the top. After pulling a pen with a built in inkwell from behind her ear, Granwin scribbled Devor's name on the parchment followed by Landersdown. "Age?"

It took a heartbeat for Devor to realize she was asking him his age. "Thirty-three," he said, taking a closer look at the document. Granwin scribbled Dorian's name followed by Athros and looked up at her.

"Thirty-one," Dorian responded.

Devor reacted with a start. Citizens of Athros were considered ageless in the Overseer Stories. Although there were some young ones and old ones, they seemed to have been born the age that they were portrayed in every story. Dorian was a teenager in the Overseer Stories. Devor was shocked to realize that the youthful Dorian Riverson had grown up. He did not dwell on the fact that the Overseer Stories were thousands of Outlander years old.

After scribbling a few more lines declaring that an Attraction had taken place and that proper steps had been made to seal the bond, Granwin pushed the paper to Devor and handed him the pen. "Please sign here." Devor wrote his name, then handed the pen to Dorian. That task done, Granwin quickly blotted the document, dropped it back into her bag and eased out from behind the table.

"Another one just happened on the other side of town," she muttered, peeking inside her bag as if checking to see if everything was still there. "Good day to you all," she remembered to say as she disappeared out the door.

"That was fun." Jac broke the silence. "I think we should all go celebrate."

Zore frowned at him. "Aren't you forgetting something? Like the fact that you plucked Devor from whatever he was doing to come here to meet Dorian." Zore folded her arms in dismay. She had done enough work on Dorian's list of coincidences to know that the person who got her interested in the subject was none other than Devor Locke. "What you thought was going to be an innocent meeting of two people interested in the same subject turned out to drastically change both their lives. They have separate lives in two different worlds."

Dorian blinked at Devor. This was going to be more complicated than the usual Attraction.

"I..." Devor rose to his feet and then stumbled back on the chair, upending both himself and the chair.

"Don't say another word." Jac shook his head as he helped Devor up off the floor. "I won't take the blame for this. This was going to happen no matter how they met. You have to admit, Zore, that a meeting was inevitable."

"You're probably right," Zore agreed.

"Devor was doing field research, and this is just a small sidetrack. As soon as he and Dorian come to some agreement on how they can deal with this Attraction, he can go back to his field work and Dorian can get back to her job."

Dorian looked up at her cousin with wicked sweetness. "I hope you're bonded to a Cridean Maid Warrior."

"What did I say?" Jac asked innocently.

"Having studied Attractions," Zore intervened smoothly, "I can understand Dorian's reaction to your little scenario. That's what would happen if they met and wanted to share their common research on coincidences. They'd be getting together as friends."

Jac shrugged. "Now they'll be getting together as really good friends."

Shaking her head, Dorian put both hands on the table and

slowly pushed herself up. She knew that the initial lightheaded-
ness faded after a few moments. Devor had remained standing
and was already much steadier on his feet. Taking slow steps,
Dorian approached the Researcher and stopped an arm's width
from him. He was maybe a half head taller, making him on the
short side by Outlander standards. At least he wasn't ugly, she
found herself thinking. Not that it mattered, but still it was nice
that he wasn't. He had to be intelligent, extremely intelligent.
That thought troubled her more than she knew was rational.

She reached out a hand, and he instinctively pulled his back.
"I was only kidding about holding hands," she said softly. Looking up and meeting her eyes, he knew that he would not have
been able to resist anything from her even if it was against
everyone's better judgment. He took her hand. It felt nice and
strangely natural.

"Before we go and celebrate," Dorian organized, "I think we
should help Devor with his field work. He doesn't have all the
time in the world like we do. Jac tends to forget that sometimes.
Although it's not going to make much difference, given how the
bond works."

"What do you mean?" Devor gave her a puzzled look.

"I'll explain it later." Dorian glanced at Zore and Jac, feeling an uncharacteristic shyness. "Where were you before Jac got
hold of you?"

"I was on Mount Windfound," Devor said.

Dorian raised an inquisitive eyebrow. That was halfway
around the world from Landersdown, the home of the Institute of
Uncommon Phenomenon. "Jac was making an appearance to the
last Outlanders who actually believe in us. If we don't do it,
they'll forget like everyone else. It must have taken you weeks to
get there."

Jac flashed a grin. "Which means that no one will miss
Devor yet. Once we get the field work done, you will be able to
spend the bonding period in Athros having long boring conversations about coincidences and whatever else happens to pop into
your heads instead of bouncing back and forth between Athros
and the Outland."

Dorian grinned at Devor. "Jac is going to make sure he's the
hero of this story. But that would dash all his hopes of ever
becoming the Overseer of Mischief. Now, what exactly were you
doing on Mount Windfound?"

"He was looking for trizwounds," Jac answered before

Devor had a chance to open his mouth.

Dorian nodded. "Oh, the Purple Ore."

"You know how to find it?" Devor's eyes lit up.

Zore winked at Jac. "A perfect match."

"I've never tried, but I saw a map showing where the veins are."

"A map?"

"It was a long time ago," Dorian said, frowning. "By your time scale, that is. I'll explain the time differential to you later. But I did see a map while I was still an Apprentice."

Jac arched an eyebrow at her. "On one of those rare occasions you showed up for work?"

"I only put up with Jac because he's my cousin and I feel sorry for him." Dorian winked at Devor.

"We are a unique kindred. Cousins with the same blood as siblings. So we tend to act like siblings," Jac explained.

Devor nodded. "I heard about that. Your mothers are twins and your fathers are twins. Twins share the same blood so the offspring of these twin pairings are the same as brother and sister, even though they are cousins."

Jac sighed. "It's so easy, yet I've spent many a long night trying to explain it to people."

"Many a long night in taverns with people so drunk they could hardly keep their own bloodlines straight much less Jac's," Dorian clarified.

"They look like twins themselves, but Jac is three years older than Dorian," Zore filled in.

"You really think in terms of years here?" Devor asked.

"The time thing is more complicated than the bloodlines." Jac scratched his head. "I'm sure Dorian will explain it to you on some pleasant moonlit night."

Dorian and Zore exchanged disdainful glances. "Cridean Maid Warrior," Zore agreed.

"I wonder what the odds would be for a Cridean Maid Warrior to be a perfect match for Jac," Dorian mused.

Jac gave his cousin a wary look. "Devor. One word of advice. She can be tricky and she can be dangerous."

"Do you think I could ever be that devious?" Dorian laughed, not even hiding the wicked glint in her eye. "That's your department. You're the Apprentice of Mischief."

"And you're the one who always gets me into trouble."

The cousins grinned affectionately at each other.

"Let's go find the Purple Ore." Dorian squeezed Devor's hand.

Chapter
Three

Apprenticeship

Janin Wiggims had never been beyond the first floor of the
Elders Hall. As she walked through the gaping entrance, she
remembered being intimidated by the chamber when she was a
child. She glanced toward the raised stone table at the back of
the chamber. When a citizen of Baniston was summoned to The
Table, it was for the most serious offenses that could be made
against the community, and the Elders were not known for their
mercy. Their staunch upholding of the laws made Baniston one
of the more peaceful villages in the district.

Nervously smoothing down her loose cotton dress for the
sixth time, Janin mounted the wide stone staircase that wrapped
along the wall. The message, delivered by one of the Elders
School Apprentices, had revealed nothing more than a summons
to present herself at Elder Gretna's chambers after the morning
meal. At sixteen, she was still too young to attend the School run
by the Elders, but they were well aware of her desire to be considered when the time came. As one of the few villages that had
a complete complement of Retired Overseers as Elders, the
School drew outstanding students from all over the district of
Larisdon.

The top of the stairs opened onto a large double storied
chamber. The lower part of the wall was lined with rounded
wooden doors behind which were the offices of the four Elders

and their assistants. The entrance to the living quarters for the Apprentices was on the opposite side of the chamber from where Janin stood. The upper story of the wall was little more than a support for tall windows that allowed sunlight to filter into the chamber throughout the day. The chamber itself was even more imposing than the magnificent first floor of the Elders Hall. Janin sucked in her breath, her senses too stunned to register everything that she saw or felt. How could she possibly have lived here all her life and never known that something like this existed within a half block of her family home?

Her attention focused on the thirty odd blue-robed Apprentices seated on hard wooden benches and hunched over small desks. The desks did not seem to follow any order or plan in their arrangement, scattered and facing every which way. The only sound from the chamber was the diligent scratching out of the morning essays on the lessons from the day before.

Realizing she held her breath, Janin let it out steadily. Her uncertainty as to where to go was eased when she recognized Soral Kinlet from the village of Rondsdon saunter through the arched opening that led to the living quarters. Resting soft green eyes on the newcomer, a wry grin spread over Soral's face as she crossed the chamber, her circuitous route expertly avoiding the student occupied desks.

"Good morning, Janin," the light haired young woman greeted in cheerful hushed tones. "I'm Soral Kinlet, Elder Gretna's assistant. Welcome to our little school." Soral cast an amused glance at Janin's obvious awe of the "little school." "Please come this way. Elder Gretna is looking forward to meeting with you."

Janin was slow to grasp this odd statement. She nearly walked into several desks as she puzzled over the words before realizing that she should be paying attention to where she was going. She focused on all the books and manuscripts haphazardly piled in and around the Apprentices. More books were in that chamber than she ever had seen in her life.

Soral knocked on the opened door of the largest office. Inside, a tall thin woman was bent over a rambling desk, sorting through a pile of papers. She looked up at the knock, smiled, and beckoned Janin to enter with a quick gesture. Although the woman's face was of indeterminable age, her hair, caught in a thick braid, was as much gray as it was brown. Her sharp blue eyes could go from comforting to steely depending on why she flashed them at you.

"Please sit." Gretna waved at the chair in front of the desk. "I'm glad you could find the time to visit on such short notice."

Soral covered a grin as she turned and left the chamber.

"Thank you, Elder," Janin stammered out. She tried to puzzle out Gretna's strange words as she sank into the chair. As far as she was concerned, when an Elder summoned, you came, no matter what you were doing.

"Are you still interested in becoming an Apprentice in our School?" Gretna's eyes rested on the slim girl's hands as they nervously played with the tassel on her belt pouch.

"Oh, yes," Janin returned. Thinking she sounded too enthusiastic, she added in calmer tones, "I look forward to it."

Gretna gave her a long thoughtful look that made Janin's insides squirm. "Are you familiar with the Athronian Talents?" the Elder asked. Janin frowned at the change in subject.

"I'm sorry." The girl shook her head, hoping that it wasn't something she was required to know to be considered for the School.

"It's usually such a minor thing that it goes unnoticed unless observed by a knowing eye," Gretna continued. "It is thought to be manifestations of talents that some Overseers develop."

Janin brightened. "Like the instant transport talent that Dorian has in the Overseer Stories." She loved the Overseer Stories and couldn't get enough of the mischievous Apprentice to Knowledge.

"Yes, something like that." Gretna suppressed a smile, savoring her own memories of the young Apprentice who had livened up Athros when the Elder was an Overseer. "I'm not one to play games, so I'll just come out with it. You stopped the Ghouls." Janin stared at her, confused and a little frightened. "I take it that I'm correct?"

"I think so," Janin stammered. "When you announced that you stopped them, I was relieved that it wasn't me."

Gretna captured Janin's eyes. "We made a quick decision to lie about that to put the village at ease." Janin was stunned at the frankness of the Elder's words. "But not before I knew who really stopped them. Please pick up that stone." The Elder pointed to a fist-sized, smooth black stone on the desk. Janin eyed it, curiosity building inside of her, but she hesitated to touch it. "Go ahead, it won't hurt you," Gretna urged gently.

Janin wrapped her hand around the stone, then took in a sharp breath as it turned to gold. "You may put it down now," the Elder instructed with a hint of puzzlement in her voice.

"Why did it turn gold?" Janin asked, warily.

"Because you have a good amount of Athronian blood in you," Gretna returned almost matter-of-factly. Janin's jaw dropped. "Much more than is common. Obviously, your parents aren't who you think they are. Am I saying anything that sounds untrue?"

"No." Janin hung her head. "I was brought to my parents when I was barely a day old. My adopted mother had just given birth to my sister, Jenne, so we were passed off as twins."

"Fortunately for you there's a family resemblance," Gretna observed.

Janin nodded. "I've always wondered about that."

"It's common practice for Athronian mothers to place their children with the families of the fathers," Gretna explained. "A common practice in the Outland, that is. These are children who are born to a pair that have not been bonded. If the Athronian and Outlander have been bonded, then the child is raised in Athros as an Athronian. Either way, the child is considered a full blood Athronian because Outlander blood strengthens rather than weakens Athronian blood. I don't think there is a single Athronian who does not have Outlander blood."

Gretna paused, making sure that Janin understood what she was saying. The girl hung on to her words as if they were lifelines.

"Of course, this is neither the Outland nor Athros, and your Athronian parent must be your father not your mother. The only Athronian women here are retired Overseers or the life companions of retired Overseers. By the time we get here, we are long past childbearing age. We're usually past that time when we become Overseers." Gretna chuckled. "The mystery of your parentage is yours to pursue if you are so inclined. The only thing that matters to us is, if you had been born in Athros or the Outland, you would be treated as a full blooded Athronian."

"But I wasn't born in Athros or the Outland." Janin shook her head, sorting through Gretna's words. "I thought the Outland only existed in the Overseer Stories."

"All the native inhabitants of this land are originally from the Outland," Gretna explained gently then raised her and to stop Janin's question. "Have patience. You will learn all about this land and about Athros because it is our duty to teach you. Do you think your family would mind giving you up a few years early so you can attend our School?"

"They would be proud and honored," Janin replied before Gretna's words permeated her mind.

Gretna nodded. "That will be the pretense for allowing you to live and work here. You have distinguished yourself in your studies enough so as not to raise too many eyebrows at our decision to let you into the School early."

"Pretense?"

"Oh, you'll certainly receive all the instruction we have to offer. That knowledge is very valuable," Gretna conceded. "But that will only be a part of what you will need to know to cultivate your Athronian blood and your special skills. No one must know of this talent or your Athronian blood until you are capable of protecting yourself from those who would want to take advantage of it."

"I understand." Janin certainly didn't want anyone to know that she had it in her to do something as frightening as stopping Ghouls dead. "Do you think my parents know that my father was Athronian?"

"I don't know, and I don't think you should try to find out as yet," Gretna replied. "If an answer is to be known, it becomes known in its own time, not ours. So be patient and let the knowledge come to you." Gretna smiled. "We are always pleased to find what we refer to as 'lost Athronians.' It is our duty to uncover your unique talents and cultivate them so we can continue the Athronian influence in this world."

"We spend the morning practicing the sword and staff. Staff to staff combat requires the most skill of all our disciplines." Captain Janvil, the muscular, leathery-skinned leader of the Banish Hall Guards, cast flinty dark blue eyes at the wide-eyed Kaston.

The young man was still numb from the news that he had been chosen to join the Guards as a reward for warning the village of the attacking Ghouls. Now on a no-nonsense tour of the Banish Hall practice fields, he followed the Captain as if he were caught in a extraordinary dream.

The two lieutenants, stripped to their light brown undershirts with the sleeves torn off for greater movement and black leather leggings, worked their staffs against each other with all the grace and skill of an intricate dance. Kaston studied the tautness of the muscles and the steely concentration on the combatants' faces as they swung their weapons with swift deftness at each other and ended in sharp clashes of wood. He was curious because the pair of lieutenants had been sparring like this for thirty years since they were comrades in the Onbersan Wars and were joined together as life companions on the blood-soaked battlefield of Luklain, thinking they wouldn't live to see the end of the next day.

When the sweat-soaked pair completed their sparring, they bowed formally to each other and approached Captain Janvil and the newcomer.

The Captain nodded in appreciation. "Nice work. This is Kaston Trint, our new recruit. Kaston, meet my lieutenants Rane and Fent Inderson-Lintan."

Rane, tall and lean, rubbed the moisture off her brow with a leather wristband and pushed short strands of soaked red hair away from her face. "It's been a while since we had someone from the nursery." She grinned as she ran an emerald eye over the young man.

Kaston straightened. "I'm eighteen."

Fent casually swept his staff against the young man's legs, and toppled him into the dirt. "He knows how to fall." The black-haired warrior flashed amused blue eyes at the Captain.

Kaston scowled but accepted the end of Rane's staff to pull himself to his feet. As he brushed off his clothes, he found himself back on the ground.

"He's got a lot to learn about being alert." Rane absently twirled her staff.

Janvil grinned. "I have every confidence in your ability to make a Guard out of him. He seems to think that this is a reward for warning the village about the Ghouls." He and the lieutenants snorted a laugh.

As Kaston climbed to his feet, the scowl deepened, but he kept his thoughts to himself. He had what it took to be a Banish Hall Guard, and he certainly could take their teasing like a man.

The lieutenants eyed him as he straightened and looked back at them, the scowl turning into a challenge. Fent thoughtfully nodded. "I think we can do something with him."

"I leave him in your care," Janvil said as his two lieutenants snapped to attention and saluted.

"You're a skinny thing," Rane commented as the lieutenants turned towards the dormitory. "Quite a runner though." Fent guffawed at this. "The next time you run like your life depends on it, it will be towards the enemy, not away from them."

"Yes, lieutenant," Kaston responded, following behind the pair. Fent and Rane exchanged amused glances.

"What do you know about the Banish Hall?" Fent asked as they strolled into the barracks.

"It's where an Athronian is banished to." Kaston gawked at the long chamber. Neatly made pallets lined one wall. The rest of the space was given over to bits of furniture, a games table, and a wall rack supporting a number of well worn weapons. This was home for a dozen Guards, and it held a bit of each of them in the decor.

"This is your pallet. Leave your stuff here." Fent nodded to a pallet farthest from the door they had entered. Kaston dropped his bundle on the pallet. Before he had a chance to take a better look at his new home the lieutenants were out the back door.

"And how often does that happen?" Rane asked as they crossed a small yard to a round stone building with smoke rolling furiously from the chimney.

"What?" Kaston looked at her confused.

"How often is an Athronian banished to this spot?"

They stepped into a cramped kitchen where Lyre Monoron and her two teenage daughters were preparing the midday meal. Kaston glanced at the girls who hid smiles behind their hands. He had danced with both of them at the Spring Festival and couldn't decide which one he liked the best. As the color rose in his cheeks, the young man turned to the lieutenants, who watched him with expectant expressions not revealing their amusement.

"There has never been a banishment since the Hall was built," Kaston answered.

"You didn't sleep through school," Fent commented in an approving tone. "Distractions are another thing. We'll have to work on that." Kaston flushed as they entered the refectory. The chamber had two long rough-hewed tables with equally rough benches.

"Meals are at the sixth, twelfth and seventeenth bell," Rane explained. "If you want food any other time, you'll have to flirt with the Monoron girls." Kaston stared at her to determine if she was kidding. The tough lieutenant only raised an eyebrow and strode to the door leading to the Banish Hall.

Fent laid a friendly hand on Kaston's shoulder. "She has a very dry sense of humor. Since there has never been a banishment to this Hall, what do you think the Banish Hall Guards do?"

Kaston frowned at this. "They guard the Hall."

"Why are we guarding the Hall?" Fent pressed as they ducked through the small door in the back of the formidable round building.

Kaston stared in awe at the large rounded chamber rising to a cupola of smooth marble. Windows wound around the upper part of the wall allowing sunlight to stream in throughout the day. Their footfalls against the dark polished flagstones broke the hanging silence as the brooding stone walls glared ominously at the intrusion. Near the large wooden double doors at the front of the building stood the ever present Guard.

"We must always be prepared for a banishment," Kaston replied. "It is the responsibility of the community to deal with a banished Athronian according to the laws of Onbersan."

"We are also responsible for protecting Baniston so it can fulfill its special duties to the Crown," Rane added.

"Why do you think there hasn't been a banishment in so long?" Kaston asked. The stark emptiness of the chamber was unsettling.

"We don't know the minds of the Athronians." Rane sauntered to the center of the Hall. "It takes a very serious crime to merit such an extreme punishment. Something that is aggressively against Athronian nature."

"Only Apprentices, Overseers, and High Overseers can be banished," Fent continued as he led the way through the heavy rounded double front doors of the Hall into the bright morning sun. "Ordinary Athronians are exiled to the Outland."

Kaston nodded. "That's where the Overseer Stories take place. You mean it's a real place?"

Fent and Rane chuckled but not unkindly. "It's a real place all right, and you should be thankful for it considering that we're all descendants of Outlanders."

"But those are just stories," Kaston protested, remembering the tales of how their civilization was born.

"It is up to you to decide what you believe or not about the past," Fent said. "To be a Guard, all you have to believe in are Athronians."

Mariet had forgotten to tell Panute that old Professor Gris was back and haunting the musty vaults deep beneath the Archives of Tanabran. Panute always enjoyed the long chats the old Professor had a talent for indulging. Of course, Panute was interested in anything to do with prophecy. A waste of a good mind in Mariet's opinion. As far as he was concerned, prophecy didn't even deserve a place in the University curriculum, but not many shared his passion for mathematics.

The Archives held many more manuscripts and books on subjects of little substance and consequence, in his opinion, than on the really important subjects such as the physical and biological sciences and, of course, mathematics. But Mariet could not fault it too much since his position as Archivist gave him the opportunity to indulge his study of his chosen subject. He was only reminded of these frivolous pursuits in the name of higher learning when he had to serve at the desk near the entrance of the Archives. The Head Archivist warned him about the consequences of being too one-sided in his intellectual passions and put him on the desk to force his interaction with the other Archivists and the Scholars who used the Archives.

In spite of himself, he found Professor Gris an interesting old character even if he went on too much about the importance of prophecy. The old man had a compelling personality, the kind that marked an excellent professor. He could pull students to him based on personality alone. Mariet half wished more professors of mathematics were as personable.

Laughter cut through the silent main corridor behind him. Panute's laughter. Several heartbeats later, a tall woman in an orange Archivist robe appeared on the arm of an amiable man sporting a black Professorial robe with a white sash tied around the middle. The insignia for prophecy was delicately embroidered down the middle of the sash. Despite his gray hair, he did not look as old as he probably was. Some people were just lucky when it came to showing their age, Mariet mused to himself.

Panute Taner, a stately woman in her forties, did look her age with gray streaks through her pile of black hair and small creases on the edge of her clear blue eyes. Around Professor Gris, she lost much of her elegant reserve and reverted to somewhere between her first and second year at the University. Mariet shook his head. Maybe the old man had been her Professor and she had a crush on him then. That would almost forgive her excessive enthusiasm for his company whenever he came to the Archives.

The Professor grinned. "There's my friend Mariet."

"It's been a while, Professor," Mariet greeted. At least he didn't have to force being amiable around him. "You know how much we all miss you." He tried to keep the dryness out of his voice as he cast an amused glance at Panute.

"I may be retired, but I still try to keep busy," the Professor returned. "I get to do all the things I couldn't do when I had to teach the likes of this young thing here." He laid an affectionate hand over Panute's, which was resting on his arm.

"Now, now, Professor." Panute smiled at him. At least she refrained from giggling. Mariet was not sure if he could take hearing a woman of her age giggle.

"I'm going to show Panute an interesting manuscript with a most intriguing prophecy in it," Gris announced. "Would you like to join us?"

"Uh. I don't think so, Professor. Although, it was nice of you to ask." Mariet was concentrating so hard on making his refusal friendly that he didn't notice the flashes of amusement flitting around Panute's eyes.

"You really should open yourself to these new experiences," the Professor gently teased. "Who knows, you may find something else that interests you."

"Thank you. But I am more than content with mathematics," Mariet returned, without realizing that he was being teased. Why was everyone always trying to get him to change? he wondered as he watched the pair saunter to the staircase.

As they plunged into the musty gloom of the Archives cellar where piles of neglected and unsorted manuscripts and books were left to take care of themselves, Panute affectionately pounded a fist into Gris's upper arm. "Why do you always tease the poor boy like that?"

Gris chuckled. "Because he opens himself up too easily to teasing."

"What would you have done if he had decided to come with us?" Panute asked.

"Someone once told me that we are only truly living when we take the risk of failing," Gris replied thoughtfully.

Panute wrinkled her brow. "Who was that?"

"Dorian. After she was pitched out of a tavern into a muddy

street not far from here in the middle of the night. She was so drunk she couldn't stand up, and I pulled her up by the scruff of her collar and demanded to know what she was doing there and was she aware what kind of trouble she could get into. She was maybe sixteen or seventeen at the time." An amused grin spread across Gris' face.

"And?"

"She simply looked at me and said that wonderful line."

"For all her youthful antics, she was never a child," Panute muttered. "What did she fail at that night?"

"What she always fails at," Gris said thoughtfully. "Figuring out what makes us happy."

Panute stopped walking and looked at him. "That's very astute of you. I hadn't thought of that."

"That's why I'm the Overseer and you're only an Apprentice."

Panute gave him an alarmed look. "Say it louder, I don't think the researcher in the corner heard you." The Outlanders in Landersdown, where the Tanabran Archives were located, had not believed in Overseers for generations and would probably take their exchange as a joke. But Panute never felt comfortable mentioning anything concerning Athros while in the Outland.

"No one ever comes down here and you know it," Gris replied.

"I've never trusted those wards that Gracion gave you."

Gris raised an eyebrow at her. "Are you suggesting that I shouldn't trust a fellow Overseer?"

"I've always been uncomfortable around Gracion. Why would anyone want to study sorcery?" Panute shuddered.

"Many people wonder why anyone would want to study prophecy," Gris teased. "Or mathematics." Panute choked back a laugh. "It's just a little farther." He held a small glowstone in front of them to illuminate the musty gloom. The Overseer took a deep breath when he stopped at an aisle of pile after pile of neglected manuscripts thick with dust and mold. He acted as if reluctant to go on. "It's down here."

"I would have never apprenticed to Prophecy if I'd known it was such dusty work," Panute grumbled, gingerly following him down the narrow aisle.

"I think you'll appreciate it when you see this," Gris said almost reverently. "Although appreciation can be double edged." He carefully lifted a filthy pile of manuscript sheets and revealed a small leather bound book he had taken the precaution of hiding there. "When I first read this, I slipped it under this pile of papers and walked away for three weeks. I needed to put what I had read into some kind of perspective."

"A prophecy?" Panute felt a chill without knowing why she should be frightened.

Gris opened the volume. The writing on the thick ancient parchment was small and neat. He carefully turned the pages until he stopped. Staring at the words, he wished that he had read them wrong but the same words glared back at him. He mutely handed the volume to Panute and with a forefinger indicated the place to read. Panute took the book, flashing Gris a curious glance. Focusing on the small script, she recognized an ancient language never widely used among Outlanders. As she read, she pulled the volume closer and closer to her eyes in disbelief.

Pale from the shock of the words, she lifted her eyes to Gris. "This can't possibly be a prophecy," she stammered out.

"This prophet is reliable. Very reliable. Even when she's wrong, it's not by much."

"What are you going to do?" Panute's words were filled with panic.

"This would land me in serious trouble with our High Overseers, I fear," Gris said sadly. "That is why I'm showing it to you. If I can pull it off, they will never find out about it."

"But the truthstone," Panute protested, devastated by what Gris was proposing. The old man held up a hand.

"The truthstone is why I cannot withhold the prophecy from them, unless I do something daring."

"What do you mean by 'daring'?" Panute was almost shaking with the desire to beat sense into this dear old man whom she loved like a father.

Gris sighed. "I'm going to make up a prophecy even more shocking than this one. I'm betting that the High Overseers will be so upset over it that I won't be given the chance to reveal any other prophecies I may have found. They will force me into retirement to prevent the made-up prophecy from being revealed. I'm close to retiring anyway."

Panute was so upset that tears threatened to break through. "But what good would it do to retire and let the true prophecy go unrevealed?"

"I can proceed with my plan better if I am out from under the High Overseers' thumbs," Gris reasoned.

"But you'll be in The Land Out of Time, and we'll never see or hear from you again." That thought alone was distressing for Panute.

"Not if the prophecy comes to pass," Gris returned quietly.

Panute took several long deep breaths while thinking on the implications of the cryptic passage. "You think its fulfillment is that eminent?"

"I think that it has already begun," Gris said.

"Because of a single event?"

"A very significant event involving a very singular being," Gris emphasized with his forefinger. "The Overseer of Knowledge has been caught in an Attraction. It is certainly unprecedented and a surprise. The prophecy is very clear about that." He captured Panute's sad blue eyes with his own. "Since you are my best Apprentice, you will be the next Overseer. You will be in the unusual position of knowing a prophecy without ever having to reveal it to the High Overseers. If you happen to be questioned about the false prophecy, you won't know the content of it because I am not going to tell you. That will get you around the truthstone. You have not set foot in Athros for over two millennia except for your brief assistance in locating our wayward Overseer of Knowledge. I think nearly everyone has forgotten that you're even an Apprentice. If I am retired, you will be recalled to take the exam. Don't be happy about it since you are deep into the Hail Ragoon Prophecy."

"Which I am," Panute put-in.

"Of course. But you don't need to let them know that you'd drop it tomorrow for a chance to be Overseer." Gris grinned knowingly at her. "You must be upset at being dragged away from your work, and if they ask about contact with me, just tell them you saw me when I made my visits to my Apprentices scattered throughout the Outland."

"What good will it do to know the prophecy and not be able to reveal it?"

"If the catalyst for change—this unbelievable act of treachery and lying—takes place, then the prophecy will have to be revealed," Gris explained. "You must learn which Overseers to trust and be prepared to draw them in so they will be able to help our victim when the time comes. You must learn the made-up prophecy when you become Overseer and after the High Overseers are satisfied that you know nothing about it. I will personally put a copy of it in the Archives next to the Hail Ragoon

Prophecy if you wish. That way I bypass Dorian."

"Why should I know this prophecy?" Panute asked, distressed.

"Because its purpose is to prod the High Overseers into making several moves that will ensure that the real prophecy comes true." Gris pointed to the volume in Panute's hand.

Panute pressed a forefinger to her lip, piecing together the enormity of what they were about to do. "It's such a terrible thing, and you want to force it to happen?" she finally asked.

Gris bowed his head. "The prophecy must come true. Fortunately, the High Overseers only call me for meetings when I visit Athros. Barring any unforeseen reasons to go there, I'll still be around for a while." The old Overseer put a reassuring hand on his Apprentice's shoulder. He felt that he would be recalled to Athros sooner than later, but he didn't want to worry Panute any more than necessary. Not envying her part in this, he had confidence in her ability to get the job done. "Let me show you the place where Dorian was dumped so long ago. The tavern is now a respectable tea shop."

Panute managed a smile. "Maybe she made a lasting impact on it after all."

"Maybe." Gris nodded, wanting to put the future out of his mind, at least for the moment.

Chapter Four

Celebrations of Sorts

A child getting caught in an Attraction was a special occasion for parents. The event usually signified the beginning of maturity and independence for the offspring. Dorian's parents were doubly shocked and delighted, as it was considered impossible for an Overseer of Knowledge to be caught in an Attraction. Lengthy treatises were devoted to the subject and the fact that it had never happened before only bolstered the belief.

Dordan and Yanos Riverson, Apprentices to the Overseers of Gardens and of Culinary Delights, received the news at their places of work and, as was the custom, were given the rest of the day to prepare for receiving the newest member of the family.

Dordan was an older version of her daughter, a finger length taller and with patches of white at the temples of her short cut black hair. The gray eyes were the same, except Dordan's did not have the sharp focus that some found daunting, even intimidating, when Dorian chose to level a gaze at them. Possessing the gentle disposition of a gardener, she was mother to all the plants in the sprawling exquisite Central Gardens.

Yanos already had a batch of the delectable pastries that were his specialty baking in the spacious stone oven when he heard the back door bang shut. Knowing Dordan's excited moods, he put down his bowl of flour and wiped his hands on his apron before she flung herself into his arms.

Yanos was a jolly man who preferred to laugh and have those around him at their ease. He had a crumple of curly blonde hair and was on the pudgy side, given his culinary specialty. Niether Dorian nor Jac had a sweet tooth, so they could not completely appreciate their fathers' work. His eyes had a blue twinkle and at the moment were brimming with moisture as he held Dordan. They felt only pride for their daughter, who was the first in either family to become an Overseer.

"I'm still numb from the news," Dordan cried excitedly. "Our Dorian is going to have a life companion. I just can't believe it. An Outlander. What are the odds that an Outlander would be a match for the Overseer of Knowledge?"

Yanos beamed. "Not enough that it's ever happened before. But that doesn't matter. It happened to our Overseer, and that's all that counts."

"How much time do we have before they get here?" Dordan's mind ran with the thousands of things that she had to do to make their home ready for the newest member of the family.

"Zore sent a note saying that Jac and Dorian were going to help the Outlander, whose name is Devor Locke, with some kind of research he's doing." Yanos smiled affectionately at Dordan's tendency to overreact when she wasn't given the time to properly plan things. "They'll be here when they return to Athros."

Dordan frowned. "Research? That could take some time."

"They didn't think it would take that long," Yanos assured her. "If they can't finish it today, they will leave it for tomorrow. Dorian knows how much we want to celebrate this great news."

A sand mark later, Deiden and Yabot Riverson threw the front door open and ran into the house. The sets of twins greeted each other in a comical dance of excitement. All talking at once, it was long heartbeats before the cacophony would have been intelligible to anyone but the foursome.

The only way to tell the sets of twins apart was by their dress. Early on, they decided to wear certain colors. Dordan and Yanos sported shades of brown and green, and Deiden and Yabot preferred blues and grays. Being identical twins with Dordan and Yanos, Jac's parents were also Apprentices of Gardens and Culinary Arts, working side by side with their siblings most of the time. Because of this, they found out the news as quickly as Dorian's parents, but they had to stay at work until their daily chores were done. Even then, their Overseers took pity on them and sent them home early. Since Jac was older than Dorian, it was probable that this would be the only Attraction in the family for this generation.

Dorian wandered in at that moment, then stood at the threshold of the great room that dominated the house, watching in amusement as the elders chattered on excitedly. The four, noticing her at once, stopped their words and stared in surprise.

"Dorian!" Her mother quickly recovered, ran to her daughter, and caught her in a hug, with the other three quickly following. After they poured repeated congratulations over her, they realized that the other half of the Attraction was missing.

"Where is the lucky young man?" Yanos asked, looking around expectantly.

Dorian smiled slyly. "Waiting outside with Jac." Jac's parents were already halfway to the door, shouting for them to come in. "Devor's an orphan, so he hasn't had any experience with exuberant families."

Dordan laughed. "I'm sure he'll get used to it soon enough."

"Here's the young man," Yabot cried as they led in a politely confused Devor followed by a grinning Jac.

"Welcome to our home, Devor," Dordan greeted, as she and Yanos stood before the Outlander. "I am Dordan and this is Yanos. We welcome you as the future life companion of our daughter, Dorian."

"Thank you for your welcome. The honor is mine." Devor stammered out the words that Jac and Dorian had instructed him to say. Dorian's parents drew him into a hug. Devor tried to take this spontaneous display of affection as casually as possible; he just wished that Dorian and Jac weren't so amused by his obvious embarrassment. Biting back a grin, Dorian finally stepped forward and rescued him by gently pulling her parents away for another hug for herself.

"Come, come, let's all go into the garden and drink a toast to the happy couple," Yanos said expansively.

Dorian moved swiftly to Devor's side and grabbed his hand. Just that gesture allowed him to let go of the unfamiliar sensation of being a part of a family.

"They make the cutest couple," Dordan gushed as the sisters led the way into the sprawling back garden. Dorian rolled her eyes and gave Devor a devastating smile. All of a sudden, the bonding idea seemed too much of a formality. He was ready to drop everything and go through the joining ceremony right then.

"In the end, it's just between us." Dorian's eyes turned

thoughtful. "We play act for the others, so they can have their celebration and receive congratulations for their good fortune, as if they had something to with it. But at the end of the day we are the ones who have to deal with what has happened to us." Devor shook his head in understanding, thankful for her thoughtfulness to reassure him. Dorian's pensive smile became an affectionate grin. "If this silly medallion would let me, I'd kiss you." She laughed ruefully. "But that won't be for another few weeks."

Devor arched an eyebrow at her.

"It's the truth this time," she said regretfully, pulling him into the garden, her mother's other pride and joy.

Huask Gruhmer scowled and nodded to the bland faced Apprentice to Truth to let the visitor in. The High Overseer took a nibble from one of the plates of delicacies laid out before him on the small table he used for his morning meal. The elegantly decorated sitting room reflected his tastes, which were both refined and expensive.

A man wearing a well-tailored cloak and tunic that marked him as an Outlander merchant strode confidently through the door. He gave the room a quick appraising glance before settling his gaze on the gaunt, white-haired High Overseer. Huask, savoring another mouthful from the kitchens of the Overseer of Culinary Delights, raised irritated dark eyes to the visitor.

"You'd better have a good reason for interrupting my morning meal," the High Overseer growled.

Fenchan Parack rubbed his thin beard but did not betray that he felt intimidated by the disagreeable old man. "I think you'll be more than pleased by what I have for you," he said in a smooth voice that swayed many a bargaining session to his favor.

"What is it this time?" Huask impatiently pushed up the sleeves of his faded gold silk robe. "If it's not the Enceland Lamp, I'll be very disappointed," he added coldly, leveling a steady glare at the merchant.

The Outlander merchant met the glare with a sly grin. "I have something even better. A piece of information."

"What kind of information could you have that would be of any interest to me?" Huask returned his attention to meal.

"Information concerning a certain Overseer who is a particular favorite of yours." Fenchan watched as the High Overseer placed his fork down on the table.

"Go on," Huask prompted, narrowing his eyes at the merchant.

Fenchan spread out his hands. "Information such as this is worth at least as much as an Enceland Lamp."

"I can see the worth of a lamp before I put money down for it," Huask returned coldly.

"What kind of information would be worth the price of the Lamp?" the merchant countered.

"Nothing short of incriminating information for that particular Overseer," Huask replied.

"That is what I have."

"I will only accept it if you have first hand knowledge of this information," Huask warned.

"My knowledge is as first hand as it can get." Fenchan flashed a grin. "I am the source of the incriminating evidence."

Huask raised an eyebrow and leaned forward. "You passed some kind of merchandise to her?"

"Is it worth the price of an Enceland Lamp?" Fenchan's eyebrow matched that of the High Overseer.

Huask carefully cut a small mouthful of asparagus, and dipped it into the delicate yellow sauce before savoring the flavor. He knew he had to take chances to meet the demands of his ambition. The challenge was recognizing which chance he could not afford to ignore. With a decisive nod of his head, he decided that whatever Fenchan had to offer was most likely worthwhile testimony. The merchant had enough integrity to deal only in merchandise of the highest quality.

"The price of an Enceland Lamp," the High Overseer agreed. "Tell me the information."

"The day before yesterday while I was in my shop in Rerdon, a young woman dressed like a typical Rerdonian came in. I immediately recognized her as the Overseer in question. Beyond the clothing, she made no other attempt to disguise herself. Perhaps she thought that Outlanders today have forgotten what she looks like. And on the whole this is true. But I've seen her enough here in Athros to recognize her." The merchant noted Huask's intense interest in his words. "When I asked if I could assist her, she placed a slip of parchment before me. It was a list of several kinds of acids and exploding powders. The quantities and variety were such that made me suspect she's working on some kind of research into explosives. I sold her everything she wanted and was surprised that she did not take the parchment back."

"Do you have it with you?" Huask's eyes glowed in anticipation.

"She proved too clever for me." Fenchan sighed, privately amused at the High Overseer's eagerness for such evidence. "The parchment disintegrated right after she left the shop." Huask collapsed his ancient frame into the delicate wood chair, his disappointment much greater than Fenchan could ever imagine. "It wasn't until later that I realized that, research or not, explosives of any kind are not allowed in Athros. Even if she is doing her experimenting somewhere in the Outland, why would she be interested in creating explosions in the first place?"

"Exactly." Huask nodded, eyes half-closed as if savoring the possibilities flooding through his mind. "Thank you, Fenchan. This is truly worth the price." He pulled out a sheet of parchment from a small drawer in the table and scribbled a few words. "Don't forget I'm still interested in the Lamp." The High Overseer managed a crooked grin as he handed the merchant the note.

"You'll have the first one that comes my way." Fenchan bowed and strolled out of the chamber.

An uncharacteristic sound emitted from the dour High Overseer. The noise was a cross between a twitter and a chuckle threatening to take over his features in a genuine grin.

Kaston was tired of getting dumped every time a Guard passed by. He sat on the ground more often than walking on it lately. If the Guards weren't so amiable about it Kaston would be angry instead of plain disgusted at having his feet swept out from under him all day.

"So, you think you're ready to try the staff?" Morna asked in the casual manner adopted by all the Guards. Kaston took the hand she offered to get him back on his feet. The Guard was in her mid-twenties, tall and lean with long supple muscles from endless practice on her weapon of choice.

"The sooner the better," Kaston muttered but flashed Morna a weak grin.

Morna grinned back. "Don't let our bit of fun get to you. We'll tire of it quick enough. Long before you'll be able to dump any of us," she added strolling casually past him.

"Is that a challenge?" Kaston demanded as he followed after the raven haired Guard, considered one of village beauties. Of course, the young men of Baniston had to admire her from a safe distance since she was never without her staff.

Morna paused to let Kaston catch up with her and cast her pale blue eyes at him, allowing a rare close view of her fine high cheekbones and flawless tanned skin. "Everything around here is a challenge," she almost purred, absently twirling her staff between long strong fingers. "It keeps us focused and alert. Otherwise, we'd be bored silly."

Kaston scratched his head. "I never thought that it would be so difficult guarding a place where nothing ever happens."

Morna shrugged. "It's not so bad. At least it gives us the chance to train to be warriors. Many of us have joined the Royal Guard. Others have gone to fight in far-off wars." Her eyes looked distant as she envisioned a battlefield before her, the clash of metal and wood echoing in her ears.

"That's what I want," Kaston responded enthusiastically. "I want to be a warrior. Fight in a great battle."

Morna laughed. "We'll have to toughen you up for that. Get some muscles on those skinny bones."

Kaston straightened. "I'm ready any time you are." The next person who called him skinny was going to see how tough he really was.

They entered a long shed opened at both ends. The walls were lined with a collection of staffs, swords, bows, and daggers, but Morna walked past them to a plain staff leaning in the far corner. "This will be yours until you have earned the privilege to wield one with the Mark of the Guard upon it." She tossed him the staff.

Kaston wrapped his hands around the wood, surprised at how awkward and unnatural it felt. He immediately feared he wouldn't be able to learn to use it. Morna's staff seemed to be an extension not only of her arms but also of her soul as well.

Noticing Kaston's perplexed frown, Morna allowed a small smile to touch her lips. "I remember the first time I picked up a staff," she mused. "I thought it was impossible to hold. It felt so solid, so unforgiving. I don't know how it happened, but after working with it for a time it became the most natural thing in my hands."

"I see what you mean about the solid feel," Kaston commented, feeling a little better about his initial reaction to the weapon.

"Come on, I'll show you some moves to get you started." Morna led the way to one of the practice fields. "To get used to it, carry it with you all the time. Make it a part of you."

"Why did Captain Janvil decide for me to learn the staff rather than the sword?" Kaston asked. Not that he was about to protest. Although he would never admit it, he found swords a bit daunting and was more than relieved when the Captain thought the staff was a better choice for him.

"You are physically more suited for the staff," Morna replied. "At least right now you are. Swords require a lot more bulk and muscles. Perhaps you may end up a sword bearer, but for now, the staff is the best weapon for you. We become proficient on all the weapons in the armory. What we chose as our favorite is up to us."

Kaston nodded. He followed Morna's example and stripped off his black leather tunic to the loose brown cotton shirt underneath.

"So, what possessed you to run from the Ghouls like that?" Morna asked, casual as ever, as she demonstrated the proper way to hold the staff.

Kaston tore his attention away from the placement of his fingers and looked into her curious eyes. "Running seemed like the best thing to do." He shrugged with a bit of humor glinting in his hazel eyes.

"You knew they would have outrun you eventually," Morna commented, as she made minor adjustments to his hands. "That's the proper grip, remember how it feels." Kaston thought that it felt even more awkward, but he knew better than to say anything. "Did you really think you could beat them to Baniston?"

"Not really," the young man admitted. "But I knew I had to try."

Morna gave him a re-appraising look, then she grinned and slapped him on the back, causing him to lurch forward. She was stronger than she looked, and she looked strong enough.

"That's thinking like a Guard." She laughed, hitting her staff against his. As expected, his staff was on the ground before he knew what happened. "Time to learn how to keep that grip once you have it. Catch this." She pulled a small object from her belt pouch and tossed it to him. Without thinking Kaston caught it. "Good reflexes."

Kaston looked at the gold stone in his hand. "What a strange looking stone."

"Isn't it though?" Morna returned, keeping her expression blank. "Toss it back. Just testing your reflexes." After catching the stone, she glanced in the direction of Janvil's quarters on the edge of the practice field. The Captain stood outside his door visiting with Elder Trudlin. The Guard gave the stone a few tosses in the air before returning it to her pouch. Noting that Kaston had the proper grip on his staff, she casually twirled her staff and swept it against his legs.

"I wish you'd quit doing that." He sat disgusted, with his elbows on his knees.

Morna stood over him. "Just a reminder that the proper grip is only a small part of fighting."

"I think I've learned that lesson well enough," Kaston responded, accepting Morna's hand to pull himself to his feet. "It'll be just my luck that my best skill is falling down."

Laughing, Morna picked up his staff and handed it to him. "Not a bad skill to have. Now, let's see what you can do standing up."

Her eyes still twinkling, the Guard nodded to Elder Trudlin as the older woman passed by. The Elder nodded back, concealing her delight in the results of her little experiment. She really needed to learn to follow her hunches more often. The Land Out of Time had more surprises in it than any of them could begin to suspect. The Elder's delicate features creased in a broad grin as she stepped onto the green, away from the curious eyes of the Guards.

Kwen carefully stretched his back while massaging the stiffness from his shoulder. Sometimes he wondered why he continued these nightly vigils hunched over piles of books and manuscripts with no lighting other than a dim glowstone. The chill of the evening seemed more intense in the dark cavernous sorting chamber, and lately, even his woolen tunic could not stop it from prickling his skin. Each chill from the breeze reminded him that he was not a young man anymore. This type of introspection usually led him to face the reality that he would never be Overseer of Knowledge because Dorian was so much younger.

Then why am I doing this? Sometimes, like this night when

the breeze had the musty scent of rain on it, he would ask himself that question enough to stop work and go over all the justifications he had made up through the years. His whole world came down to the fact that someone had to be prepared to step in as Overseer. Orvid, the previous Overseer, had simply disappeared. The idea frightened the controlled Athronians almost beyond reason. Overseers did not disappear without a trace of foul play or intent. A shiver having nothing to do with the now gusting wind fluttered through him.

Kwen blinked at a flickering light outside of the chamber. A glowstone swaying on a short chain illuminated a fellow Apprentice stepping into the chamber. Bary Jolner paused just within the walls as his eyes adjusted.

"I thought I'd find you here." His grin could be heard in his naturally jovial voice.

"Just catching up on a few things." Kwen self-consciously brushed his hands on his woolen leggings. Although his nocturnal work habits were well known, he still was embarrassed when caught at it.

"Whatever you say." Bary waved his hand. "A bunch of us were having an ale at The Silver Mountain, and we got to talking about Dorian's bonding."

"What else?" Kwen jokingly rolled his eyes.

Bary shrugged. "It is an unprecedented event. Anyway, we thought it would be nice to pitch in and get her a joining gift."

Kwen nodded. "Good idea. We should let her know that we don't have any hard feelings that she got caught in an Attraction."

Bary shook his head. "I think we got over not being able to get caught in an Attraction years ago."

"As did she," Kwen reminded him. "I can imagine her surprise."

"No kidding." Only a few Apprentices to Knowledge had ever been caught in an Attraction, and these bonded few spent the rest of their lives knowing that they would never be Overseer. Everyone believed the quote from the writings on Athronian life by Orvid that was repeated so often in treatises and history books that nearly every Athronian had it memorized. It said that an Overseer of Knowledge could never be caught in an Attraction, and the fact that it never happened proved the statement as truth. Never happened until that day.

"Let me know how much for my share."

Kwen turned back to the piles of knowledge before him and the reason why he was there came painfully into focus. He had nothing else to live for.

Chapter
Five

Choice of Weapons

"How did you ever start making the connection between events?" Dorian looked up from the papers she was signing.

Devor pulled his attention away from his surroundings. He had taken a week to persuade Dorian to let him see the celebrated place where all the knowledge of his world was brought to be sorted and memorized before being housed in the equally famous Athros Archives. He was delighted to discover that the cavernous chamber that was depicted as a white marbled temple of knowledge in the Overseer Stories was just a large open-sided structure in the courtyards of Palmathon University.

Devor shrugged. "I don't know. It started with one, then the others just became clear."

Dorian smiled. "Spoken like a true Researcher. Do you think what happened to us is a part of this phenomenon?"

"Do you really think it all adds up to a phenomenon?"

"Or just a lot of coincidences," Dorian replied. "It's hard to prove one way or another. That's what makes it so irresistible."

A muffled explosion and a flash of bright light yanked their attention to a corner of the chamber where the Apprentices rummaged through the knowledge. The Apprentices jumped back, too alarmed to even think, as a cloud of smoke puffed out from where Kwen had just picked up a stone tablet.

Dorian was on her feet and at Kwen's side before the dust cloud settled. "Are you all right, Kwen?" Dorian was trembling. The blast pulled up memories of the time she got caught on the losing side of an Outland war. That war was one of the few times she wished she had not followed her need to experience what she read about.

"I'm fine," Kwen gasped. "When I picked up this tablet, the book underneath it smoldered and exploded."

Dorian studied the remnants of the book, wisps of smoke still rising from it. "Someone get Lincim. It may be a demented practical joke, but we must be sure everything is safe before we continue work."

Their attention turned to a half-dozen gray robed students running through the wide openings where the walls were pulled back to let in the fresh air. Blinking at the confusion in the chamber, they stood for a heartbeat trying to find Dorian. Motioning to Devor to follow, Dorian approached the breathless students.

"There was an explosion in the chemistry lab," an older student panted. "Strange markings were etched on the table. The Overseer of Language cannot decipher them."

"Explosion?" Dorian reacted in confusion. Two explosions at once? In a city where explosives were prohibited? Something very strange was going on. "Tell Lincim what happened when he comes," she yelled over her shoulder to her equally confounded Apprentices as she ran into the sunlight to the chemistry building. Devor and the students followed close behind.

Dorian ran a hand through her thick hair as she stared at the wildly engraved figures on the long, ancient worktable in the chemistry classroom. The small group of gray robed students and professors hovering near the door knew better than to disturb the Overseer of Knowledge. Wanian, the Overseer of Language, stood staring out the window, pushing out all distractions while trying to place the angry markings.

"Do you have any idea what this means?" Devor had never seen such a script, if it was indeed a script. Its fierceness was almost horrific.

"No," Dorian returned quietly and simply. That admission in itself was both shocking and frightening. She thought she knew every language, both living and long dead. Stunned, Devor stared at her. "I know. I'm supposed to know these things," Dorian muttered, glancing at the lanky chemistry professor. "Professor. I'm afraid we're going to have to remove this table to the Archives for further study. You see, a small explosion happened in the sorting chamber not too long ago." The students murmured uneasily. "If this is the work of a prankster, then we must leave the evidence intact."

"But what does it say?" Professor Tibbits pressed.

"That's the mystery. The fact that it seems made-up makes me think that this is a prank," Dorian commented as she felt Devor's curious eyes on her. Sometimes the Overseer of Knowledge had to hedge around the truth until what may be a serious problem could be worked through without setting off undue alarm. "It looks like script but could be random scribbling or a code."

"It must be a prank," Wanian murmured, feeling a little better that he couldn't decipher the script.

Two explosions going off in Athros, where the materials to create explosives were banned, was certainly a mystery. And the script. The only way the script could have been created was through sorcery. No doubt every Apprentice to Sorcery would be put to the truthstone, but something told Dorian that they were not the source of the script or the explosions.

"Are you disappointed?" She asked, feeling Devor's silence as they navigated the twisting corridors of the chemistry building.

"You handled it very well," Devor responded. He was startled by her question.

Dorian glanced back at him trying to read his expression. "But that's not the way the Overseer of Knowledge behaves in the Stories."

Devor grinned. "Nothing I've seen here is how it is in the Stories. Besides, you're not the Overseer of Knowledge in the Stories. You're the lazy, undisciplined Apprentice who is always getting the Apprentice to Mischief into trouble."

Dorian grinned back. "It's good to know my image will stay its lovable tarnished self even after I've moved on to more respectable things. Are the people in Landersdown aware that Orvid disappeared and that I've replaced him?"

"It was announced by the Royal Scribes a millennium ago, but that doesn't change the old stories," Devor returned, blinking at what he just said. A millennium, yet in Athros she was younger than he.

"A millennium," Dorian mused. "I was very young when Jac and I added our bit to the Overseer Stories. A millennium. They still believed in Overseers then," she added thoughtfully. "The Chroniclers always said that if there weren't a Jac and Dorian to liven up the Overseer Stories the people would have made us up."

Devor chuckled. "You're probably right."

"Yet, it wasn't enough to keep the Outlander's interest in us." They stepped into the chaotic sorting chamber. A challenge to occupy her mind was refreshing. Sighing a little, she glanced at Devor. The timing could have been better.

At this time of day right before the evening meal, Trudlin knew that Gretna spent some quiet time in her tiny parlor. She also knew that Gretna wouldn't mind being disturbed with the kind of news that she could barely hold inside. Deftly threading her short slender frame around the almost empty Apprentice desks, the Retired Overseer of the Body could not keep a silly grin off her face. After strolling through the opened door of Gretna's office, she turned to the doorless passage that led to the snug parlor.

"Out collecting Athronians?" Elder Gretna, relaxing in her favorite chair, asked as Trudlin plopped down onto the soft couch.

"Found two." Trudlin valiantly tried to suppress a smug expression.

Gretna sat up startled. "Two? How can this be?"

Trudlin absently tapped the wooden arm of the sofa. "I've been thinking this over. We've always thought that the Outlanders were just Outlanders. It never occurred to us to routinely test them for Athronian blood."

"If there were hordes of Athronians running around, there would be Attractions," Gretna countered. "I have never heard of any instance of an Attraction, at least not in this district."

"There aren't hordes of Athronians running around but a very small percent," Trudlin reasoned. "There can't be too many. Only a few Athronians here are capable of having children."

"Finding three in the same village without even trying

doesn't sound like a small percentage." Gretna leaned forward and poured a cup of tea for her friend.

"The three display extraordinary abilities," Trudlin reminded her.

"So you're suggesting that we watch out for unusually gifted Outlanders." Gretna arched an eyebrow at her.

Trudlin grinned. "Something like that."

The Head Elder handed Trudlin the delicate cup. "So, who else besides the boy?"

Trudlin shrugged. "Morna."

"Morna?" Gretna frowned. "What made you think of her?"

"I didn't. When I handed her the stone, it stayed gold in her hand." The Overseer of the Body couldn't hide her delight. "To cover the true purpose of the stone, I told her I was experimenting with how different bodies react to a mineral in the rock and that it may turn black or gold. I saw it remain gold in Kaston's hand, and she confirmed it with the signal we worked out."

"What do we know about their backgrounds?" An interesting idea was forming in the back of Gretna's mind.

"Kaston's a member of the Trint clan."

Gretna nodded. "The Trints. Well off and extremely clannish. Who claims to be his parents?"

Trudlin shook her head. "That's the strange thing. I don't think any of them do. He seems to be everyone's nephew or cousin. But he's definitely a Trint. There's no mistaking the family resemblance. Now Morna's a different story. As you know, Rane and Fent took her in when she was a child. The lieutenants rescued her from a battlefield right before they came here to join the Guards. No one has any idea who her parents are or where she's originally from. The only thing that might be a link to her past is the ring that was on a chain around her neck when she was found."

"The ring she now wears."

"It has an unusual design," Trudlin mused. "She's been in the Archives on more than one occasion going through our volumes on family insignias trying to track it down."

"So she's curious about her ancestry."

"Wouldn't you be?" Trudlin asked. "I doubt she could have found a life she's more suited to, and I don't think she would trade being a warrior for anything else. Not to mention her devotion to Rane and Fent. But she wants to solve this puzzle in her life."

"You think being proficient with a staff is an exceptional skill?"

Trudlin took a long sip of tea. "That's not her only skill. She can read a body as easily as we can read a book."

"She does seem to have a knack for anticipating her opponents' moves," the Head Elder mused.

"Observe her sometime when she's not sparring."

Gretna chuckled. "You mean when she's asleep?"

"She's taken me by surprise a number of times with her eagerness to discuss various injuries suffered by her comrades," Trudlin continued. "She seems to know the injuries in a little more detail than I would expect. I just thought she was extra observant and had run across some of the anatomy books during her visits to the Archives. Sometimes her knowledge and observations were a little unexpected but not quite enough to make me suspicious."

"Are you going to tell her? And Kaston for that matter?" Gretna asked. "Having the gifts and not developing them is against Athronian principles. True, we're not in Athros, but we're not in the Outland either. The Land Out of Time is a study in the unique development of social and political structures. The idea of actually cultivating Athronian blood here may be a worthwhile pursuit."

"I think we should have a plan before springing this news on them," the smaller woman stated. "It was a shock for Janin and would have been even harder for her if we couldn't provide her with a safe environment to develop her talent."

"Maybe our school can be for more than training Elders," Gretna said as the radical nature of the idea took hold.

"Our own little Athros? It's an interesting thought." Trudlin caught Gretna's look. "The Queen may not be pleased with the idea."

None of the Elders could figure out how the Queen of Onbersan's mind worked. Royal meddling in other districts kept the Elders alert to the political undulations that occasionally rolled from the capital city of Praen. So far, their sleepy district, having nothing to offer in natural resources and being geographically remote, remained untouched by ambitious speculators.

"Who knows how she would react, given her hobby of collecting Athronian artifacts." Gretna wrinkled her brow.

Trudlin shook her head. "Not just any kind of artifacts. Only those that are a part of an Overseer's trade."

"She thinks that they'll bring her power," Gretna scoffed. "They're tools for those who already have the power to use them."

"She'll never understand that." Trudlin rested her thoughtful brown eyes on Gretna. "Which means we have to keep our Athronians a secret. At least for a while."

"Here's to secrets." Gretna raised to cup.

"And you were afraid being an Elder wouldn't be challenging enough." Trudlin grinned as she lifted her cup.

The Overseer of Mischief was an expert on the art of getting into trouble by prankish behavior. When the behavior broke the law, it became the domain of the Overseer of Crime. Causing explosions or leaving cryptic messages was not in itself breaking the law as it was currently written in the legal tomes. Damaging property was. In the case of the mysterious explosions, the issue of who oversaw the case was a question of intent. Were the explosives set off with the purpose of damaging property or was the damage an unintended result? Motive always determined who performed the primary investigation in a case.

The question of whether causing an explosion in Athros was a violation of the law had never been debated, so it was not in the massive tomes of judicial interpretations. That was one of the peculiarities of Athronian law. A legal declaration added to the law by the Society of Overseers did not become a law until it was broken. Only then was it debated by the Society of Overseers. The law concerning explosions had never been broken. Something a cunning mischief-maker could take advantage of, given the trend of rarely receiving a conviction for the first challenge of a law.

By gathering and piecing together the evidence, Lincim Sonterly, the Overseer of Mischief, conducted a methodical investigation. The placid lean Overseer with graying wisps of blond hair and dark blue eyes possessed the right combination of knowledge and deductive skills for solving puzzles like the explosives case. Patient and unruffled, he could whittle away at a knotted mystery until the solution was all that was left.

Jac spent two days following Lincim, helping him take samples from the burnt book and table and scribbling down eyewitness accounts. Beyond discovering a common explosive material, they were not any closer to solving the puzzle. The most interesting discovery was that the acid solution used by Professor Tibbits in his experiment was partially responsible for the etched script. Jac mused to himself that this was a mystery for the Institute of Uncommon Phenomenon. For Athronians, it meant calling upon the Overseer of Magic.

Jac rolled his eyes when Jadrick Kant, Overseer of Magic, arrived with his entourage of Apprentices. Jadrick sported a garish red and gold cloak that hurt Jac's eyes. Each Apprentice, basking in the certainty that they were to be the next great Overseer of Magic, had equally appalling cloaks in as many unique color combinations as the lack of tasteful imagination could produce. This group rivaled the Apprentices to Theater in ego and an unabashed need for attention.

All the items touched by the explosions were in one of the work rooms in the Archives. The low ceiling chamber had far too many Apprentices idling about, certain that their very presence would give their Overseer the edge needed to solve this mystery. For Jac, it was bad enough having all the Apprentices to Mischief engaged in hot debates, but with the arrival of the Apprentices to Magic, the interactions rapidly deteriorated into boasting and posturing matches.

Jac, never possessing the ambition to become an Overseer, stayed quietly at Lincim's side, taking notes for him and holding the palette of picks and tweezers and sample bags. The Overseer made his selection from these tools with the seriousness of an Overseer of the Body. As usual, Jac's attempt at not being ambitious set him up to become the next Overseer of Mischief. By remaining at the side of the Overseer, he received a good grounding in how an Overseer of Mischief's mind worked. Lincim was aware of this and had the good sense not to mention it to Jac. The last thing he wanted to do was scare him off. Besides, he made an invaluable assistant and never tried to make suggestions or impress the Overseer with what he knew. Jac didn't need to distinguish himself. That had been done long ago when he was under the influence of his cousin. If anything, he was trying to live down his notorious youth.

The Overseer of Magic approached them and flourished a bow. "Where's your cousin, young man?" Jadrick squinted at Jac. Jac tried not to grin at the poorly dyed black hair that hung in clumps around the Overseer's pudgy shoulders.

"At work?" Jac raised an eyebrow as Jadrick steadied his

watery blue eyes on him.

"Why isn't she here?" Jadrick demanded theatrically. "She was on the scene for both these incidents."

"She's made her reports," Lincim stated calmly. This occasion wasn't the first time Jadrick wanted to have Dorian around to make up for his shortcomings. The skill level for the Overseer of Magic was not as precise as that for some of the positions that required good solid knowledge. Even the ability to put on a performance rated higher than being a scholar of magic. "It isn't her place to be involved in the investigation. She knows that."

"I just thought..." Jadrick stumbled around for a few heartbeats. "You're right. I've got so much on my mind, I wasn't thinking."

Lincim flashed Jac a stern warning look before a less than reverent response popped out. Jac sighed and straightened the implements on the palette.

"You've got the next best thing," Lincim deadpanned. "Our very own Dorian look alike." Jadrick smirked at the old joke.

The Overseer of Magic took a slow stroll up and down the length of the table. "What an angry looking script," was all he could manage until he saw the expectant looks of nearly everyone in the chamber. That was the problem with this kind of situation. Everyone expected an on the spot analysis. Whereas Dorian had a gift for it, he always felt like an idiot. "Professor Tibbits was performing an experiment for his class." Jadrick's voice took on a dramatic air to cover the lack of substance and originality behind his words. "He placed the flask of an acid solution in the middle of the table. It exploded, the solution spread across the table, and when it burned off, this script was etched into the table. It is clear that the table was prepared beforehand with several coats of different solutions that control the destructive action of the acid."

"Professor Tibbits told us that there was nothing in the flask that would cause it to explode, no matter what it happened to interact with on the table," Lincim informed him steadily.

"Meaning, either the flask itself had been prepared before the experiment or it was set off by some airborne stimulant..."

A commotion from the surrounding group revealed a brown robed Apprentice to the Overseer of Geology pushing her way through to Lincim and Jadrick.

"The Rock of Teyerbom," the young woman gasped, trying to catch her breath.

"What about the Rock of Teyerbom?" Lincim asked patiently.

"It somehow jumped so that it is teetering on the Pinnacle of Enra," the Apprentice finally stammered out.

"Jumped? Teetering?" Jadrick's jaw dropped. "I didn't feel any seismic activity."

"There wasn't any," the Apprentice exclaimed excitedly. "It just moved on its own."

"This is the Banish Hall." Soral and Janin walked through the gaping double doors. Their footfalls died against the brooding black stone walls. "We sometimes come here to study and read. It's so peaceful."

They paused to watch a shadowy Guard perform a graceful dance with a staff on the other side of the floor. Concentrating on the drills that were as natural as breathing to her and creating new moves to challenge her skills, Morna reached out with a practiced sense in the direction of the newcomers. *Always be aware of everything around you. Your survival could depend on it.*

"A Guard is always here, day and night. They usually work on their drills to pass the time. It's the secret to why they're the best skilled fighters in the Royal Guard. They have plenty of time to practice."

Morna, coming out of her meditation, brought her movements to a halt. "Good morning, Soral." Casually leaning on her staff, she grinned at the Elders Assistant. "I heard there was a new Apprentice."

"There are no secrets around Morna," Soral said to Janin. "Fact or rumor, Morna hears it before anyone."

"Hello, Morna," Janin greeted.

"Hello back, Janin." Morna absently twirled her staff. "Some Apprentices balance sitting all day at a desk with learning a weapon or two."

"Morna's always looking for new sparring partners," Soral explained with a twinkle in her emerald eyes.

"I can't help it if I kill them all," Morna returned casually, catching Janin's widening eyes. "Figuratively speaking, that is." Soral grinned harder to keep from laughing out loud. The Guards were entertaining neighbors for the Apprentices. A surprising number of friendships resulted from their having to share the Banish Hall grounds.

"It's not that unheard of for those with a scholarly bent to become proficient in this kind of sport," Janin mused. "Dorian is supposed to be a master of the staff."

"That's only according to the Stories," Morna said, thoughtfully. "The Chroniclers had to think of some way for her to get out of those impossible scrapes."

"You don't think the Overseer Stories are true?" Janin asked, her curiosity piqued.

"They're probably based on things that really happened," Morna conceded. "But I'm sure they're exaggerated to make them more entertaining."

"Perhaps." Janin slowly nodded. "Why do you think it improbable that Dorian could be proficient with the staff?"

"She's just sixteen or seventeen in those stories. Not even old enough to develop that kind of skill," Morna reasoned. "It takes long years of steady dedication to be that good."

Soral gave Morna a wry look. "Weren't you considered a master at that age?"

"Yes, well..." Morna colored a little. "I began training at a very young age and didn't have other distractions."

"Rather, you didn't let anything else distract you," Soral clarified, knowingly. The Guard was just too striking looking, and the staff was one way for her to say without words that there was something beneath the physical beauty. Of course, the grace and muscle tone only increased her attractiveness. In time, she learned to deal with the admiring glances of others and even used her attractiveness to her advantage on occasion after Rane pointed out that it was just another weapon to use.

"So how do you know that Dorian did not learn the staff when she was young?" Janin pressed. "She only became an Apprentice to Knowledge by accident, after all."

"Is this discussion leading somewhere?" Morna's eyes sparkled with the recognition of a challenge in the making. Her staff swept the air in her deft hands.

"I think I could master the staff without having to give up my studies or my life."

"In five or six years, maybe." Morna was intrigued but would not think of betraying it.

"In five or six months, more like it," Janin countered.

Morna chuckled, even more intrigued by the challenge.

"You'd still be learning how to stand up from being dumped on the ground all the time."

"That would just depend on how good my instructor is, wouldn't it?" Janin kept her expression smooth as she noted a little tension underneath Morna's casual facade.

"An instructor's only as good as the pupil," Morna countered, raising an eyebrow.

"Then that would make us about even." Janin allowed a small smile to touch her lips.

"Do you know many Overseer Stories?" Morna asked, momentarily resting the staff against the back of her neck.

"I know them all. Or as many as I could find," the Apprentice returned. "I could never get enough of them when I was younger."

"I've only heard the ones told by the other Guards when there wasn't anything else to do on a cold night," Morna admitted with a hint of regret. "The ones about the battles or the amorous adventures but not many of the Dorian stories, except the real popular ones."

"I could tell you Overseer Stories in exchange for instruction with the staff. I mean real instruction. Not just what it takes to be a sparring partner," Janin bargained. "Do you think that is a fair enough trade?"

"Fair enough for me," Morna agreed.

"Bashing about with sticks isn't something you'll find me doing." Soral shook her blonde head. "I guess that's why I'm at the Elders School instead of guarding an empty hall."

"I believe in trying to experience things when possible," Janin explained. "It helps in my understanding."

"Just experiencing and becoming a master are two different things." Morna cocked an eye at her.

"I want to experience being a master," Janin rejoined, folding her arms with a wry expression on her face.

"I'll keep that in mind." Morna twirled her staff casually. "Five or six months from now when you finally figure out how to stay on your feet."

Chapter
Six

Challenges

The Rock of Teyerbom's incredible jump from the solid plateau to the pointed top of the Pinnacle of Enra was the kind of news that traveled almost instantly, and the park was already overflowing with curious onlookers. By the time Lincim and Jadrick, accompanied by their entourage of Apprentices, arrived at the Rock of Teyerbom's new home, a good number of Overseers, exchanging a cacophony of ideas and suggestions, were gathered below the Pinnacle. Apprentices loitering nearby in a much larger group echoed their Overseers. The rest of the Athronian citizenry were content to stay at a respectful distance.

Lincim and Jadrick were quickly pulled into the group of Overseers and pounded with questions, theories and suggestions before they even had a chance to look up at the Rock. "Magic. It can only be magic." Shawndoc, the Overseer of Geology, shook his finger at the Rock above them. "Nothing can move in nature like that. Nothing."

"If it is magic," Jadrick looked up, trying to stay calm and appear thoughtful, while actually feeling terrorized by the thought that it might be up to him to solve this puzzle, "it would mean that the magician is a master of the highest rank. I see hints of an obscure Outlander Branch of Physical Magic practiced several centuries ago." He made the mistake of casting a furtive glance at Dorian, who was observing the Rock from a different perspective several paces away from the group. She stared at him like he had grown an extra head. "Uh, yes. In other words, it's not your everyday magic."

Dorian shook her head and returned her gaze to the Rock above her. The sun sank a fraction lower in the sky, illuminating a protruding rough area on the underside of the Rock.

"Jadrick. In which century did these Outlanders practice this obscure kind of magic?" Dorian asked.

The group of Overseers gathered around Dorian and looked up. Jadrick gasped and rubbed his forehead with a loudly patterned handkerchief to recover himself.

"That looks like the same writing that's on the table," Lincim observed steadily. Jac squinted at the fierce writing etched into the bottom of the Rock and exchanged an expressionless glance with his cousin.

"Surely, something like this has happened before in all our long history," Lons Gudry, the Overseer of Art, commented as she shook out her rainbow colored shawl before resetting it onto her shoulders.

"If it has, it's never been recorded," Dorian responded quietly.

Lons settled a thoughtful gaze on the young Overseer. Much to the surprise of the regular citizenry of Athros, the Overseers had accepted this extremely young, notorious Apprentice into their society with a graciousness and goodwill that had the High Overseers raising a collective eyebrow. The High Overseers were more than prepared to deal with protests and appeared a little disappointed when one never erupted. After seven years, the Overseers still had problems seeing past her youth but never doubted Dorian's abilities as the Overseer of Knowledge. She did, after all, get the highest score ever achieved on the most difficult of the Overseer exams, taken under extreme circumstances.

Lons was intrigued by the contradictions that co-existed within Dorian's psyche. She was intellectual but worked her body into the tautness of an athlete. She was restless and mischievous yet possessed more sense, Lons always suspected, than the whole lot of them combined. And then there was the most recent twist in the life of Dorian Riverson.

The theory accepted as fact was that an Overseer of Knowledge could never be caught in an Attraction because it would only be a cerebral compatibility. Dorian shattered that myth when it was clear that her attraction to Devor was as much physical as cerebral. She was obviously as in love as anyone caught in an Attraction, with all the hand holding and staring into each other's eyes and not a discussion of volcanic ash deposits or Landersdown brewing techniques to be heard. With a faint smile touching her lips, Lons shifted her gaze to a nearby stone bench. Devor sat observing the scene with curiosity but never letting his attention stray from Dorian for very long.

"I thought Jadrick just said..." Shawndoc cut in.

Jadrick looked so distressed that Dorian stepped in without even thinking. "He said that it had hints of the magic performed several centuries ago by this obscure Outlander Branch of Physical Magic. He didn't say they did anything quite like this," Dorian clarified smoothly. The Overseer of Magic gave her such a look of relief and thanks that she was sure that alone would give him away, but everyone was too caught up in the stone balanced above them to notice.

"So what are we going to do about it?" Lincim finally asked. As far as anyone knew, this was the first time the Overseers had been confronted with a problem that none of them knew how to solve.

Dorian turned a puzzled eye to him. "Everything is new at some time or another. We can't expect to have encountered all the mysteries in the world."

Lons grinned broadly. She was right about Dorian having more sense than the rest of them.

"She's right, you know." Interwood Jincl, the Overseer of Mathematics, nodded vigorously. "The probability that there is only a set number of mysteries is very low, and the probability that we have found all of them is ever lower..."

"In other words, we simply need to put our minds together and work it out," Shawndoc stated, and they all talked at once, caught up in the idea of actually having to solve a mystery.

Jac watched his cousin and frowned as she slipped away from her colleagues and continued to scrutinize the Rock. He knew that something so great that she couldn't mention it to the others was troubling her.

Finally, Dorian sighed, walked to the stone bench, and sat next to Devor. He watched her just as intently as Jac. When the Overseer of Knowledge was deep in thought, it was certain that those thoughts had never been pondered before.

"What do you think?" Dorian asked, pulling herself away from the problem enough to smile at him.

"I think you've got some idea of what it is, and it's not a pleasant discovery," Devor replied.

Dorian quickly recovered from her startled expression before responding in a normal voice. "Can you really read my mind or is this just a trick you picked up from Jac?"

Devor looked at her with a flash of surprise before returning her steady thoughtful gaze. "I'm beginning to think that I can read your mind sometimes." He held her gaze until the heat rose in his cheeks.

Looking back at the Rock with a small, amused smile, Dorian murmured, "Perhaps you can at that."

Chuckling softly, Devor followed her gaze at the Rock. "What do you think?"

"I think you're right," she replied in a troubled voice.

The four Elders stood around the three large trunks sitting in the middle of the prison floor. A large chamber across from the prison cell had been used as a storage closet for centuries. Recognizing the need for more space for the Elders School, Gretna had decided a part of the third floor could be used without compromising the purpose of the area. They spent several days moving all the age encrusted remnants from the past into newly excavated cellars. Everything, that is, except for the three trunks.

When they had been pulled out of the chamber, Gretna had recognized the fine workmanship that could only be found in Athros. Such work was so rare in the Land Out of Time that she had actually gasped when she saw them. She had directed the trunks to be set aside and now there they were, covered with dust and mildew but not as aged as the other things removed from the chamber. The sides were fashioned from hard wood panels. The corners and locks were of tarnished silver etched with distinctive Athronian design and craftsmanship. The locks were keyless. Enigmatic smooth silver latches without a clue as to how to release them.

"Let's clean them off. Maybe there's an inscription or a symbol or something," Gretna suggested.

Carefully rubbing the grime from the locks, each Elder was

filled with emotions and sentiments they kept carefully packed away. This was too strong a reminder of the home that they loved and were to never see again.

"We need Janin up here," Gretna decided as the clean locks presented as much of a puzzle as they had when they were hidden behind the dirt. "Maybe her talent for making things happen by just thinking them can help."

Janin had visited the prison floor only once before when Soral had given her a tour. The idea that a place was maintained to hold an Athronian criminal made it seem more frightening than it actually was. The light color of the stone and the airy calm one felt belied the darker purpose. The ceiling curved into a simple, elegant dome and long, narrow windows sliced through the thick walls. A round stone table stood in the middle of the floor surrounded by neatly placed stone chairs. Dusted and swept every day by an Apprentice, the chamber felt like a museum. On the Banish Hall side was a door of metal bars. The door hung open because the key had been lost generations past and the lock removed in case someone was fool enough to get shut inside the chamber. The small room was about twice the size of an Apprentice's cell and was as immaculate as the rest of the floor, but empty of all furniture. No one knew if the cell ever had been furnished.

"These are special keyless locks," Lanler explained as Janin stared in curiosity at the three large trunks. "It's not magic, just knowing the trick to release the latch. To prevent accidental opening, a combination of pressure points usually have to be touched all at once."

"I don't know if I can open them."

"We know," Gretna reassured her. "Just give it a try."

Janin knelt down in front of the closest trunk, studying the shiny silver plate. The surface was smooth without blemish or even the slightest indentation. Nothing seemed available to make it give up its secret.

The Elders held their breaths. They didn't tell Janin that she had only one chance to get it right. The magic woven into the locks did not allow for fumbling attempts even if one eventually released the latch. They didn't want to scare her but did want to test how true her talent was.

Janin, not getting any feeling one way or another by just studying the lock, thought that if she felt the silver something would come to her. She reached out her hand and stopped short of touching the cold metal. Knowing she was just going through an exercise and too embarrassed to tell the Elders she had no idea how to unlock the trunk, she pressed her fingers against the cold metal without thought. The apology was on her lips as something moved beneath the metal plate. She raised confused eyes to the Elders, who looked resigned that she had done her best but failed. Janin returned her attention to the trunk, placed her hands on the lid and slowly lifted it.

"You did it!" Gretna caught her breath.

"I don't know what I did," Janin confessed. "I didn't feel anything at all."

"It's not always a feeling," Enle said. "Sometimes you just know."

"I didn't know what I was doing," Janin mumbled.

"Knowing doesn't have to be with the mind. Sometimes the body knows," Trudlin mused.

"But that doesn't change the fact that I don't know if I can do something until after it's been done." Janin looked down in frustration, then frowned at the contents of the trunk. Neatly stacked small leather bound books beckoned to her curiosity.

"Interesting," Gretna commented, as the Elders looked over Janin's shoulder into the trunk. "It seems we've uncovered a treasure."

"Remember, we must not let on that we suspect anything," Lektle twittered, casting a bright eye to the other High Overseers seated at the long stone table at one end of their receiving hall.

"Yes, we remember," Usaf grumbled. That was, after all, the purpose of this meeting. To act like nothing was the matter and give a certain Overseer a false security about her secretive activities.

"But we can't behave any differently than usual," Huask reminded them, "which means we'll have to display the usual amount of suspicion."

"Of course," Usaf agreed. "But no truthstone."

"Of course. She's here. Wake Trandle," Huask growled under his breath.

"Do you think we'll actually see her squirm?" Lektle whispered, unable to let go of the look of delight on her ancient face. Huask shot her a dark glance. Lektle had enough sense to pull herself together and put on a solemn expression.

Dorian never enjoyed her meetings with the High Overseers, and this one promised to be worse than usual. A blank faced Apprentice to Truth stood in the doorway of the small hall, lined on one side with a wooden bench. Dorian sighed and rose to follow the green robed servant of the High Overseers.

The High Overseers Hall was an endless cavern of cold white stone and magnified echoes. Dorian always thought that it reflected claustrophobia to the extreme. The High Overseers weren't known to entertain more than a few visitors at a time. She hadn't heard of them ever inviting the entire Landersdown army over for tea, for instance. Suppressing a smile at the image, she focused her attention on the four figures behind the imposing granite table at the far end of the hall.

Any citizen of Athros could become a High Overseer, being one of the few positions that did not require Apprenticeship before the examinations. So that Athros would not be without a High Overseer for even a short period of time, a citizen of Athros could take a High Overseer position exam any time they desired. The length and depth of the exam was enough to deter the most casual interest in the job. Eight sand marks of intense questioning by the High Overseers with a jury of an equal number of Retired High Overseers. Just facing the High Overseers for a quarter sand mark at a time was more than enough for most.

The sitting High Overseers were all but retired Apprentices when they passed the exams and grew more ancient during the time they served these positions. The two women and two men would have blended right into the bleached granite table and columns behind them if their clothing weren't so colorful. Their sense of fashion was outdated by several millennia, reflecting a time when Athronians had sported clothes splashed with bright colors, in sharp contrast to the present trend toward black and brown leathers or subdued colors. Many of Dorian's generation adopted the tunics and leggings worn by the Outlanders, mostly because they spent more time in the Outland than their ancestors had.

"Come sit," piped Trandle, the oldest High Overseer. Dorian slid onto the stone bench at the table, facing the four. "Busy few weeks," Trandle murmured as she shuffled a stack of papers in front of her.

"Not much knowledge coming in," Lektle squeaked as she shakily poured a cup of tea.

"Too little," Dorian replied, blandly. "I don't quite know what to make of it."

"It could be just the natural flow of things." Lektle's voice cracked as the tea warmed her throat. Dorian said nothing and kept her face expressionless. She knew that the High Overseers probably checked and double-checked that the knowledge wasn't being swept into corners or conveniently forgotten. Dorian was long resigned to the fact that they would never trust her.

"Explosions." Usaf tapped the end of his quill pen on the sheets of paper in front of him. "Your presumption is that someone is pulling pranks. Lincim has come to the same conclusion. Are we talking about pranks here?"

"Yes and no," Dorian answered slowly. "If they are pranks, they have another purpose than to satisfy someone's demented sense of fun." The four shifted and exchanged glances. "I think someone is trying to let us know that they can do things and get away with it, leaving us uneasy about what they might try next."

"What about the writing on the table?" Usaf pressed.

"It's a script I've never seen before," Dorian admitted.

"You told Professor Tibbits that it was meaningless scribble," Usaf challenged.

"I told him it looked like a script but could be random scribbling or possibly a code," Dorian corrected.

"Then how do you know it's a language?" Lektle pressed.

"I said script, not language." Dorian concentrated on keeping her growing temper from boiling over. "Why are you trying to trick me into saying that I know more about it than I do?"

The sound of four robes shifting against granite echoed in the chamber.

"You misunderstand our line of questioning," Huask said smoothly.

"It's only fair since you misunderstand my answers." Dorian gave him a cold stare. She had little patience with their games. "And you've misunderstood my reports." She nodded to the papers on the table.

Huask sighed. "The book."

"It had residue of the mineral Surfite, which when mixed with a little Blackite can explode when friction is applied. My guess is that the mixture was on the inside cover of the book and was placed under the heavy stone tablet that could only be moved by dragging before lifting."

Huask nodded. "Very clever. You don't think that these incidents are just the work of an Apprentice to Mischief who is getting a little too enthusiastic about his or her work?"

Dorian stared at him for long heartbeats. All the Apprentices had already been thoroughly questioned by the Overseer of Truth. They were baiting her about something. She tried not to frown, but she had never been in a position where she couldn't even guess what the other person was thinking. "You must ask the Overseer of Mischief about that," she finally answered. They could imply that they didn't trust her all they wanted, but she would fight any attempt to implicate Jac.

The High Overseers exchanged looks. The meeting wasn't getting the responses out of Dorian they thought it would.

"Thank you for meeting with us. That will be all for now." Usaf nodded. "Wait. What's that?" His eyes focused on Dorian's neck.

Dorian frowned, confused. "What?"

"That thing around your neck." Usaf waved a shaky hand. The others squinted at her.

"It's a bonding medallion!" Trandle squeaked in disbelief.

Huask glared at Dorian. "What kind of prank are you playing?"

"No prank." Dorian stared at them. "I got bonded three weeks ago. Don't you look at Granwin's reports?"

Ignoring Dorian's question, Huask rose to his feet, a rage building within him. "Are you saying you were caught in an Attraction?"

Dorian shrugged. "Yes."

"Who's the other half of this Attraction?" Huask demanded.

"He's from the Outland," Dorian replied steadily.

"An Outlander?" Huask held her eyes for long heartbeats. Dorian just folded her arms and stared nonchalantly back.

"If you wish." She wasn't going to tell them anymore than that. They could read Granwin's report if they were that interested. "Sorry if you find it so difficult to believe. So do I, but I can't argue with what happened." She then slid off the bench, leaving the astonished High Overseers staring at her back as she angrily crossed the endless chamber.

Once free of the cavernous place, she quickened her pace to the narrow winding stairs that took her to freedom from those conspiring, secretive, doddering misfits. Every meeting always ended with her gasping for fresh air once she cleared the cloistered overhangs of the High Overseers Hall. This time there was a wonderful difference. Seated on a stone bench in the middle of the courtyard, Devor waited patiently. After three weeks, she was still both surprised and amused at how absolutely happy she was to see him after even a short separation. She had never given the Attraction much thought before, mostly because she knew it was a fate she would never have to face. Now she wondered how she could have been so indifferent to it.

"An enjoyable meeting?" Devor greeted wryly, rising to his feet.

"Sometimes I'm tempted to meet Jac's challenge and take the High Overseer's examination just to rile up those old fools," Dorian muttered.

"Doesn't a High Overseer have to retire first?" Devor asked, wrinkling his brow.

Dorian mirrored his confused look. In a heartbeat, she realized that there wasn't any way an Outlander could know about the inner workings of the Athronian political structure.

"Any Athronian can become a High Overseer any time they want. All they have to do is pass the High Overseer's exam," she explained. "There isn't a limit on the number of High Overseers who can be in office at the same time."

"Any Athronian?" Devor repeated. "You mean, you don't have to be an Overseer first?"

Dorian nodded bitterly. "Right. It's a tradition to be an Overseer first. And useful, since a first hand knowledge of being an Overseer is an important thing to have."

"I would think so," Devor agreed.

Dorian arched an eyebrow at him. "Ever wonder why we're not very respectful of our current High Overseers?"

"I was kind of surprised. But I only know the High Overseers from the Stories, and they were always fair and benevolent."

Dorian grinned. "Lucky for me. They were usually rescuing me from big trouble. The misfits we have now conspired to become High Overseers when they were only Apprentices. They were greedy for power, and one of them was clever enough to figure out how to make them all High Overseers."

"Greed has a way of bringing out amazing skills that could be better used for good," Devor mused.

Dorian gave him a wry look. "It took only the best of them to finally make it as High Overseer and the others followed quickly."

"How?"

Dorian shrugged. "They cheated on the High Overseer's exam."

"Isn't that against the rules?"

Dorian shook with laughter wanting to throw her arms around him but knew the bond medallion would protest. "Unfortunately, it's extremely difficult to prove these things when the upholders of those rules are the ones breaking them."

"Kind of a tricky situation," Devor agreed. "How do you know they cheated?"

"Because there isn't any other way they could have passed," Dorian stated simply.

Devor scratched his beard thoughtfully. "What happened to the High Overseers already in office?"

"They retired rather quickly."

"Oh." Devor wasn't sure he wanted to know any more about the current High Overseers. "So, why don't you take Jac up on his challenge?"

Dorian grinned. "The last time I did that I ended up an Apprentice to Knowledge, and we all know the mess that got me into."

"Being Overseer of Knowledge is a tough job." Devor all but invited the playful jabs Dorian gave his arm. "Hey, you're strong."

"You've watched my workouts," Dorian returned.

"I didn't know they made you that strong."

Dorian laughed. "That'll teach you to watch who you pick a fight with. Anyway, no Athronian has tried to become a High Overseer because they would be alone against those greedy monsters. They forced the previous High Overseers into sudden retirement, and I'm sure they would force that on anyone who tried to invade their little domain."

"And this is the way it is after every meeting with them?" Devor asked wryly.

Dorian gave him an apologetic smile. "I'm sorry. They don't bring out the best in me."

"Just the side you've been careful to keep hidden from me," Devor teased. "That famous Dorian temper."

"It hasn't been any effort to keep it from you." Dorian gave him another one of those devastating smiles before turning in the direction of the delicate metal gates that opened onto the street. Devor had to restrain from spinning her back around and kissing her. "Don't even think about it." Dorian turned to him slyly before continuing down the path.

Devor came up beside her. "Can you really read my mind or is this just some kind of trick you picked up from Jac?"

Dorian grinned. "I'm just guessing that you're getting the same ideas I am. I take it I'm guessing right."

"More or less, I think." Devor took a deep breath. Remembering all the stories about her, there was no telling what Dorian was thinking.

"There isn't any way that she could have done that." Kaston, absently twirling his staff, shook his head. He had been on his way to the practice field when he got caught up in the story that Janin was telling Soral and Morna. The three young women lounged on the large stone steps that rounded the base of the Banish Hall. "There isn't any way she could have that kind of strength."

"She caught him off balance," Morna explained, a little irritated.

"That explains how she knocked him over but not how she kept him from getting up," Kaston returned, puzzled by Morna's uncharacteristic annoyance.

"Oh really?" A dangerous tone colored the Guard's voice as she rose to her feet.

"I don't think this is worth getting into a fight over," Soral broke in nervously.

"I'm just going to correct Kaston's thinking, that's all," Morna purred. "First, we need someone about Dorian's age." She stared at Janin.

"Oh no. Leave me out of this," Janin protested good-naturedly.

"You've had a few lessons on the staff." Morna studied the tip of her own staff casually. "It's not like I'm going to ask you to do anything particularly difficult. Just dump Kaston and pin him so he can't move."

"Is that all?" Janin asked wryly.

"That's all." Morna grinned wickedly and turned to Kaston. "Are you game?"

"Sure, why not." Kaston imitated her casual stance.

Morna led the group away from the building and handed

Janin her staff. Whispering into the younger woman's ear, the Guard laid out the planned attack. Kaston looked on, leaning on his staff and was surprised at the nervous tug in the pit of his stomach. Janin's uncertain expression changed to understanding and even confidence under the influence of the Guard's words. Kaston's stomach jumped causing his forehead to react with a frown. As Morna whispered, Janin's face brightened with a grin followed by a chuckle of delight. By this time, Kaston's agitated stomach had worked into his disposition, and he scowled impatiently at the pair.

Without warning, Morna straightened, strode to the young man, and knocked the staff he was leaning on out of his hands as she passed. At that moment, Janin stepped forward and swept her staff against his legs and tumbled him to the ground. Before he could even think, she stood over him with the end of her staff firmly placed against his throat. Any movement would have unpleasant consequences on his windpipe. Staring at Janin in wide-eyed shock, he tried to make some strangled noises of protest before realizing that he was beaten. Satisfied, Janin stepped back.

Kaston slowly rose to a sitting position and gingerly fingered his throat.

Soral grinned. "That was fun."

Morna used Kaston's staff to pull him up before returning it to him. "That wasn't fair, you knocked away my staff," he protested.

"To get you off balance," Morna reminded him.

"What was all that grinning and laughing about?" he demanded, still feeling like he'd been tricked.

"To create a diversion?" Morna shrugged.

"What?" Kaston gave her a puzzled frown.

"You became distracted by how your stomach was reacting to our actions," Morna explained.

"How'd you know what my stomach was doing?" Kaston straightened, indignant at the thought that they knew he'd had a large attack of the flutters.

Morna smirked. "Experience."

Janin twirled the staff, eyeing Kaston. "So you think you're better than I am? Even though we've had about the same amount of training?"

"Of course I'm better..." Kaston began before stopping himself.

"You think just because you're studying to be a Guard you're going to learn faster and be better?" Janin pressed.

"Well, I..." Kaston knew that he had been caught.

"Or don't you think that a person who spends all day with her head in a book can be good at anything else?" Janin playfully tapped at his staff with her staff. Kaston returned the taps on reflex, engaging in a few casual thrusts and parries.

"I will wager that Janin can disarm Kaston." Morna turned to Soral, who was curious about this competitive side of the young Apprentice.

"You're taking Janin's side?" Kaston turned to Morna startled, nearly getting whacked by Janin's staff. Fortunately, both trainees had quick reflexes.

"Do you think she can disarm you first?" Morna asked.

"No, of course not," Kaston returned.

Morna shrugged. "It's never fun making a wager on the sure winner."

"In that case, since I don't think that Kaston is the sure winner, I'll put my wager on him," Soral joined in. She knew that Morna was playing some more of her mind games on the young man. "What are we wagering, anyway?"

"Mmmm." Morna rubbed her chin in thought. Before she had a chance to answer, a familiar clanking rang out from the other side of the Banish Hall. Mealtime. Being late meant getting the scrapings off the bottom of the pans. "I guess we'll have to continue this some other time. Unless you two want to back out of the challenge."

"I'll take her on anytime she wants," Kaston responded.

"Just let me know when you feel up to it," Janin countered as she tossed the staff to Morna.

Morna grinned wickedly at Soral. "We're going to have to think of a really good wager, I think."

"Just don't wager on something you're fond of." Sorel waved as she and Janin turned towards the Elders Hall.

Chapter
Seven

To the Truthstone

The Overseers Hall, unlike that of the High Overseers Hall, was a warren of mismatched chambers constructed and reconstructed through the many generations of Overseers. Chaos was the word that best described the halls connecting the chambers where hundreds of Apprentices spent more time than the Overseers, taking advantage of the privilege of being allowed into the building. The Overseers themselves treated the Hall as an occasional refuge from the rest of Athros.

Although the fifty-six Overseers had regular meetings, it was rare that more than half were ever present at one time. Between work, travel and plain disinterest, many Overseers never made the effort to be actively involved in the Society. Mostly, they were content with letting a few make sure the Society's bylaws were not violated and its good name wasn't insulted.

On this clear summer evening, bylaws and good name were just the beginning of the Overseers' rage at the High Overseers. Rumor had it that all fifty-six would be in attendance that night. No one could remember the last time that had happened, if indeed it ever had.

Dorian looked up at the thick wooden double doors to the palatial stone building and sighed. "I leave Devor in your capable hands, Jac," she said with great reluctance. "Try to stay out of trouble."

Jac folded his arms. "In case you haven't heard, I only get into trouble when you're around."

"Then how come I only get into trouble when you're around?" Dorian gave him a pained look.

Jac squinted at her but held his ground. "There are plenty of times you've gotten into trouble without me."

"But none of those stories are true." Dorian smiled sweetly before turning her attention to Devor. "I hope this isn't going to take all night. I'll find you when we're through. If it's too late, I'll see you tomorrow."

Reluctantly, she turned and sauntered into the vestibule along with a crowd of Apprentices and Overseers. Before she even had time to think, Lons was at her side.

"I need to have a few words with you," the Overseer of Art murmured in Dorian's ear. Dorian shrugged and followed Lons into one of the small chambers used for quick private conferences.

Readjusting her ever present multi-colored shawl, Lons took a deep breath. "I just thought someone needed to warn you." She bent her head to the shorter woman. "The High Overseers have put many, if not all of us, to the truthstone about the strange incidents that have been happening lately." She straightened at the indignity they all felt. "How dare they not trust us. It makes me angry just thinking about it."

"Why are you warning me?" Dorian asked.

Lons blinked at her in surprise. "Because they think you are behind these things."

"Then why haven't they put me to the truthstone?" Dorian asked steadily as her insides tried to lurch forward without the rest of her body.

"You weren't put to the stone?" Lons almost laughed with relief.

"Is that the reason so many Overseers are here?" Dorian raised an eyebrow. She had been wondering why they were giving her odd looks as they passed by the chamber.

"Yes. That's the reason for the meeting. Since everyone else had been put to the same humiliating inquiry and due to the delicacy of the situation, no one thought there was a need to mention the reason for the meeting when it was called." Lons rested sympathetic eyes on Dorian's troubled face. "I'm sorry you had to find out this way."

Dorian shrugged, trying for a casualness she didn't feel. "It's better than finding out inside the Chamber. And to tell the truth, I wouldn't have thought much about it if I had been put to the stone. So this would have been just as much a surprise. The High Overseers seem to delight in trying to catch me up on anything they can. I've been accused of having something to do with every little incident or irregularity that has happened in Athros since I was elevated. I've held the truthstone in their presence as often as I ever did when I was an Apprentice."

Lons stared at her stunned. An Overseer's word was accepted as being above the need for the truthstone. The acceptance was a matter of respect and trust. That more than anything was what upset the Overseers. "Most of us don't have the, uh, experience you've had with truthstones."

"I was surprised I wasn't given the stone at our last meeting. They all but accused me of having something to do with those incidents," Dorian confessed.

"Something very odd is going on here," Lons muttered absently. Dorian gave her a patient look. "Excuse me, I must talk to Lincim." The Overseer of Art hurried after the Overseer of Mischief, who had just passed the doorway.

Dorian stood for a few heartbeats, pulling her thoughts together. So the Overseers had not only been questioned about the incidents but also about whether she was involved in them. She shook her head. How did the High Overseers think they could get away with all but accusing her and yet not taking the final step to prove it beyond a doubt? She didn't mind making them look foolish; she just wondered why they thought this strange ploy would work. Musing on this, she walked to the Overseers Chamber.

The chamber was a high domed half sphere. The curved section of the hall was lined with raised rows of benches for the Overseers to sit in full view of each other. In front were the long bench and table for the Overseers Council, an honorary group of three who acted as representatives for the rest of the Overseers and mediators when the need arose.

As she entered at the floor level, Dorian looked up at the rows of benches, already nearly full. Never had she seen so many Overseers in one place. Some of them hadn't set foot in the Hall since she had become Overseer, much less attend a meeting. The other members of the Council were already seated as Dorian climbed to her place at the end of the bench. The Overseer of Knowledge along with the Overseer of Justice and the Overseer of Prophecy comprised the Council.

Gris stood next to her, waiting politely for her to be seated. Looking down with an uncharacteristic grimness, he gave her shoulder a paternal squeeze. "We'll get you through this," he murmured as he sat on the bench.

Dorian gave him a wane smile and nodded. So this was how the strange but brief career of Dorian Riverson was to end. Not very dramatic but real life rarely was.

Tigren Iocene, Overseer of Justice seated on Gris' other side, rose to bring the meeting to order.

"I am glad to see that all the members of our Society found the reason we are gathered here important enough to attend this meeting," Tigren began dryly after he had the Overseers' attention. He looked at the doors wide open to the corridor where Apprentices gathered quietly to observe a meeting of the Hall. Attending Overseer meetings was considered a part of their education, and the presence of a full complement of Overseers drew an overflowing number of Apprentices. "I move we seal the doors." Tigren glanced about the chamber. "Any objections?"

The Overseers assented by tensely watching him. The Apprentices were stunned. They had heard of closed meetings, but none had happened in a long time.

"Please close the doors," Tigren directed. The Apprentices hesitated before pushing on the heavy doors. The Chamber felt small, catching the echoes of the doors snapping shut. "I turn the meeting over to Overseer Twaene." Tigren nodded to Gris as he sat back onto the bench. Gris rose, not at all happy about the task before him.

"We are gathered here to determine the veracity of a recent inquiry made by the High Overseers to each of us concerning a member of our Society. It appears that the High Overseers have evidence that Dorian Riverson, Overseer of Knowledge, was involved in the recent destructive incidents in Athros. Have you prepared a statement in your defense, Overseer Riverson?" Gris turned to Dorian, whose expression betrayed no emotion.

Dorian rose to her feet. "I just heard of the accusation right before the meeting, Overseer Twaene. I have no statement in my defense."

"Just heard?" Interwood, the Overseer of Mathematics, jumped to his feet. "How is this possible?"

Lons stood up before Dorian had a chance to reply. "I approached Overseer Riverson before the meeting to give her a few words of friendly advice. She had no idea that we had been put to the stone about the explosions or that we were questioned about her possible involvement."

"How could she not know?" Interwood pressed. "The High Overseers would not have questioned us if their evidence was not straight from her holding the truthstone."

"The High Overseers never put her to the stone for this," Lons declared.

"Is that what she told you?" Interwood was just too logical to think that things weren't as black and white as the world of mathematics.

Lons straightened. "Yes, it is. And I believe her. She has no reason to lie about this. The High Overseers have been in the practice of putting her to the stone ever since she was elevated to Overseer." A gasp of disbelief came from more than a few.

"Will you verify this statement, Overseer Jandor?" Gris gazed at the Overseer of Truth, his heart nearly ready to burst with the realization that not only was Dorian innocent, beyond doubt, but also that they would be able to prove it.

Kerit Jandor, Overseer of Truth, rose to his feet. "It is true."

The Chamber erupted in a fit of angry shouts with half the Society on their feet. Gris took several long heartbeats to settle them down.

"The issue of making Overseers use the truthstone will be dealt with when we have taken care of this present problem," Gris said smoothly when they were silent. So, he wasn't the only one not trusted by the High Overseers. How interesting.

"Why would the High Overseers go to the trouble of holding the inquiry if they did not have the evidence?" Shawndoc demanded.

"We'll be long retired before anyone can figure out the actions of these particular High Overseers," Jadrick responded bitterly.

"I will take the truthstone now." Dorian held a hand out to Kerit, who slowly rose, bowing his head to hide his humiliation. Everyone in the chamber not only sucked in their breath but also turned pale. Dorian cast a puzzled eye around the room. "What have you neglected to tell me?"

Gris sighed. "It's all right, Kerit. How could she have known if she hadn't been put to the stone? In case there was lingering doubt in anyone's mind." He swept cold blue eyes across the rows of tense Overseers.

"What would I have known?" Dorian kept her temper even, but she could not conceal the fury building up inside her, not with so many defined muscles to reflect her tension.

"They didn't even trust Kerit to do his own job. The High Overseers performed the inquiry themselves, shutting Kerit out." Inhga, Overseer of Gardens, jumped to his feet, fists clenched, practically spitting the words. Everyone turned to him in astonishment. Inhga was the gentlest amongst them. No one had ever seen him exhibit dismay much less any kind of anger. Realizing his outburst and how strange it felt, he looked around embarrassed but continued to stand his ground.

Dorian was almost oblivious to who said the words. The words themselves sent her plummeting into depths of concern. Forgetting her own anger, she stared at Kerit with compassion. "This is more serious than the High Overseers trying to remove me from Athros, once again."

Kerit raised his head to meet her sharp gray eyes. He had been the Apprentice to Truth who had sat through nearly all her encounters with the truthstone when she was constantly getting into scrapes. He probably knew her better than anyone there, having seen her strength at telling the truth even when it was not always in her best interest. Never had he witnessed the truthstone even flicker while in her hands.

"Overseer Riverson tells the truth," he said as a simple statement of fact. "She has never lied or hedged around the truth while holding the stone. I know none of us here or anyone else in Athros who can make that claim." Dorian's jaw dropped in surprise. He knew that, more often than not, Dorian took the blame when it would be more disastrous for whomever she was protecting to be caught. She had been in the better position to get into trouble without consequence because of the dubious distinction of being the highest ranked Apprentice to Knowledge. "No, Dorian. This time it's your turn to be blameless." She blinked at him. "The High Overseers took advantage of our dignity and honor by leading us to surmise that they had overwhelming evidence that you had something to do with the recent prankish incidents. I refuse to give the High Overseers the satisfaction of thinking that they can use us to get their way. They are confident enough in whatever evidence they think they have to insist that we hold an Inquiry for Impeachment against the Overseer of

Knowledge. Are you confident enough to withstand this Inquiry?"

"Of course," Dorian responded. "But I still don't understand what they are trying to achieve from this futile exercise. They may have something even worse for us if you disbelieve their word that they have evidence against me and clear me of the charge." Dorian, realizing that her eyes had tears in them, quickly brushed them away. The heightened emotions caused by the bonding could be inconvenient at times.

"We would never sacrifice a member of our Society under any circumstance," Gris resolutely stated.

"I'm just one Overseer. If I have be to sacrificed to protect the Society from the continued assault of the High Overseers, then you need to seriously consider it." Dorian swallowed down her grief at the idea. "I don't care what other people think I've done as long as I know that I am blameless or innocent. The heavens know I've let more fiction than fact pass without comment." She flushed in astonishment at her own words. Never had she made such an admission except when joking with Jac. The bond was affecting her judgment. "Overseer Jandor knows what I'm talking about. As far as I'm concerned, with the worst of these fictions accepted as truth, there isn't much left of my honor or reputation to defend. I truly believe that the more serious problem here is that the High Overseers don't trust the Overseer of Truth. This strikes at the very foundation of what our society is built upon."

Kerit was flushed, not only from the fact that the focus had been turned back to him, but also by some of these untruths that he was, under oath, sworn to keep secret. He had spent many sleepless nights after a session with the young Dorian Riverson, doubting his abilities to do his job with the required impersonal detachment. The hardest thing for a truth seeker to deal with was that the truth could do just as much harm as an untruth.

Before Kerit could say anything, Gris straightened and signaled him to sit, then gently put a hand on Dorian's shoulder, easing her back down onto the bench.

"Let's put it to a vote," the Overseer of Prophecy suggested patiently.

Dorian felt foolish with the tears trickling down her cheeks as the count of the vote was read. Fifty-five Overseers in favor of proving Dorian innocent of all suspicions against her. No one seemed to notice or care that she had lost control of her emotions. Gris absently handed her a large cotton nose rag as he stood at the end of the vote. Granwin rose at the same time.

"Permission to have a pot of bondroot brought to the chamber," the Overseer of Attractions requested.

"Granted." Gris, along with all the others in the chamber, managed to hide his amusement. Nearly all of them had been caught in an Attraction when they were younger, much younger than Dorian since Attractions usually occurred when Athronians were in their twenties. The number of Overseers caught in an Attraction while Overseer was small, if it had ever happened at all, given their older ages when elevated to the position. Unfortunately, it made her seem even younger to them, and the request for bondroot was something akin to asking for baby food. An amusing precedence in that Hall of Athronian maturity. But none doubted that the request for actual baby food would follow soon enough. Imagining Dorian as a mother was difficult, but it had been just as hard imagining her caught in an Attraction.

Dorian was not only aware of her colleagues' thoughts as they watched her with a touch of amusement around their eyes, but also she knew that a request for bondroot had never been made in that Hall before. How will the Chroniclers twist this story around, she wondered.

"Dorian Riverson, Overseer of Knowledge, has been implicated in a number of destructive incidents that have occurred recently in Athros," Gris began dryly. "It is our duty according to the Law of Athros to get to the truth as expediently as possible. Since the High Overseers do not trust our Overseer of Truth and since the High Overseers neglected to put Overseer Riverson to the truthstone, we have no choice but to place before the High Overseers a Question on how to go about our duty of trying a member our Society in a way that they will accept as truth."

"They could stall forever in making a reply," Lincim warned.

A helper of the Hall placed the pot of bondroot tea and a mug in front of Dorian during Gris' speech. She poured the steaming liquid into the mug and took a deep sip, grimacing at the bitter taste, but the effects were almost immediate. She felt in control enough to talk some sense into her misdirected colleagues, and she rose to her feet.

"Please, sit back down, Dorian," Gris said in his most fatherly voice.

"I will not—"

"Andora. Will you join us for a moment," Gris interrupted smoothly. Dorian stared at him. What did he want with Andora?

The Overseer of the Body climbed down to the floor with the calm, no-nonsense expression she always carried. She touched her fingers to Dorian's hand resting on the table. Dorian jerked her hand back. "This isn't fair," was all she could manage to mutter.

"Please place your hand back on the table," Andora requested steadily. Dorian did as she was told but not without her temper rising. Andora pressed her fingertips against the back of Dorian's hand for a few heartbeats as her mind filled with the details of Dorian's physical well-being. "I will allow her to stay as long as she continues to drink the bondroot and sits quietly."

Dorian's body tensed like she was exploding from the inside out. Allowed to stay? What kind of nonsense was that? And to have to sit quietly. She was not a child. The soundless explosion died as quickly as it happened. In present company under the present circumstance, she was a child. She sank to the bench disheartened at this revelation.

"It's good to know our Overseer of Knowledge can still make sensible decisions," Gris mused, ignoring the look of disdain Dorian shot at him. "Thank you, Andora."

"My pleasure." Andora gave Dorian a wry look. She held one or two of Dorian's secrets herself, although hers were obviously more amusing than the ones known to Kerit.

Gris cleared his throat. "As we all know, once we begin an Inquiry of Impeachment, according to the written law of Athros, we can choose to remain in this chamber until the Inquiry has been brought to a satisfactory conclusion." Dorian stopped herself from squirming by planting her forehead into her palms with her elbows on the table.

"May I make a statement before you begin?" she asked the table.

"Speak," Gris said with a sigh and sat down.

Dorian raised her head, choosing her words carefully this time. She rose to her feet, keeping her hands on the table. The bondroot had some unsteadying side effects. "I just want to state for the record my observations on the manner in which the High Overseers conducted their inquiry concerning the recent destructive incidents in Athros. Since my words may include an admission of innocence, I am required by the Law of Athros—that you've suddenly taken such a great interest in—to hold the truthstone." When Kerit hesitated, Dorian looked to the other Overseers. "The need for me to hold it will become apparent once I've said what I have to say." Gris nodded to Kerit.

Kerit dug a pair of palm-sized, dull gray stones out of his belt pouch and climbed down to the floor. As he put the stones on the table in front of Dorian, he gave her a look of apology and agony.

"I do know what I'm doing, Kerit," Dorian reassured him. "Not all of my experiences with the stone have to put truth seekers convictions into turmoil." Kerit's eyes widened before recovering from his surprise.

Dorian placed her fingertips on each stone.

"Please give a false statement to the stones," Kerit directed, taking comfort in the ritual.

"My cousin Jac always wears mismatched boots," Dorian replied. The dull grayness of the stones burst into a deep blue. Kerit picked up one of the stones and returned to his place in the circle of Overseers.

"Make your statement for the record," Gris directed.

"I couldn't figure out why the High Overseers were so clumsy in this plan to extricate information from each of you about these recent incidents and neglect to put me to the stone," she began in a steady calm voice. "They gave the impression that they already had the truth of guilt from me and were looking for accomplices or at least those withholding knowledge from them. It made no sense because they had to know that you would find out that I hadn't been put to the stone. I believe they wanted you to find out and be outraged, thereby forcing me to take the stone and reveal my guilt before this Society. In other words, they wanted to place the burden of removing an Overseer on you, leaving them blameless." Dorian held her free hand up to stop the immediate angry murmuring. "Let me finish. They made a rather large error." Dorian looked puzzled as she re-examined her thoughts. "By performing the truth seeking inquiry themselves, they are suddenly in the position of not trusting what comes out of this chamber."

"Knowing them, they would conveniently overlook that little detail if we found you guilty." Shawndoc's face scrunched in irony.

"That's the gamble they're taking. I don't know why, but they're sufficiently convinced that I'm guilty of these charges that they created this elaborate ruse. Maybe they thought, if nothing else, they could plant a seed of distrust towards your wayward but well meaning Overseer of Knowledge. I am not guilty, and I am ready to state it to the stone. With your permission, Overseer Jandor."

"Say the words," Kerit directed, holding up his stone in the palm of his hand.

"I, Dorian Riverson, Overseer of Knowledge, declare that I am innocent of causing the explosion in the sorting chamber, the explosion in the chemistry classroom, and the movement of the Rock of Teyerbom. I am also innocent of causing a script to appear on the chemistry table and the bottom side of the Rock of Teyerbom. Do you need more detail?" She looked up at the stunned Overseers. The stone didn't flicker during the entire time she had her fingers on it. That rarely happened even when the truth was spoken.

"That is sufficient," Gris said, staring at Kerit whose face reflected his relief. The truth was always more complex with Dorian. This simple statement of fact was like a miracle to him. She had no one to protect but herself this time.

"The truth has been spoken," Kerit announced, and climbed down from his place in the circle to retrieve the stone from Dorian.

"I'm sorry. When I was younger..." Dorian said softly. Kerit was caught off guard.

He straightened. "It made me a stronger Overseer."

"But not necessarily a happier one," Dorian murmured as she lowered back onto the bench.

"We will take a quarter sand mark recess before we start the Inquiry," Gris announced. "You know the Law. No one is to leave the building or speak to anyone about what has come to pass within this Hall."

What was most disconcerting to Dorian, as she watched her colleagues return to the Hall after the recess, was not that they were about to embark on one of the most serious activities an Overseer can engage in. Or that the Inquiry was made on her behalf whether she wanted it or not. What she couldn't keep out of her reasonable and rational mind was that she wanted to be with Devor. That very moment. The intense longing to be with him swelled within her until it was almost physically painful.

She shook her head and took another swallow of the awful tasting tea, breathing out in relief that its effects were almost immediate. She knew that it was going to be a long night.

Chapter Eight

Revelations

Once they recovered from the astounding revelation that the Athronian trunks found in the third floor chamber belonged to Orvid, the Overseer of Knowledge, the Elders decided to entrust Janin with the task of studying the trunks' contents. Maybe they contained a clue on how the Overseer got them to Baniston and, more importantly, how he was planning to retrieve them.

A long table and bench were moved to a corner of the prison floor of the Elders Hall for Janin to perform her special assignment. Since it was unusual for a new Apprentice to be given such a task, Soral was brought into the secret of Janin's heritage to keep down the questions and idle talk. Soral had a way of placating people, a desirable skill for an Elder. Instead of being jealous of the special privilege Janin received, the amiable Elders Assistant recognized it as a unique opportunity to study a young Athronian develop her special talents. In fact, all she asked, in return for the Elders trust in her and for her promise to protect Janin from any negative reaction from the other Apprentices, was to be allowed to observe Janin's growth as an Athronian.

Janin's charge was simple. She was to learn as much as possible about the articles in the trunks. After systematically sorting the items onto the long table, her attention fell to the journals. The assortment of stones wrapped in soft leather, neatly engraved medallions and badges and curious small mechanical devices were interesting, but she was a reader and words were what she craved.

The small books were Orvid's journals. Written in a neat script, they depicted his day-to-day life as the Overseer of Knowledge. Janin arranged the journals into chronological order to read them from beginning to end. Entries were interesting but uneventful, until she came to the first mention of a twelve-year-old who had gotten the highest score ever achieved on the Apprentice examination. Although considered too young for any Apprenticeship, Orvid had taken on the precocious child for fear of losing her to the Overseer of Mischief to whom her fifteen-year-old cousin had already been accepted as Apprentice.

Janin, forgetting the evening meal and even bedtime, read deep into the night, unable to pull herself away from the true everyday life behind the infamous character in the Overseer Stories. She sympathized with Orvid's frustration that his most prized Apprentice spent all her time in the Outland and was only brought to Athros to take the truthstone. When he did get her to work, she displayed an incredible talent for knowledge, picking through the work by memorizing at a glance and spilling many times more information into the knowledge stone than the other Apprentices. He devoted endless passages to wondering how he could put a rope on his restless protegee. As she got older, she strayed longer and farther, with new temptations capturing her dangerous curiosity. He wrote of the usual antics from the Stories, such as romance and spirits. More disturbing for Janin were the accounts of Dorian exploring all aspects of life including the intensely dark sides. Many a time, the young Apprentice had to be found and dragged out from the underpinning of this darkness.

Janin shivered as she read about the black side of Dorian Riverson. Never had she imagined the happy-go-lucky Apprentice fighting in battles, crawling through thieves' dens and disreputable taverns, getting shot at, beaten, left for dead on battlefields—all this and being not much older than she.

Instead of feeling disappointment at these revelations about her hero, Janin felt reassured that Dorian was real and not, as some people insisted, a character from the imaginations of the Chroniclers. This new knowledge made Janin want to reread the Overseer Stories.

Devor woke with a start, realizing that a warm shaft of sunlight crossed his bed. Squinting through a jungle of plants, he saw that Jac was still asleep in the other bed. Both Riverson homes overflowed with vegetation as a consequence of living with an Apprentice to Gardens.

The sand mark was late. Much later than he or Jac had been allowed to sleep in the three weeks that Devor had spent in Athros. Usually, as dawn cracked, the mischievous Overseer of Knowledge crept into the room and tried out creative ways of waking Devor. According to Jac, Dorian never needed much sleep. She went days without closing her eyes and then crashed for a sand mark or two wherever she was.

Slowly sitting, Devor frowned at the strange fuzziness in his head. After a few moments of unfocused thoughts, he realized that his body felt vaguely out of sorts, a sure warning of a nasty illness coming on. Just what he needed, he sighed as a movement from the other bed caught his attention.

Jac opened his eyes and wrinkled his brow as if trying to think what was different. He rubbed his eyes, and pulled himself to a sitting position. "Where's Dorian? Isn't it awful late?" He blinked at the sunlight.

"I guess she had better things to do this morning," Devor replied, feeling his head for fever.

Jac squinted at him. "What's the matter? Coming down with something?"

Devor sighed. "I hope not." Best to not even think about it.

"Dorian never gets sick. It's disgusting, really."

"Would she have told us if she had something else to do this morning?" Devor asked.

Jac eyed him thoughtfully for a moment before displaying a wide grin. "She certainly wouldn't tell me, but she would tell you."

"Do you think we should be concerned?"

"Possibly." Jac ran a hand through his hair. "Come on, let's go put our minds at ease and find her."

Devor got out of bed, not liking how his body felt at all. Sighing, he pulled on his clothes and followed Jac through the house.

"Have you seen Dorian?" Jac asked as they wandered into the airy kitchen. Deidan yawned at the table, not quite paying attention to the day yet.

Yabot looked up from preparing the morning meal, surprised that Jac and Devor were still in the house. Dorian usually dragged them away long before the rest of the family was up.

"She hasn't come by?" Yabot frowned. "Want some food?"

"Sure." Jac nodded absently as he and Devor sat at the table with Deidan. "She never showed up after that meeting last night."

"The meeting." Deidan scratched her head. "Someone said they closed it."

"They had a closed meeting?" Jac wrinkled his brow. He couldn't remember the last time that happened.

"She could still be asleep if it went too late." Deidan stifled another yawn. She hated getting up in the early morning.

Jac shook his head. The old intuition that allowed him to find Dorian no matter where she was, nagged at the edge of his consciousness. "She can't stay away from Devor that long."

"Are you feeling all right?" Deidan eyes rested on the Out-lander.

Devor blinked up at her. He was by that time feeling shaky. What kind of viruses did they have in Athros?

He shrugged. "I'm fine. Maybe catching a cold or some-thing."

Deidan turned to Jac. "You shouldn't keep him out so late. He doesn't have the constitution of an Athronian."

Jac rolled his eyes. "Talk to Dorian about that."

Dordan, raising an eyebrow at the young men, strolled in through the back door. Unlike her twin, she enjoyed the early morning. "Jac, Devor. What a nice surprise. You're usually long gone by this time. Where's Dorian?"

"I was about to ask you," Jac replied.

Dordan frowned. "She wasn't in her room." She had the habit of checking Dorian's room each morning. Sometimes the bed had been slept in. Sometimes her daughter was even there. "Her bed hadn't been slept in."

"And she's been making it home to sleep nowadays," Deidan commented, winking at Devor.

"Her habits have been uncharacteristically regular thanks to Devor." Dordan smiled at the Outlander. "You don't look well. Are you feeling all right?"

"Probably just catching a cold." Devor gave her a reassuring look.

Dordan gave his shoulders a motherly squeeze. "We need to toughen you up. So you really don't know where Dorian is?"

"She never came back from the meeting."

"The meeting." Dordan's expression was touched with concern. "They closed it, I hear."

Jac sighed. "I guess we should go to the Overseers Hall."

Jac knew something was wrong by the greeting of silence as he walked into the building. His apprehensive rose when the large gathering of Apprentices in front of the closed doors of the Overseers Chamber mutely parted for him.

A document was posted on the Chamber's door. A proclamation that an Inquiry for Impeachment was in progress. An impeachment against his cousin. Jac read it three times. Not only did it feel like the blood drained from his face but also from his whole body.

He turned to the gathered Apprentices. "Does anyone know what this is about?"

"We only know that this was posted before we got here this morning," Liyla, Apprentice to Culinary Arts, offered. She was the same age as Dorian and Jac and had played with them when they were children. "And a delegation of three Overseers went to the High Overseers Hall not long ago."

If Jac's face had been pale before, it was like ash as he stared in shock at his old friend. A delegation already. "Which Overseers?" By tradition, the members of the Overseers Council were the ones to do official business with the High Overseers. That would not be possible in this case since Dorian was a member of the Council.

"Lons, Interwood and Shawndoc," Kwen answered. "No members of the Council."

Jac rubbed his chin. "Strange. So it was not an official delegation."

"The document they carried had a purple seal," Kwen agreed. Purple was the everyday color for the Overseers. Official documents were sealed with white. Jac let his breath out in relief. Whatever the Inquiry involved, it was not a simple right or wrong decision. "They've sent out for food and drink, including bondroot." Jac looked up at him.

"What's the outer boundary for a three week old bond?" Jac

turned to Nema, Apprentice to Attractions.

"Three hundred strides," Nema mused.

"At least I can help Dorian by making her more comfortable," Jac muttered.

"The Hall Tea Shop ought to be close enough," Nema suggested, placing a sympathetic hand on his arm. "Whatever it is, it has to be a misunderstanding."

"You know Dorian." Kwen clasped Jac on the shoulder. Jac gave him a wane smile and nodded.

"I know Dorian," he said in a way that indicated that he knew her better than any of them and that knowledge did not make him feel better. After casting an apprehensive glance at the closed door, he turned and left the Hall as quickly as possible. He didn't want their sympathy. He wanted Dorian to walk out that door as the Overseer of Knowledge.

He stepped into the bright morning sun, and he stopped as Devor looked hopefully up at him from a nearby bench. Noting Jac's expression, Devor rose as the morning meal tumbled nervously in his stomach.

"You'd better sit back down," Jac muttered bleakly, collapsing onto the bench.

"What is it?" Devor asked, trying to abate the apprehension overtaking him.

"Dorian's in some kind of serious trouble," Jac stammered out.

Devor frowned in puzzlement. "Trouble?"

"The session was closed last night before it even began," Jac explained. "So no one knows what it's about."

"Then how do you know Dorian's in trouble?"

"A proclamation is posted on the door of the Chamber." Jac swallowed hard. What could she possibly have done? "An Inquiry of Impeachment is in progress." Devor paled as he clutched the Athronian's arm in mute alarm.

"Against Dorian?" The unbelievable words somehow came out of Devor.

"Yes."

Devor stared at the Hall doors. "Doesn't an Overseer have to do something really bad to be impeached?"

"That's an understatement." Jac dropped his head into his hands. "This isn't a question of some little mischief. This is a question of serious consequence to the entire Athronian community."

"What can we do?" Devor watched as several Apprentices stepped through the door for some air.

"We can't do anything to help with whatever this Inquiry is about, but we can help Dorian in another way." Jac straightened, resolute to hold himself together until this ordeal was over. "She's been in need of bondroot."

"What's that?"

"It's an herb that helps ease the effects of a bonding separation. You don't have to worry about it because the separation doesn't have the same effect on an Outlander," Jac explained. "Right now, there's only heightened emotions, sudden tears, bouts of uncontrolled thoughts, feeling out of sorts, things like that. Not the best of conditions to be in when you're fighting for your place in the community. If we can keep you within three hundred strides of the Chamber, that will be one less thing for her to deal with."

"I'll stay here as long as it takes," Devor responded without hesitation, frowning a little at the description of the symptoms.

Jac nodded. "The Hall Tea Shop is close enough and more comfortable. We'll be able to watch everything without bringing attention to ourselves."

"Why would it matter if we brought attention to ourselves? It's only natural that we would be concerned." Devor's frown deepened at his future cousin.

"When Dorian gets into trouble, I'm not far behind," Jac said bleakly. "It's an unwritten Athronian law."

"But you don't even know what this is about."

Jac gave him a wry look. "That's never mattered before. I love my cousin, but I always stumble into the middle of the most improbable situations when all I'm trying to do is rescue her out of them."

"I've read the Stories," Devor said blandly.

"Those stories are true," Jac responded defensively. "No matter what she says." He relaxed a little. "At least, most of them are. Maybe the details aren't quite exact." He realized he was babbling to hide his fear of the nightmare that unfolded inside the Hall.

"Let's go settle into this tea shop," Devor said steadily. "Then you can tell Dorian's parents what is going on if they haven't learned of it already."

Jac nodded as Devor helped him up and led him across the green to the Overseers Hall Tea Shop.

The delegation from the Overseers had difficulty keeping a solemn demeanor as they strode down the long cavernous High Overseers Hall. The four ancient beings frowned a bit when they noted that none of the delegation was from the Council. Their frowns deepened when the Overseers were close enough to be recognized. A strangely mismatched group: Art, Mathematics and Geology.

"You have an announcement for us?" Huask almost demanded, trying to keep his impatience down. Interwood stepped forward and placed the sealed folded papers on the High Overseers table. Huask glared at the purple seal. "What's this?"

"It's a document explaining why the Overseers are currently in a closed meeting and a list of questions we need answered before we can proceed," Interwood responded in the blandest possible tones.

Flickering an irritated eye towards the delegation, Huask shakily broke the seal and read through the document, his mouth tightening as he read. The Overseers maintained calmness, ignoring the nervous jumble of their insides.

Huask locked cold eyes on the Overseers. "Please wait out-side," he barked with a tense impatience. The trio refrained from exchanging glances before they turned around and made the long trek out of the presence of the High Overseers.

The other three High Overseers had the document read by the time the far door echoed shut.

Usaf grimaced, emitting an unpleasant sniffle. "They're stalling. They don't want to condemn one of their own."

"Too soft hearted," Lektle muttered.

Huask angrily waved the document. "They have a lot of nerve. Look at this. They're confused because they have not received any Inquiry against the Overseer of Truth. They have decided the only reason we would keep him from doing his job is because we have lost confidence in his abilities."

"Not using him might have been a mistake," Trandle voiced hesitantly.

"You know that we can't trust any Overseer." Huask wished he didn't have to keep explaining the same things over again. "They're playing games with us. We simply placate and reassure them that they have misunderstood and that we have every confi-dence in the Overseer of Truth's abilities and faith in their judgment in this serious matter. We will accept anything that comes out the Chamber."

Usaf shuffled a few papers before voicing that single fear that hung in the air. "What if we're wrong?"

"We are not wrong," Huask gasped out, using fear rather than confidence to seal his commitment to his words. They couldn't risk the humiliation of being wrong in this case. Their credibility must remain intact in order to attain their ultimate goal.

Soral's duty of watching over the newest Apprentice to the Elders School was an interesting assignment. She marveled at Janin's drive to devour everything she focused her attention on. That had to be a demonstration of the same kind of determination that pushed Athronians to become Overseers. The dedicated Elders Assistant kept a journal of her own on the rare phenomenon of a young Athronian. The duty, unfortunately, also forced her to play "mother" at times when Janin forgot about meals and bedtime. She quickly adopted the habit of fetching Janin when the mealtime bell rang or when the sand mark got too late.

Visiting the prison floor in the middle of night was not something Soral ever had the inclination to do before. The purpose of the place colored her perception too much, and she was the first to admit that it unsettled her a little. Even after several weeks, she could not cast off an irrational response the moment she stepped off the last stair and felt the brooding impact of the ghostly stone.

As expected, Janin sat with elbows on the table and cheeks in her hands, intently devouring one of the journals by the light of a single lamp. Soral took a deep breath and walked swiftly across the shadowed open floor to the table in the far corner. The older Apprentice always wondered how Janin did not jump at her presence, so absorbed was she in her reading. Soral knew that every little shadow or twig scratching on the window would have her off the bench constantly.

The young Apprentice glanced up just as Soral stepped into the circle of light. "Did you know that there are fifty-six Overseers and they keep offices so anyone can consult with them?"

Soral grinned at her friend. "Unfortunately, you have to be in Athros to take advantage of that little service."

Janin grinned back. "Details can always be taken care of. This trunk is more than just journals; it's like a compendium of life in Athros. The customs, the laws, anything you can think of."

"Really?" Soral looked down at the piles of books with interest. Elder Enle had mentioned that the Overseer of Knowledge had penned a definitive work on Athronian life. "The Elders will be happy to see that since they refer to Orvid's compendium all the time."

Noticing that the objects from the trunks were arranged according to sameness, Soral's attention rested on the heap of leather wads at corner of the table.

"Those are stones," Janin explained, observing Soral's interest. "I've only peeked at a couple. No telling what they're used for."

"I've always wondered how the stones worked." Soral picked up the largest bundle and carefully pulled away the leather. "Rather plain looking. I wonder if the stones contain the magic or if it is added to them."

"Maybe Orvid says something about that in here," Janin mused. "I haven't gotten very far yet. It's dense reading." Her attention was drawn to the stone that Soral had liberated from the soft leather.

Soral shrugged. "Feels ordinary to me."

"Let's see." Janin held out her hand. Much to their surprise, she dropped it the moment it touched her skin. The thud against the thick wood of the table bounced once against the dense walls and died.

"What happen?" Soral watched her friend with intense curiosity.

"It was like a thousand words slamming into my brain at once," Janin stammered out, staring at her shaking hands. Soral reached out and hesitantly touched the stone. Nothing. Just a cold smooth stone.

"What kind of words?" the older Apprentice ventured.

"Words about everything," Janin said slowly. Concentrating, she discovered she could scroll through the words at her own pace, one following the other without effort. "By all the Overseers in Athros." Swallowing hard, Janin stared at Soral, stunned by her realization. "It's a knowledge stone."

"That would only make sense," Soral responded, distracted by the bewilderment in Janin's eyes. "What doesn't make sense is how you can hear the knowledge." The impact of her words impaled her as she said them. The two Apprentices stared at each other for long heartbeats.

Janin's gaze returned to the stone. Frightened and curious at the same time, she deliberately reached out her fingers until they barely touched the smooth brown surface. She pulled her hand back as if it had been burned. "I think I can learn how to use this," she murmured, wholly focused on the relic.

"But what are we going to do?" What a secret. It was worse than knowing that Janin was an Athronian.

Janin looked up at her. "The Elders must be told. Only they can help me work with it."

"Isn't this the kind of skill that is learned once an Apprentice becomes an Overseer?" Soral couldn't believe how calm Janin was. "Apprentices can't use stones."

"I don't know why this is happening," Janin responded quietly. "I only know that it is. Orvid writes of instances when the talent to read stones sometimes happens naturally. He had Dorian take the Great Stone once. She would not tell him if she could read it but from then on she seemed to hold knowledge that could not have come to her any other way."

"Just be careful." Soral wasn't quite sure what she was concerned about. Perhaps it was only the unknown.

"One step at a time," Janin agreed. "That's what my life has been since learning about my heritage. I just wonder when the revelations will stop and I can feel I really know who I am."

By midday, the Overseers Hall Tea Shop overflowed with idle Apprentices, family members of Overseers, and quite a few curious citizens. Jac was thankful they had gotten a sizable table early in the day. Even Zore deserted the office to join the Riverson clan, miserably huddled around a table in the back of the shop.

Both sets of twins unconsciously twisted and arched to watch the constant activity around the door. The green outside the shop was just as crowded, so a clear view of the Overseers Hall was gone.

The little group gathered around the table, littered with remnants of the mid-day meal, were the quietest souls in the place. They couldn't even speculate on the trouble Dorian was in. Since becoming Overseer, Dorian had displayed a diligence in her work that no one, even herself, had thought was possible. After seven years, she was almost respectable by Athronian standards.

"You seem to be feeling better," Dordan commented, resting a motherly eye on Devor.

"Yes, I am," Devor responded, realizing that he had forgotten about the rocky start to his day. "Maybe I just needed some tea."

"I'm glad you're not coming down with anything," Dordan returned thoughtfully. "Dorian will need your strength when this is over."

The others went to a deeper level of stillness at the words. Devor read more in the silences than shouted words could express. An Impeachment was apparently more than just stripping an Overseer of the title. He was near crazy from needing to know the truth, but he didn't want to upset the others any more than they already were.

"It can't last much longer," Zore sighed. Waiting was far worse than knowing.

The late afternoon sun just reached the front windows when a commotion near the door caused the seven people in the back to jump to their feet. Pushing through the agitated throng, they were able to determine that the meeting was over. Finally breaking free of the shop, their first instinct was to look for the personal guards of the High Overseers. If the Impeachment was successful, Dorian would be put into immediate custody.

"No guards." Yanos let the tension flow out of his body as he reached for Dordan's hand.

"You know, Jac," Devor turned to a visibly relieved Apprentice to Mischief, "I'm going to want to know the truth behind all this sometime."

Jac nodded. "I know. I just didn't have the heart to tell you how bad it really was."

A number of Overseers were trying to escape the confines of the Hall through the crowd of Apprentices. By their exhausted, but relieved, expressions, it was apparent that no Impeachment had been successful that day.

"Where's Dorian?" Zore tried to look over the crowds swelling around the doors of the Hall.

"I'll go get her," Jac volunteered and was pushing his way through the people before the others had a chance to respond.

By the time he entered the Hall, he found it was nearly

deserted. While scanning the large main chamber, his eyes fell on a lone figure sitting on the floor with her back against the wall and knees to her chin. Even from that distance, he could see the haunted expression on the exhausted face. Hesitantly approaching her, he visited a fear that he was going to find a stranger in his cousin's eyes. Standing several foot lengths away, he waited for her to come back from wherever she was. Finally, she took a deep breath and looked up at him, surprised that he was there.

"Jac." She frowned as if she had forgotten something important, like her family was possibly worried about her. Bracing against the wall, she got to her feet. "It's been a long night. Day. Whatever. It was long."

"Come on." Jac was so relieved that she seemed to be all right that he fell into his role as the one who pulled his cousin together when mischief got the better of her. "You really ought to stop scaring the life out of us."

"I thought I had," Dorian mumbled as she slouched into step next to him.

"What was it all about?" Jac turned to her, not hiding his concern.

"Forget it ever happened." Dorian gave him a sidelong glance before returning her gaze to the floor in front of her.

Jac stopped walking, staring after her before rushing to catch up. "What do you mean, 'forget it'?"

"It would not be in the High Overseers' best interest if the details of this little incident got out." Dorian sighed, beyond exhaustion, almost beyond caring.

"Wait. Stop." Jac tried desperately to assimilate what his cousin was telling him. "No one outside the Chamber is ever going to know what you were accused of?"

"Right, Jac," Dorian returned, blandly. "Where's Devor?"

"And the High Overseers agreed to this?"

"That's right, Jac." Dorian leveled a discussion's over look at him. "Let's just say it would be more embarrassing for them than for me. Now, where's Devor?"

"He's outside." Jac sighed and hurried after his cousin.

Chapter
Nine

Best Laid Plans

"Attractions," Huask muttered darkly as he rummaged through the pile of thick leather bound books in the small room that passed for a study. "Orvid said something about Attractions. Must get someone to straighten this mess." He carefully studied each volume trying to decide which one would most likely contain the information. It could be anywhere. He glowered in frustration as he opened the first book.

The time was closer to sunrise than sunset when Huask crowed in satisfaction. At last he had found the passage he knew he had read when he was a young Apprentice. Orvid, the previous Overseer of Knowledge, had made a special study of Athronians and Athronian life, sifting through manuscripts from the most ancient to the near present time. From these studies, he had gleaned a series of consistencies that were pretty much accepted as indisputable facts.

Huask jabbed his finger at the words on the page. Embedded in a treatise on Attractions was a quote from one of the endless tomes on Athronian life that Orvid had penned. He had determined that an Overseer of Knowledge could not be caught in an Attraction. Huask was relieved that it was a direct quote, because finding the original text in the fathomless archives would be two steps south of impossible.

The ancient High Overseer still fumed over Dorian getting around the truthstone about the explosions in Athros. He had no doubt that she was behind them. The materials she had bought from Fenchan and those used in the explosions were the same. But according to the Overseers, she had sworn her innocence to the truthstone and passed. He made a mistake not to anticipate that they would close the meeting. The High Overseers had been too lax in keeping up their knowledge on certain things, so he ordered Usaf to read the bylaws of the Society of Overseers. Trandle almost got her nose bloodied from the argument the High Overseers had had about whom was responsible for reviewing Granwin's reports.

Huask beat on the opened volume with his bony fist. They could have been rid of that dangerous Overseer of Knowledge weeks ago if they had paid more attention to life outside their cocooned existence. Attraction indeed. How did she think she could ever get away with that? The fact that Overseers of Knowledge could not be caught in Attractions was so well known that he didn't understand why there hadn't been challenges or even questions about it. Not one Overseer had even brought it up when they were questioned about the explosions. The answer was simple. They were protecting her.

A sly grin that looked more like a gaunt grimace took over Huask's features. His dream to have the Overseers condemn one of their own was still alive. The fact that they were obviously protecting her simply made his goal more difficult to accomplish. As he drummed his fingers on the volume, an idea slowly wove through his twisted mind.

Strangers were rarely seen in the district, much less a Royal Guard leaning casually against the Banish Hall grounds gate. He watched an Elders Apprentice in a blue tunic and a black-garbed Guard battling each other with staffs. The spectacle was so riveting that it was long moments before the stranger noticed the tall Guard looking on with another Elders Apprentice. Now there was a face not easily forgotten. The stranger remembered that this Guard had won the all-Onbersan staff competition several years in a row. So this was the tiny backwater where the mysterious Morna kept herself. This beautiful, lethal warrior had turned down the opportunity to join the Royal Guard more times than he could count. Why did she choose to remain in this out-of-the-way place?

The stocky Royal Guard raised an eyebrow as the young Guard-in-training grasped air where his staff had been just moments before. Morna stepped forward and held up her hand.

"Three out of five. That's what we agreed to." The statuesque Guard pinned Kaston with a no-nonsense glare. "There's always the opportunity for a rematch," she reminded, softening her stance a little.

"You're teaching her new moves," Kaston complained.

"She's just more focused and more inventive." Morna added the last with a glint in her eyes. "She knows that she has to be in order to beat you."

"So you're saying I have to be even more on my guard when going against someone with less skill." Kaston puzzled out.

"Not less skill." Morna held up a quick finger to Janin, who was about to attack the young man, this time with strong words. "Less body size and, at the moment, less muscular strength. You keep forgetting that the mind is the best weapon in any fight."

Lazy clapping came from the direction of the iron gate. All four straightened in surprise as a solidly built, middle-aged man wearing the maroon and blue uniform of the Royal Guard sauntered towards them. "Well spoken, Morna. I'm beginning to understand why so many excellent staff wielders come from this district. They have the best instructor in the country."

The others turned to Morna, surprised that this man knew her and that he was familiar with her formidable skills. Morna had never mentioned her victories in the yearly competition in the far-off capital city. The other Guards who also tried their luck in competition respected her request to keep her accomplishments to themselves. She hated the attention but needed to participate to keep her skills at their peak.

"What brings you this far off the well-traveled road, Langton?" If Morna was surprised to see a Royal Guard in her district, she did not betray it as she casually leaned on her staff.

"Not you." Langton smoothed back his shoulder-length brown hair, revealing blue eyes with a softer expression than one would expect from a career soldier. But these days, his work was more as a peacekeeper than a warrior. That very reason was why Morna had no desire to join the Royal Guards. If she was going to be a peacekeeper, she felt her skills could serve the village of Baniston better. "Although, if I'd known you were here, it would have been a good enough reason to visit." The Guard bowed graciously.

Soral raised an eyebrow at this touch of gallantry. Those were not the kind of words she was used to hearing said to Morna's face, without the risk of having the poor soul trounced as a return compliment. Morna imperceptibly nibbled her lip and nodded back. Langton had, on a few occasions, pulled his comrades away from making the mistake of approaching Morna with too much familiarity. He had even taken it upon himself to apologize for the behavior of his companions. Of course, Morna suspected that he was just saving them the humiliation of being taught a lesson in the proper way to treat a young woman bearing a staff. She also sensed a deeper, more basic presence of civility in him. That essence that made him a peacekeeper rather than a warrior.

"Captain Langton Renor, these are my friends, Soral and Janin, who are Apprentices at the Elders School, and Kaston, who is training to be a Banish Hall Guard," Morna introduced.

"It's a pleasure." The Royal Guard smiled at the group, and winked at Kaston, who was in a speechless stupor. "So, this is the Banish Hall that produces all those talented Guards in the sixth regiment," he mused, gazing at the brooding round building.

Morna nodded. "The very same. Now back to my question."

Langton shrugged. "I pulled artifact duty for a while. Got a shoulder injury that's going to take some time to completely heal."

"Artifact duty?" Janin, who could never contain her curiosity, stepped forward.

"Yes. Queen Ketric's hobby is collecting Overseer relics." Langton turned to the young woman who had beaten a Guard-in-training with a staff. "She always has someone out searching the countryside for these things. I've done a pretty good job of avoiding artifact duty up to now. This time my luck ran out."

Another reason not to join the Royal Guard, Morna mused to herself. "We have four retired Overseers here. They were here long before Ketric became Queen. I'm sure they've already made their contributions to the Queen's collection."

"I've got a list of the Overseers in this district who have already been visited." The Royal Guard patted a leather side pouch. "It's a lengthy list. You seem to have a lot of retired Overseers in this part of the world. But, as you say, most of them have been visited already. So far, this duty has turned out to be little more than a stroll through the countryside."

"I can, at least, offer you the hospitality of our barracks." Morna waved to the back of the Hall. "We are always hungry for news of the outside world."

"I would be most pleased to learn more about the infamous Banish Hall Guards." The stocky man favored them with a genuine smile. Perhaps this diversion would make this routine exercise to keep the Royal Guards busy worthwhile for him.

Kaston was already pestering the man with questions about being in the Royal Guards before Morna led the newcomer out of earshot of Soral and Janin.

"I thought you were ready to squeeze the life out of that," the older Apprentice commented, pointing to the white knuckles from Janin's grip on her staff.

"We'd better get to the Elders before he does," Janin responded urgently, setting a good pace to the Elders Hall.

"I don't think he's going to go out of his way looking for these artifacts." Soral grinned at Janin's panic as she followed after the girl. "I think a few well placed rugs over the trunks will do just fine."

"Perhaps you're right." Janin slowed down, trying to focus her thoughts. She realized that she had almost drawn attention to herself over the fear that Orvid's things might be taken from her. They were more than just a new and exciting world for her. They presented a lifeline to a reality she felt more of a kinship with than her own.

Soral knew how obsessed Janin was with the treasure of relics with which she had been entrusted. Janin may say that her obsession was from the need to come to terms with her own identity, but Soral knew better. Even the newfound talent to use the knowledge stone did not compare with the true reason Janin selfishly guarded Orvid's treasure. Janin worshipped the wayward Apprentice to Knowledge and a glimpse into the real Dorian through Orvid's journals just compounded that worship.

"Don't worry. He'll be gone soon enough without ever being the wiser," Soral cheerfully predicted as they bounded up the Elders Hall steps. Janin absently twirled her staff. A good sign, Soral smiled to herself. She's back in control.

Dorian pushed Devor through a low rounded opening in a thick brick wall overgrown with ivy. "This was how we always got into the Gardens when we were young," Dorian explained. If there was a disingenuous way of doing something, Dorian found it. Devor thought that it was a way of keeping everyday life interesting.

After crashing through a small forest of miniature trees, they finally found one of the many paths that wound through the vast Central Gardens cascading up and down tight, steep hills in the middle of Athros. At the first clear view of a large portion of the Garden, Devor simply stopped walking as his senses tried to take in the endless variety of vegetation extending before them.

Dorian laughed. "These are my mother's other children."

"Unbelievable," was all Devor could manage.

The Overseer raised a curious eyebrow at him. "You like plants?"

Devor shrugged. "I had a garden when I was young. I was curious about how things grew."

Dorian gave him a knowing look. "And being the budding Researcher, you exhausted every source of information you could find on the subject."

"Something like that."

"I could never get things to grow," Dorian admitted, a little sheepishly. "I'm a poor offspring to my parents. I can't grow anything and I'm a terrible cook."

"Fortunately for you, I can do both," Devor conceded. "Learned both out of necessity."

"Necessity is an underestimated motivator," Dorian mused as they tramped a delicately carved wooden bridge across a rocky stream. "Jac usually fixes my lunch for me. I think he does it because he likes to. Oh, look. They're over there." Dorian shaded her eyes and nodded in the direction of a fern-covered, rocky overhang.

Dordan and Deidan were so intent on a patch of green on the rocky escarpment that they didn't hear the mischievous Overseer and her companion come up behind them. Dorian motioned for Devor to be quiet as she stealthily pulled the back ties that held the twin's heavy work aprons in place, successfully untying them in a single move.

"What the..." both women responded at once before spinning around.

"Incorrigible," was all that Dordan could mutter as she tried to keep from laughing at her daughter. She knew she shouldn't encourage her impish behavior. The grins on the twins faded a bit. Since the attempted Impeachment, they had trouble keeping their concerns to themselves. Every moment that Dorian was with them was treasured.

"So what brings you here?" Deidan asked, trying to bring her thoughts to the present. "And why aren't you at work?"

"Because I'm here?" Dorian raised her eyebrow in a question. "We've got much more important things to do than soak up the world's knowledge."

Laughing at this, Dordan gave her daughter a hug. "And what could that possibly be?"

Dorian shrugged. "Last minute details on our joining."

Dordan winked at Devor. "You're right. That is much more important."

Dorian grimaced. "Some of the other Overseers have been hinting that since this is an historic occasion we should do something special to set a precedence. We're going to set a precedent no matter what, so history will just have to deal with it."

"I take it you'll be wanting something simple and private." Deidan knew her niece very well.

"What about your Apprentices?" Dordan asked.

"I haven't decided yet." Dorian shifted, a little uncomfortable. Only two of her Apprentices had been caught in an Attraction. That alone was enough for them to accept that they would retire as Apprentices. The other Apprentices were equally resigned to the fact they would never be caught in an Attraction, just as Dorian had been. She wasn't sure how they really felt about her miraculous good luck, considering that her life seemed to be a string of miraculously lucky occurrences. "I don't know how they feel about it."

"Attractions have always been a rather touchy subject around Apprentices to Knowledge. Even you went through a period of despair about it," Dordan gently mused.

"We all do at a certain age." Dorian scuffed her foot in the loose gravel path. "Would you try to find out what they're saying among themselves? I don't want to do anything to break down what little respect I've been able to cultivate from them."

Both women scowled at the young Overseer. "They were beside themselves during that Inquiry. I'd never seen a more disheartened group."

Dorian leveled a steady gaze at her mother and aunt. "That's only because none of them are prepared to become Overseer."

"You can believe that if you want, but that is not what I saw or heard." Dordan returned the gaze. Dorian finally gave in and looked away at the path.

Dorian sighed. "Maybe you're right. Sometimes it's easier to believe that they aren't as loyal as they ought to be."

Her mother grabbed her by the shoulders and held her until Dorian raised her eyes. "There are obviously a lot of things going on that we know nothing about. But if you're still in trouble, we need to know. You can't go through life keeping these awful secrets to yourself."

"I have to," Dorian whispered. "I have no choice. As far as still being in trouble, I'm always in trouble. I have been for years. I just haven't been caught yet. And if I am, I hope I am prepared to save myself." Dordan's hands fell off Dorian's shoulders in shock. "You wanted the truth. It's best to know it now because the High Overseers are getting serious about removing me from the Society of Overseers."

"I don't believe you could have done anything serious enough for that to happen." Dordan straightened. She knew all about the High Overseers games with her daughter.

"I haven't done anything wrong," Dorian assured her. "I am simply a victim of circumstance."

Both Dordan and Deidan let out sighs of relief. If the truth were as evasive as that, then these High Overseers would never discover it. "We appreciate you trying to prepare us for another nasty surprise, but I think the High Overseers learned their lesson with that last one," Deidan said. "They're going to have to be certain of their accusations to impeach you. It's obvious that the evidence they had did not stick."

"Obviously." Dorian could not confirm or deny, just agree. It killed her to have to keep a secret from her family, but the decision to stay silent was to keep her credibility intact as much as the High Overseers. "I just hope they'll leave me alone once we're joined."

"I'm sure they'll finally tire of their games with you once you're settled with a family." Dordan smiled as Dorian tried not to blush.

Dorian grinned. "Me with children. Kind of a scary thought. Fortunately, Devor has a domestic side to him."

"More mischievous intelligent children to keep track of." Deidan rolled her eyes. "Athros will never survive."

"So you won't be disappointed if this thing doesn't turn into a public spectacle?" Dorian asked her mother.

Dordan laughed. "I'd be worried if you decided to make it a big deal."

"Devor suggested a huge celebration afterwards for anyone who wants to come," Dorian added.

"What a great idea," Deidan said with delight.

"It's an Outlander tradition," Devor explained.

"Then it's only right that we do it," Dordan decided. "We should have something from your world."

Dorian grinned wickedly. "Now that that's settled, we can go tease Jac into neglecting his work."

"You are a terrible influence on him," Deidan scolded good-naturedly.

"He's too diligent," Dorian returned. "I keep warning him that that can only lead to no good. Like becoming Overseer someday."

Deidan beamed. "One Overseer in the family is a delight. Two would make us the envy of the neighborhood."

"At least it would make up for our notorious pasts."

Dordan straightened. "That was only a sign of how exceptional you both are."

Dorian turned to Devor. "That's the family excuse for us." Devor laughed. "It's getting late. We'd better get to Granwin before she decides she knows what's best for us."

The twins thoughtfully watched the pair until they disappeared into the dense vegetation. Both tried to push down all the feelings of uncertainty about Dorian, but their not knowing what was hidden deep within the Overseer was almost too much for them to take. They knew that Dorian only got into trouble when she was protecting a person or a promise. A "victim of circumstance" she called it. Life was never going to get any easier for the Overseer of Knowledge; they could only hope that it didn't get any worse.

"You've been holding out on me." Soral had heard enough from their visitor during the evening meal with the Elders to track down Morna as soon as she could get away. The Guard's habits were regular, and Soral knew she would be working with a set of iron weights to keep her strength built up. "I learned more about my best friend from a total stranger than I ever learned from her."

Morna shrugged. "You knew I was good with the staff."

"Every year you go to Praen to compete, and you return with only a shrug and an admission that it was an interesting experience. Your comments are always that Praen is a huge, crowded city and that there are a lot of skilled warriors out there," Soral ranted, exasperated at her calm friend. "Not once did you mention winning anything, much less top prize. Every single year. And being offered a place in the Royal Guards. Repeatedly." The Apprentice stopped her verbal assault and rested curious green eyes on the tall figure lifting a heavy piece of iron. "Why didn't you join the Royal Guard? Most of them," she waved her hand in the direction of the barracks, "would tackle their grandmother for the chance and never look back."

"Can you see me doing artifact duty?" Morna raised an eyebrow as she held the iron over her head for several heartbeats before slowly lowering it to the ground.

"You're too clever to get injured," Soral returned.

"Onbersan is not at war." Morna stopped her exercises and looked straight at her friend. "Do you know what a Royal Guard does?" Soral shook her head not wanting to do anything to prevent her reticent friend from opening up to her. "They are peacekeepers. Stationed in the bigger cities and in key places along the borders. Since there isn't enough real work to do, the Queen has devised all kinds of wonderful activities to keep them out of trouble. They get to help the local farmers with their planting and harvest, help repair the city buildings, help the teachers instruct the children in survival skills." Soral covered her mouth with her hands to stifle a chuckle. Morna did not mix well with children. The Guard rolled her eyes to the heavens. "Artifact duty is sheer excitement compared to peacekeeping."

"So were you disappointed?" Soral knew her friend well. "When you first realized that being a Royal Guard was not the kind of life everyone around here thinks it is."

Morna bent over and picked up her staff, giving it a few twirls before approaching the Apprentice. "I was devastated," she answered softly. "I was sixteen. My first time in the capital. The first time to match my skills against the best in the country. Royal Guards were everywhere in their polished armor and maroon and blue uniforms, looking ready for battle. You have to remember I was put to sleep every night with stories of the campaigns my foster parents fought in alongside the Royal Guard. But I saw the Guards in peacetime, and they weren't as strong in the competitions as I expected them to be. They were lax and sloppy. I was dazed with disbelief and felt like an idiot for idolizing them all my life. It's the Queen's fault. She's taken away their pride. That's the thing inside that keeps you battle ready. I was suddenly lost. The future I saw for myself had been yanked away. I owe it to Rane and Fent for setting me right." Morna stared at the single light hanging from the kitchen, then focused her attention on Soral. "Do you know why my foster parents came here to settle?"

"I suspect it was because of the Banish Hall Guards."

"That's true," Morna agreed. "But their world was suddenly at peace and they realized that they weren't the farmer or merchant type. The Royal Guard was hounding them, offering high ranks just to have them. Fortunately, they were acquainted with Captain Janvil, and he offered them a chance to not only pass their skills to a new generation but also be a part of a Guard that performed an important duty to the Crown. It took a year or two for me to realize that being a Banish Hall Guard was more noble and ultimately more satisfying than being a Royal Guard in peacetime."

"The other Guards don't seem to feel that way," Soral commented.

"People see what they want to see." Morna leaned on her staff. "They refuse to believe that the Royal Guards are not the same great warriors who won the battle of Fanstaph. The fancy uniform and the gleaming armor are strong seductions for those of us who crave adventure. But if we ever go to war, I'll be the one ready to fight."

"Why didn't you ever tell me this?" Soral asked more out of curiosity than anger.

Morna sighed. "I always seem to think I have to fight my battles alone."

"It's good to remember that reinforcements can sometimes make a difference in whether a battle is won or lost." Soral was heartened by a soft chuckle from her friend.

"I'll keep that in mind." The Guard nodded. Sometimes, her scholarly friend had better sense than she did. Sometimes, she even believed her.

Chapter
Ten

Realizations of Power

The Retired High Overseer strolled unhurried down the wide corridor, oblivious of the young Royal Guard next to him trying hard to walk at such a moderate pace. Rubnic Siderling was not tall but his lean frame attested to a love of hiking and belied his advanced years as a long-retired Athronian. He was not happy about this summons to the Queen. Her interest in Overseer relics brought shivers to the Athronians living in Onbersan. Sometimes, relics had the tendency to come to life, especially when handled by someone with latent Athronian talents.

The palace at Praen was a work in progress. The previous structure had been destroyed during the Onbersan Wars. The tapping of the artisans' tools echoed through the nearly completed wing of the palace as they added ornate touches to the thick stone walls. Rubnic shook his head at the irritating noise, wondering if the palace inhabitants were being driven mad by it.

"In here, sir." The young Guard led the old man through a rather treacherous course of stone blocks, scaffolding, and oblivious cutters and masons. The pounding of chisels against stone was enough to create a new level of irritation in the already put-out High Overseer.

Finally emerging free of the construction, they ducked

through a temporary half door into a modest-sized hall. "Close the door," a woman's voice called from a cluster of chairs at the far end of the hall.

The Guard turned and pulled the door closed, successfully shutting out all but the faintest echoes of the construction work. As they neared the circle of plush blue chairs, Rubnic's observant eyes took in the added thickness around the Queen's middle since he last saw her. Of all the schools in the country, Ketric, then still a princess, had decided to send her only child to the one he presided over as headmaster, forcing him into an uneasy familiarity with the future Queen of Onbersan.

Queen Ketric rose, looking every bit the doting grandmother that she was. Her short, thick blonde hair was streaked with gray and her green eyes were more watery than he remembered, but her pleasant understated bearing hadn't changed since becoming Queen.

"Rubnic! It's been much too long." Her voice always had a cheery ring to it, making everyone feel like this woman was not just their Queen but also their trusted friend.

"I don't travel as much as I used to, Your Majesty," Rubnic apologized with a bow.

"Sit, sit." Ketric waved a hand at a chair across from the one she had chosen to sit in. "Cedic. Be so kind as to have Farlan bring us some tea."

"Yes, Your Majesty." The Guard bowed and disappeared through an open archway on the nearby wall.

The Queen smiled graciously at her visitor. "I've been wanting to have you visit for some time now. Too many things always come up. Never a heartbeat's rest, as they say. But I just had to make time to see my old friend Rubnic. So here you are. I miss those chats we used to have when I visited Loral."

All that Rubnic remembered of those chats was her incessant probing about Overseers and their special skills. "And how is the Princess?" he inquired politely.

The Queen beamed. "She's doing wonderfully. She's expecting her third child. Imagine, three grandchildren. I'm so pleased. I'm afraid I get too much enjoyment from spoiling those youngsters."

The High Overseer chuckled. "It's the privilege of being a grandparent." His own grandchildren had been distinguishing themselves in Athros by the time he retired.

"There is one thing I remember from our chats that I found

most interesting." Ketric sat back and folded her plump hands in her lap, her face still beaming with delight. Rubnic wondered if she spent long years practicing that expression so it always looked sincere. "I remember you mentioning that you had been the Overseer of Sorcery before you were elevated to High Overseer."

"That's correct, Your Majesty," Rubnic responded, fighting a wariness in his voice and expression.

"I've always been fascinated by the magic that controls nature," Ketric replied in a delighted twitter. Rubnic had no doubt of that. "What a valuable resource to have."

The High Overseer shifted as a blank-faced young man, clad in the royal blue and maroon livery, entered with a tray laden with afternoon tea. So, collecting artifacts was no longer enough for the good Queen. She had discovered what every Overseer knew, that their knowledge and skills added up to power and control. Why just collect the artifacts when she could collect the actual Overseers without having to raid the streets of Athros? He could read it in her as easily as he could read a book. Reading people's intent was his special talent. A very valuable asset for someone entrusted with the knowledge of Sorcery.

"I'm afraid it's been ages since I've been a practicing Overseer," Rubnic stated conversationally. "We have a tendency to forget much of what we once knew. I, myself, am shamelessly rusty."

"I'm sure you're just being modest," the Queen gushed. "After a few days, it would be like you never left it."

"When we retire, we're ready to concentrate on just being retired." Rubnic gave her a gracious smile. He didn't like the direction of the conversation. "Being Overseer is such an intensive job that not doing it any more is a relief."

"I guess that's something I'll never understand." Ketric reached for a cup of tea. "I could never imagine not being Queen. I enjoy it so much." She gave him a radiant smile. "There's nothing more satisfying than to make a difference in other people's lives. My projects have brought food to the tables and shelter over the heads of those caught in less fortunate circumstances. And the schools. No longer will the common people be uneducated. I am so grateful that this peace has lasted, giving me a chance to build our country into something we can all be proud of."

Or, to speak the truth, you enjoy the idea of power too

much, Rubnic thought as he raised the teacup to his lips. After a long sip, he returned her smile. "I guess being a monarch is different from being an Overseer."

"I suppose it is," Ketric mused. "Yet, I think there are a great many similarities. You each have your own little kingdoms to rule, and you are the complete rulers without having troublesome relatives or greedy usurpers lurking around."

"That's an interesting observation." Rubnic nodded, admitting to himself that she was good at this game she was playing. "I've never quite thought about it that way."

"I've got an idea." Ketric clasped her hands together as if she thought of it right at that heartbeat. The High Overseer could only marvel at the control she had over her performance. "Now, it's just an idea but I think it might be worth considering. What if I gave any Overseer who was interested the chance to get back to practicing their specialty? Some Overseers might not be as content in their retirement as you are. They might enjoy the chance to get back to using their expert skills once again. And, of course, Onbersan would benefit from having this expertise used for, shall we say, creating a new aqueduct for Praen, enhancing the curriculum at the Universities, creating parks for the children to play in." The Queen leaned forward in her excitement.

"There may be some Overseers who might be willing to participate." Rubnic kept his voice light and amiable, while the back of his mind shouted in panic. She had no idea what kind of danger she wanted to dance with.

"I'll have to think more on it." Ketric rubbed her chin thoughtfully. "I hope you'll allow me to consult with you on this little idea from time to time."

"It will be a pleasure." Rubnic bowed his head. So she knew when to back off. He already dreaded those subsequent little get togethers when she finally let her ambition take over. She wanted his sorcery skills, and she was willing to set up a charade to get to them. He was too old to get involved in this kind of dangerous sport.

The shock hung over the four Elders seated at the round table in Gretna's spacious new office. Janin, relieved to give her burden over to the Elders, had bounded out of the office to her lesson with Morna, oblivious of the bleak reactions from those left in the chamber. The Elders focused on the echo of Janin's footfalls on the steps, each hoping she would come back and tell them it was just a joke that she and Soral thought would be amusing. Not amused, the Elders sat in silence long after the echoes stopped bouncing up the stairwell.

"What do we do now?" Gretna finally found her voice.

"At least she told us," Enle ventured.

"She thinks we can help her deal with it." Lanler stared out the newly cleaned window. "Manipulating knowledge stones is the most mysterious and powerful of all our skills."

Enle stared into her teacup. "I don't think she realizes that, if her mind can retain it, she will hold more knowledge than anyone in The Land Out of Time, with the exception of the Retired Overseers of Knowledge."

"You don't think that's possible, do you?" Gretna reacted with a start. "She's bright, but she's no Kwen or Dorian, for that matter."

"You hope." Trudlin shifted in the pliable chair.

"We'll find out soon enough," Enle predicted. "It won't be long before she figures out how to control the stones."

Lanler focused her attention on the other Elders. "It's still not possible for her to retain everything in those stones."

"Unless that's a part of the talent." Trudlin's words silenced the others for several heartbeats of thought. "What was Orvid thinking? Leaving knowledge stones here."

"Why did he leave anything here?" Lanler voiced the question they had been asking themselves since they discovered the trunks.

"I just hope our other Athronians don't have similar talents," Enle murmured. "We won't be able to contain them or teach them properly."

"As long as we don't tell them, they won't know to explore for talents," Trudlin reasoned.

"I think we ought to tell Morna," Gretna said thoughtfully.

Trudlin rested curious eyes on the Head Elder. "Why?"

"That was an interesting story Captain Renor told us about her accomplishments in Praen and how she did not want to become a Royal Guard," Gretna mused. "I had a talk with Soral, who was more than a little put out that her best friend had never told her any of this. It seems Morna has decided that her destiny is to stay in Baniston and keep herself in shape in case of war.

She suffered a great disappointment when she found out that the Royal Guards were no longer the warriors they had been in wartime. I think it would give her life more direction if she were aware of her talent."

"Perhaps you're right," Enle agreed.

"You know, I think Orvid was right in his observation that Athronians always find each other," Lanler commented. "Have you noticed how our little group spends a lot of time together?"

Trudlin cast a speculative glance at Gretna. "Soral's always with them."

Gretna shook her head. "That's only because she's friends with both Janin and Morna. I tested Soral by leaving the stone out on my desk, so she had to pick it up while tidying the office. She's just an outstanding Outlander."

"Three Athronians are quite enough," Enle replied. "So who's going to tell Morna."

"I think we ought to have Janin tell her." The words sprang from Gretna's lips without thought. The others paused before voicing their initial contrary response. A few heartbeats of thought turned reservations into acceptance of the suggestion. "Janin has a better handle on how Morna will react to the news and will know what to do to help her accept it."

Trudlin nodded. "Agreed. Janin seems to be finding her own way. Perhaps Morna will also."

Lincim stared at the chemistry table and the ruined book on top of it. He had been staring at them for sand marks. Jac had gone to his mid-day meal and returned, doubting that the Overseer even noticed he hadn't been there. The workroom in the Archives was dark except for a few dim glowstones around the evidence, allowing the Overseer of Mischief to concentrate without distraction.

The High Overseers' attempt to blame Dorian for the explosions returned his investigation back to the beginning. The other Overseers seemed more than willing to put the incidents behind them, but he realized that Athros would never be wholly safe until the prankster was found. He had to determine what evidence the High Overseers had against Dorian and why it had turned out to be false. Someone was trying to frame Dorian. He blinked, and straightened. Turning around, he spotted Jac, cross-legged on the floor next to a glowstone, reading.

"I have a puzzle for you, Jac." The Overseer moved the chair around so he faced his top Apprentice. Jac looked up, and closed his book.

"I love puzzles," Jac responded a little warily.

"Let's say that there have been a number of unexplained explosions," Lincim began.

"I think I can envision that," Jac replied dryly.

"Let's say that no one has a clue as to who caused these explosions or how they could do it without being seen," the Overseer continued. "The materials used in the explosions are not allowed in Athros and certainly cannot be acquired here. On top of that, mysterious script appears at the site of one of the explosions and at the site of another unexplained phenomenon, the moving of the Rock of Teyerbom. To add to the puzzle, someone has what they thought was positive evidence against a specific person, but it turned out to be false." Jac froze and met Lincim's steady gaze.

"I won't let Dorian know that I know," Jac whispered, lowering his eyes and focusing on nothing but his own troubled thoughts.

Lincim nodded. "Good, because I need your mind to help me solve this. Sometimes I think you were meant to be the Apprentice to Knowledge and she to Mischief."

Jac smiled weakly. "You have no idea how many times we've said the same thing."

"Now, let's forget about the Rock of Teyerbom and the mysterious scripts for a moment and concentrate on the explosions." The Overseer pressed his fingertips against his temples. "We know explosives cannot be found in Athros, so they had to have been acquired in the Outland. That means a merchant was involved."

"How many merchants deal in that sort of thing?" Jac leaned forward, being drawn into the puzzle.

"More than you might think," Lincim returned. "It would have to be a merchant known to an Athronian. An Athronian had to have something to do with the explosions. Even if it only meant helping an Outlander."

"Why would an Outlander want to cause explosions in Athros? How would the Outlander find an Athronian willing to go along with the idea?" Jac shook his head. "It would be too many coincidences. It has to be the work of an Athronian."

"Now, how does an Athronian go about making a purchase from an Outlander merchant?"

Jac shrugged. "In this day and age, we just walk into a shop and buy whatever we want. No one recognizes us as Athronians."

"What if the merchant did recognize the patron as an Athronian?" Lincim pressed.

"There are very few Athronians who could possibly be recognized by an Outlander. Even Dorian roams the Outland undetected these days." Jac pursed his lips, unconvinced. "Assuming for a heartbeat that a merchant knows he sold explosives to an Athronian, how can he or she report this to the High Overseers? How does the merchant even know that explosives are against the law in Athros?"

"What if the High Overseers happen to be dealing with that particular merchant?" the Overseer mused. "Several Outlander merchants are known to regularly visit Huask. There are many merchants who have spent enough time in Athros to know certain Athronians by sight and to pick up on some of our laws and customs."

"Another coincidence," Jac scoffed. "All right, let's say that our mysterious Athronian who looks like Dorian buys explosives from a merchant who just happens to be doing business with a High Overseer. If this Athronian is clever enough to create these incidents, he or she would know which merchants have dealings in Athros and shop somewhere else."

Lincim rubbed his chin. "Unless that was a part of the plan."

"What are you saying?" Jac asked.

"I'm saying it sounds like a setup."

Jac's eyes widened. "So these incidents were created to get Dorian into trouble? Where does the wild script and the Rock of Teyerbom come into this?"

The Overseer frowned. "I believe that whoever is behind this couldn't resist letting us know that he or she is just playing with us. That they have skills beyond our understanding and control."

"That's a pretty scary thought." Jac re-crossed his legs. The idea that someone could strike at anytime and do inestimable damage to Athros was beyond his comprehension.

"We start with what we have and put the puzzle together piece by piece." Lincim rose to his feet decisively. "Are you with me?"

"You know I am." Jac jumped to his feet. He had felt so helpless not knowing the trouble Dorian had been in. Now he had a chance to solve the mystery. Maybe this time he could get her out of trouble and not be dragged into it himself.

The confused donkey tossed irritated glances at the small man on his back. This same man had always let the beast travel at his own pace. Now he was in a hurry to get home. On top of that, he was muttering unkind words such as "dumb beast" and "worthless creature." The scowling animal knew that if his master wanted him to go faster he shouldn't feed him so much and let him laze around in the pasture with the cows.

When the donkey finally stepped into the lane that wound through a thin woods to a tiny cottage on the edge of Waynsfare, Rubnic slid off its back and pulled the methodical beast the rest of the way.

"Greenar," Rubnic shouted as he struggled to pull the donkey to the opened front door. "Greenar. I need help with Crik."

"What has he done?" A calm voice came from a calmer looking woman. Small and thin with an ageless smooth face, only her thick gray hair betrayed her age. "What are you doing to that poor beast?" She stood in the doorway, all but laughing at the sight of her life companion trying to get the indignant donkey to move much faster than he was willing to go.

"I was in a hurry to get back," Rubnic grumbled through clenched teeth as he leaned back on the rope. "I must get in contact with the other Overseers. Right away."

"The Queen up to her old deceits?" Greenar patiently took the rope from a grateful Rubnic.

"New deceits. New troublesome deceits." The old man shook his head.

"I'll take care of Crik." Greenar already had the rough blankets off the grateful animal's back. "You can tell me about it later."

"Thank you," Rubnic remembered to say before running into the cottage.

The musty study was actually a room built onto the back of the original structure. The older floor dipped and lurched onto the new flooring, making it treacherous for visitors. Between Rubnic and Greenar, who was a Retired Overseer of Justice, they had an envious collection of books and manuscripts. More importantly, they also stockpiled a good number of those precious artifacts that so enamored Ketric.

Several Overseer objects were actually indigenous to the Land Out of Time, created for the special circumstance of being Athronian without an Athros. Athronians were scattered across the sizable world and suffered from the need to be with their own kind. Through the ages, they had devised ways of detecting when another Athronian arrived from Athros and how to keep in quick contact with each other.

The aged High Overseer pulled a weighty ornate bookend from one of the shelves that lined the chamber from floor to ceiling. The books it supported magically stayed put—a little display of Rubnic's Overseer specialty. He carefully placed the bookend on a small table. Twisting off the top half of the object, he exposed a large polished white stone. He laid two fingers on the stone and sent his message to similar stones throughout the Land Out of Time by simply thinking the words. The next time the Overseers checked their stones, they would receive the message. A simple but efficient communications device. He expected to hear quite a lot of reaction the next time he checked the stone. Outlanders meddling in the ways of the Overseers was not a popular subject amongst the Athronian population.

After putting the bookend back on the shelf, he finally relaxed, flexing his strained fingers. Pulling on the rope of a stubborn beast had done nothing to improve his aged joints or his mood. Sighing, he turned to leave the chamber when a turquoise stone he used as a paperweight caught his attention. The stone was more translucent that usual. Another Athronian had arrived in the Land Out of Time.

Chapter
Eleven

A Lesson in Truths

"Summoned to the Overseer of Truth." Dorian absently crumpled the slip of paper. "When was the last time I heard those words?"

"It used to be all the time," Jac replied, not feeling very jovial.

Dorian gave Devor a wan smile. "The Truthseeker's office was my second home."

The Outlander watched the interplay between cousins and knew that this summons was something too serious for them to voice. "Do you know what this is about?"

Dorian's expression turned thoughtful as she gazed at him. "I have no idea."

"None?" Jac eyed her, puzzled.

Dorian gave him a flat look. "None, Jac."

"I have a bad feeling about this one," Jac whispered. Dorian's flat look slid into a troubled one, then she shook it away.

"It'll be all right. I've done nothing wrong, and I've nothing to hide." Faced with two sets of uncertain eyes, she turned away frustrated. "Well, not too much. I'll see you later." The brusqueness was so out of character that she immediately turned back, afraid that she had hurt them. All she saw was a sad helplessness. Without thinking, she stepped forward and kissed Devor on the cheek then hurried away.

Devor lifted a hand to his cheek, wondering at the shock of warmth produced by such a brief touch of her lips.

Jac frowned. "She's never kissed you before?"

"No."

"She must be really frightened." Jac's stomach tightened. "Forgetting the bond like that." Devor looked at him, trying to swallow his own rising fear. "I hope she regains her focus before she faces Kerit."

As Dorian turned the corner, she crashed into several empty metal juice containers lining the paved walk. Muttering all kinds of colorful curses in a wide range of Outlander languages, she managed to get back on her feet and set the juice containers upright. Leaning with one hand against the wall, she took several deep breaths, trying to pull her scattered thoughts together.

She must be losing her mind forgetting the bond and kissing Devor like that. Bonded pairs always pushed the limits of the bond as a part of the fun of getting to know each other. But that was a conscious pursuit, wary of the consequences if they went too far. She had just forgotten about it.

By the time she stepped through the unadorned door with a simple shingle reading "Truth" hanging overhead, Dorian had regained her composure. The outer room was large with a high ceiling, and empty. Not even an Apprentice was there. Just Kerit sitting on the bench that lined the back wall.

The Overseer of Truth's face was drawn as he raised miserable eyes to Dorian.

Sitting down next to him, Dorian matched his dejected posture. "So I take it this is a private encounter?" Dorian ventured.

Kerit put his miserable head into his hands. "Please. I need your forgiveness."

Dorian looked at him bewildered. "For what?"

"For what the High Overseers have directed me to do." Kerit lowered his hands and looked at her. "No Overseer, no Athronian, should have to go through what they are putting you through."

"If they've put me through an Outlander's underworld, Kerit, they've dragged you right down there with me," Dorian muttered.

"Why do you always do that?" Kerit asked in frustration. "You've got to start thinking about yourself. I thought the

Impeachment hearing finally forced that into your head. It's not going to be so easy this time. The High Overseers are looking for a lie, any lie, from you. They are going to keep this up until they have it or you're completely broken."

"I'm not that easy to break." Dorian straightened but could not hide the haunted looked that pulled at the edges of her eyes. "What is it this time?"

"It's the Attraction," Kerit muttered, putting his head back into his hands. Dorian looked at his dejected, hunched over shoulders for several heartbeats before sighing and slumping against the wall.

"So they finally figured it out," she mused quietly. "I guess if you're going to be caught in a lie, it should be a big one or else the Chroniclers won't be happy."

Kerit jerked his head up and stared at her. "We can't save you if you're not willing to save yourself." His frustration was pushed to the limit. "And we want to save you. We need to save you. Any one of us would sacrifice everything to prevent something from happening to you." Realizing he had said too much, Kerit turned away, muttering much milder curses than Dorian had been known to use but shockingly strong for him. Dorian stared at him, feeling as if he had just slammed her head with a quarterstaff.

"I didn't hear it, Kerit." Her throat tightened from her reaction to his words. "I won't betray your trust." How had they come to this wild idea that she was so valuable to them that they were willing to go to such risks to help her? She realized Kerit was staring at her with mouth gaping, open hands still where they had held his head. Saying she didn't hear his words was the first time he had ever heard her tell a lie. "Do you want me to say what I really think about what you just told me?" Her voice was edged with a menace that Dorian could sharpen to a frightening point.

Kerit, realizing he held his breath, let it out raggedly. "No."

"Have they put Granwin to the stone?" The fury rose in her. What the Overseers were doing behind her back and how the High Overseers were putting them through humiliations because of her was too painful to contemplate.

"Yes, this morning," Kerit said miserably.

"Now they don't trust the Overseer of Attractions."

"You're doing it again." Kerit, beyond exasperation, jumped to his feet. "You must learn to think of yourself first."

"What have the High Overseers charged you to do?" Dorian looked up at him, eyes cold as stone. He knew she was angry, and it would do no good to push it further.

"I have to put you to the stone."

She raised an eyebrow at him for stating the obvious. "Not in the High Overseers' presence? Are they trusting you now?"

"About as far as they can throw me," Kerit returned bitterly. "They want me to put you to the stone before the Overseers. They really think they've got you this time. So if you—"

"I haven't done anything wrong, Kerit." Dorian stood, bringing herself as close to eye level as she could, being a head shorter, and gave him a cold steady look.

"But, the lie—"

"*I* haven't done anything wrong." Her voice was as hard as stone. "Being caught in a lie is not the same as creating one."

"I hope you can manage to convince the stone of that," Kerit replied. "The meeting has been called. We are to be escorted by a group of High Overseer Guards."

"I didn't know the High Overseers had a taste for the dramatic," Dorian muttered as she followed Kerit to the door. "Are they afraid I'll try to run away?"

Kerit looked back at her. "We won't go into that special talent."

"I don't possess that skill," Dorian replied steadily. "As you well know."

"But no one else knows that," Kerit returned.

"And you have been sworn to protect that secret," Dorian reminded him.

"I would never betray your trust," Kerit said softly. Dorian stopped, startled, but he had already opened the door. Four guards in black tunics and armed with overly large swords came to attention as the pair of Overseers walked into the street. A small crowd gathered, keeping a curious respectful distance.

"Dorian." Jac's voice came from behind her. Turning around, she saw Jac and Devor pushing through the people. "What's this all about?"

Dorian shrugged. "I'm in a little trouble again."

Jac scowled angrily at the guards. "In the old days, you actually had to do something to get into trouble."

"Times have changed," Dorian said softly. "Devor. Stay close by. I wouldn't want to bother the Overseers for bondroot again."

"I will." Devor found a voice. Dorian held his gaze for long heartbeats. Only after she and Kerit started down the street that he realized that she had been studying him as if she may never see him again. "Jac," he said, as the little crowd pushed them along. "I think she thinks she really is in trouble this time."

"I know," Jac responded, bleakly.

The Overseers were already seated. Dorian looked around the Chamber of somber faces with new insight. They have been working to protect her all this time. Shaking her head, she stepped to her place on the Council bench, surprised to see Panute Taner seated there.

Dorian frowned. "Where's Gris?"

Panute looked up at the Overseer of Knowledge, as always, startled by her youthfulness. The last time she had seen her was the day that Dorian stood for her Overseer examination. Now she was confronted with a young woman with sad, mature eyes. "Gris has retired," Panute said dryly.

Dorian nodded without betraying any reaction. "I see. Rather suddenly it seems."

"Yes. Rather suddenly," Panute returned steadily.

Dorian looked around the Chamber. Was this one of those sacrifices that Kerit hinted at?

"Welcome to our Society, Overseer Taner." Dorian made a small bow with her head. "I hope to spend many long years working on the Council with you, but that's not likely if the High Overseers have any say in it."

Panute was taken aback by Dorian's frankness concerning her position. "I also look forward to a long and fruitful relationship." There was something in the way Panute emphasized the words that caused Dorian to wonder what she was actually saying.

"The meeting will come to order," Tigren, Overseer of Justice, announced. He looked longingly at the gaping doors crowded with Apprentices. "As much as I would like to close this meeting, I have received orders from the High Overseers to keep the doors open." The Chamber erupted in angry outbursts. Tigren turned to Dorian. "I apologize that this has turned into a public spectacle."

"Do not apologize for something that is not your fault,"

Dorian said.

"Thank you for your understanding." Tigren bowed to her. He looked around the Chamber and took a deep breath before embarking on the troublesome task before him. "We are here at the request of the High Overseers to be witness to Overseer Riverson being put to the truthstone by Overseer Jandor—"

"This nonsense has gone too far," Lincim broke in, springing to his feet. "The High Overseers are creating these spectacles just to show off their power. They are pulling and pushing us like puppets, submitting us to public humiliation. The stronger we are, the greater the humiliation." Lincim looked straight at Dorian, who stared at him, astonished. "And what happened to Gris? Retired? Forced retirement, more like it."

"May I remind the Overseer of Mischief that we are in an open session," Tigren said steadily.

"I don't care. The High Overseers don't need any reasons with substance to make accusations or to force retirements." Lincim cast his eyes about the Chamber. "Dorian's too young to force into retirement." The unspoken implication of these words hung thickly in the Chamber.

"We must not forget why they are doing this to her," Interwood reminded them.

"May I again remind the Chamber that this is an open session," Tigren said more forcefully this time. "I think Overseer Riverson would appreciate certain things remaining unsaid." The Chamber settled down as the Apprentices pressed around the door murmured loudly.

"Thank you," Dorian, with head bowed down, whispered to the table, after letting out a long held breath.

Panute looked at her young colleague. Gris had filled her in on this ongoing subject among the Overseers.

Tigren signaled the Apprentices to silence. "The High Overseers have prepared a set of questions for Overseer Jandor to ask Overseer Riverson. If she fails to answer any of these questions truthfully, we are allowed to close the session." Again the unspoken words echoed louder than the spoken ones.

Dorian, head still bowed, shifted her eyes to the door. Jac had pushed through to be right in the doorway. Their eyes met, Jac's wild with concern, Dorian's unreadable. She wasn't going to reassure him this time.

A small commotion behind Jac gave way to the rest of the Riverson clan. She pushed back tears as she saw their frightened and concerned faces. Jac looked behind him and pulled his distraught aunt and uncle forward in front of him. Maybe their presence would give Dorian the steadying influence she desperately needed at that moment.

"Overseer Jandor, you may proceed." Before sitting down, Tigren glanced in Dorian's direction. Her attention was on something at the door. Her parents. Tigren's heart went out to the young Overseer of Knowledge.

Kerit, doing his best to hide his agony, approached Dorian and placed both truthstones on the table in front of her, avoiding her eyes. Dorian rose and laid her fingertips on each stone.

"Give a false statement to the stone," Kerit intoned.

Dorian looked steadily at him. "I have lied to the truthstone."

The blood drained from every face within hearing. The gasp at the door was from her mother. The stunned tension was so tight in the air that it seemed ready to snap. Both stones blazed with an intense blue.

"May I request that you refrain from scaring the morning meal out of us." Tigren looked past Panute to Dorian, who stared, as shocked as anyone, at the stones.

"Sorry." Dorian raised sheepish eyes to him. These kinds of situations always brought out her penchant for mischief. That was one of her special talents, and that's why she could never keep herself out of trouble. The deeper the trouble, the deeper she was compelled to drag herself into it.

"You may begin the Inquiry," Tigren said, wariness and uncertainty reflected in his face.

Kerit picked up one of the stones and took it back to his place in the circle of Overseers. He shuffled a thick stack of parchment sheets in front of him. Staring at the first question, he prayed for the High Overseers to render him useless at that moment so he would not have to go through with this ordeal. Realizing that he had paused too long, he cleared his throat and placed his fingertips on the stone. "Overseer Riverson. Did you pass the Overseer of Knowledge exam through the use of counterfeit?" Kerit did not raise his head from the parchment. His was the only set of eyes not riveted on Dorian.

Fury rushed through Dorian so rapidly that it even frightened her in its intensity. Everyone caught their breaths at the anger flashing in her eyes, tensing her well toned muscles like a cornered jungle cat. Strong emotions could push the truthstone in strange directions. She pulled her fingertips from the stone.

"I apologize," the Overseer of Knowledge gasped after several tense heartbeats. "I found the question insulting and demeaning. I hope you will forgive my show of temper." She held her hand under her arm for a few heartbeats to stop the uncontrollable shaking. Telling the truth was difficult when one could barely remember the event. And Dorian had very little memory of taking the exam. The only relief she felt was at the way the question was worded.

The collected release of tension rippled through the Chamber.

Dorian carefully replaced her fingertips on the stone. "I, Dorian Riverson, Overseer of Knowledge, did not use counterfeit to pass the Overseer of Knowledge exam." The relief on Kerit's face was reflected in the other Overseers. Letting out a long breath, Dorian was certain that this was one of the easier questions on the list.

"Is it true that you have been caught in an Attraction?" Kerit continued.

"Yes. It is true that I have been caught in an Attraction."

Kerit watched her closely. "Is it true that Orvid said that an Overseer of Knowledge could not be caught in an Attraction?"

Dorian paused, that old need for mischief rising within her. "No. It is not true that Orvid said an Overseer of Knowledge could not be caught in an Attraction." The stone did not even flicker.

Fighting hard to keep from grinning at the stunned expressions around her, she knew she was going to get into serious trouble one day. But maybe not today, she mused. She sent a prayer to the author of the treatise for not checking the original source for exact wording or including the whole statement for that matter. Leave it to the High Overseers to be too lazy to check the original.

Kerit tried to regain his focus. The logical line of the questions just lost its thread. Dorian was supposed to say that the statement was true. According to the High Overseers' perspective, that was the correct response. Most confusing. But he knew that the truth was only what was known to whoever held the stone. Everyone in the Chamber thought they knew what Orvid said about Overseers of Knowledge and Attractions. Dorian, of course, knew exactly what Orvid had actually said. "Take your hand off the stone, Dorian." Kerit let the formality drop.

"What?" Dorian started.

He sighed wearily. "Remove your hand and tell us what Orvid really said." She could have at least warned him of this. Of course, she had no way of knowing what the questions were going to be. This was the old Dorian from the days when the truth had many shades to it and she could manipulate it down to the words she chose. Dorian removed her fingers from the stone.

"Why don't you want my hand on the stone?" she asked, more out of curiosity than anything else.

Kerit straightened. "Because we're to report everything you say to it. I am not willing to give them one word more than they ask for." Dorian was taken aback by Kerit's strange sense of honor.

"What Orvid actually said was, 'according to the Ancient Book of Overseers, an Overseer of Knowledge cannot be caught in an Attraction.'" She stopped herself from finishing the statement. What else Orvid said was no one's business but her own, even if it could invalidate the present proceedings. The fact that it never made it into the treatises reflected the tendency to ignore the possibility of exceptions to these kinds of sweeping declarations.

Kerit gave Dorian a look of disdain as he picked up on the fact that the question he asked was still true in substance. A matter of a single word turned it into a falsehood. Dorian gave him a weak quirky smile. The statement would have been true for everyone else in the Chamber, but for Dorian it was false.

"What's the next question, Kerit?" Dorian pressed.

"They were assuming you would answer the previous question as 'true' and that would be the correct response," Kerit stammered.

"The correct answer is 'true,' generally speaking. I chose to answer it as 'false.'" Dorian folded her arms in a challenge. "The results are the same either way." This caught the Chamber off guard, but no one got to their feet in protest. Their collective protection of Dorian pulled in around her even closer. She was playing some kind of dangerous game. They only hoped it was for a reason other than plain mischief.

The Riverson clan was struck dumbfounded that no one challenged her statement. They knew that the vaguest hint of irregularity in a formal proceeding was enough to trigger, at the very least, a debate. Yanos was so pale that Jac was ready to catch him if he collapsed. The young Overseer brought herself within a breath of closing the doors of the Chamber, yet no one even shifted, much less made a move to press her into a corner. They could easily start a dizzying line of questions that would eventually break her down.

Kerit visibly swallowed. He knew why she did it. She wanted to get the Overseers to show her the truth that she had denied hearing from him. He was no longer burdened with betraying the trust of his colleagues.

"The next question," Dorian prompted.

"I don't have to ask it you know. The line of logic has been broken." Kerit was almost pleading. "You don't want to jeopardize—"

"I have the truth on my side," she interrupted.

"You've been too lucky so far." Kerit gazed at Dorian, all but forgetting where they were. "The odds are going to go against you eventually."

"But not today. Because I have not done anything wrong," Dorian returned, steadily. "There is truth even in those caught in a lie."

"But it may not be a lie." Interwood jumped up. The entire Chamber stared at him until he sank back to the bench. "Of course, the odds are so improbable that it must certainly be a lie," he babbled, realizing that he let logic get the better of him and this was not about logic.

"You have been charged with asking those questions until I give a false answer to the stone." Dorian met Kerit's eyes. "As far as the stone is concerned, I've told the truth. The fact that it is not the truth the High Overseers were hoping for does not invalidate their instructions to you."

"Even if it increases the chance of you faltering?" Kerit implored. "Even if it means you'll never walk out of this Chamber a free Athronian if you fail?"

The silence hung like fragile glass. No one dared voice it before, but Kerit had to get Dorian to face the final truth of her situation.

"Ask the question, Overseer Jandor." Dorian's voice lost the ominous tone to something much colder, much more frightening.

Kerit gave her one last look before returning his eyes to the parchment. "Given that all the above questions were answered true, isn't it true that you have been caught in a lie."

Thanking the heavens for the wording of the question, Dorian, without hesitation, placed her fingers on the stone. "It does not mean that I've been caught in a lie, just that I've been caught between truths."

The air crackled from the tension, but again the stone did not even flicker. Dorian could have answered the question any way she wished because the question itself contained a falsehood.

Tigren shot her a look. "A simple restatement of the question would have sufficed."

"Sorry." Dorian turned an innocent face to him. "I've always had a problem following protocol." Several Overseers cleared their throats at this understatement.

"Is that the answer you really want to give?" Kerit asked.

"It doesn't matter since you have to report everything I say to the stone anyway," Dorian came back with that quirky smile. "What's the next question?"

"The next question is based on the assumption that you agreed that you have been caught in a lie and that it is a true statement." Kerit sighed. Questioning Dorian always made his head feel like it was under water. "If you have been caught in a lie, how can the circumstances creating the lie be true?"

Puzzled looks were exchanged, then all eyes rested on Dorian. The Overseer of Knowledge almost laughed before she realized she was the only one who saw the humor in the question.

"Since, according to the High Overseers' definition, I have not been caught in a lie, I do not need to explain any circumstances that can turn truths into lies." Dorian looked at Kerit. The relief on his face told her that this ordeal was over.

"That is all the questions for speaking truthfully to the stone. These are the questions if you had not spoken the truth." Kerit picked up the pile of parchment. "It would not have been pleasant."

"And this was?" Dorian raised an eyebrow at him before sinking onto the bench.

"That concludes this Inquiry," Tigren rose and announced, the relief heavy in his voice. "Overseer Riverson has answered the High Overseers' questions truthfully and has acquitted herself of any impeachable offense. Unless anyone has more to say, this meeting is adjourned."

Dorian lifted her head and then stood. "I have one small thing to say." She looked around the Chamber. "If we are gathered again for one of these quaint little meetings, just impeach me and put us all out of our misery." Gasps escaped several throats. She bowed to her colleagues, whose stunned shock was frozen on their faces, slid off the bench and hurried to the door. Head down, she pushed past her family. The Riversons, understanding her better than anyone, shrugged off her brusqueness and followed after her through the suddenly active crowd of Apprentices. Dorian did not stop until she was out of the Hall and practically ran into Devor.

"Devor," she gasped, realizing she almost gave the bond another jolt. By that time her family had her cornered from behind, the concern in their eyes not lost on the Outlander. Dorian looked up at her future life companion with a newfound knowledge searing through her mind. The person she had protected this time was him. She almost got herself banished because of what she had left unsaid of Orvid's statement. But she would have gladly faced it if she were sure they never found out. "I need a drink. And not tea." She finally let the tension flow out of her. She turned to her family and hugged each one, trying to avoid their questioning eyes. "Sorry you had to witness that."

Before they voiced their admonitions, Kerit broke through the crowd of Overseers and Apprentices spilling into the courtyard and walked straight to her.

"You came too close this time." Kerit didn't know if he was furious or frustrated, but it all equaled the same thing. "I don't know who it is you were protecting this time, but it is not in anyone's best interest if anything happens to you." He tried to swallow some of his anger. "Just remember that." He bowed to Dorian's family and stalked away.

All sets of eyes were riveted on Dorian. "He's just a little upset, that's all." The Overseer of Knowledge pulled herself away from them, and headed for the nearest tavern. An Outlander tavern would have suited her better, but convincing Jac of that was not a good idea at that moment.

Chapter
Twelve

Trading Secrets

Morna trudged up the staircase in the Elders Hall, more than a little curious about why Janin wanted to see her and that it was something that required privacy. The sand mark was late, but nearly every desk on the second floor was illuminated with the distinctive soft light of glowstones. Blue robed shadows were hunched over manuscripts and books. The only sound was the scratch of pens and the turning of crisp pages. Morna paused to stare at this study in intense concentration. She could never understand how they sat still for so long at one time. Absently twirling her staff, she was thankful that she had been a fast learner in school. She had fidgeted too much, and as long as she passed all her lessons, her teachers were more than happy to let her burn off her extra energy practicing the staff.

She had only been to the prison floor a few times in her life. Each time, it took her breath away as she focused on the open cell door, the stone interrogation table, and the narrow windows. If there ever were a banishment, this floor would become the domain of the Banish Hall Guards.

Several glowstones illuminated the table near the far wall. Seated behind it, half hidden by piles of journals and relics, Janin was bent over a book. Morna was halfway across the floor before the young Apprentice pulled her eyes from the words that held her captive.

"Interesting." Morna nodded, running a finger across the tops of the mechanical objects gathered in a corner of the table. "They let you stay up here all night, studying these things?" She picked up one of the stones. Frowning a little, she tossed it into the air a few times.

Janin grinned. "Yes. But Soral usually makes sure I get to bed at a decent hour."

"What kind of rock is this?" Morna turned it over in her hands.

Janin sat back. "Why do you ask?"

Morna held it up to study it closer. "It has a strange weight to it."

"Lighter or heavier?"

"Off balance," Morna returned.

Janin arched an eyebrow. So Morna had the ability to recognize Overseer stones. "It's a knowledge stone."

"Knowledge stone." The Guard put the stone down and picked up another one. "Used by Athronians." She remembered that from school.

"Yes. These belonged to the Overseer of Knowledge," Janin explained.

"How do you know that?" Morna scrutinized the stone. "There isn't anything to distinguish it from any other rock. Except it doesn't seem to balance right."

Janin pulled a small smooth brown stone from her belt pouch. "Try this one." The moment Morna touched it, she let it go like it was a fiery coal.

"That is definitely no ordinary rock," Morna stammered out, staring at the offending stone.

Janin picked it up. "I don't feel anything," she said steadily. "But the first time I picked up one of these stones, I had the same reaction as you had to this one."

Morna eyed her with a mixture of confusion and skepticism. "Are the Elders teaching you Athronian tricks now?"

Janin met Morna's eyes and held them. "These are tricks that no one but Athronians can learn."

"I was never any good at riddles," Morna finally said, warily.

"What happened when you touched that stone?" Janin pressed.

"Nothing happened." Morna swallowed. In truth, it had

shouted her secret through her brain. She realized, in that brief instant, she had been in tune with every body in the Hall. Not only in tune, but also given knowledge of diagnosis and healing.

"You possess what they call a 'skill' in Athros," Janin went on steadily. "If you were there, you would be an Apprentice to the Overseer of the Body."

Morna laughed. "What are you talking about? That only applies to Athronians. Besides, how do you know what kind of skill I might possess?"

Janin pulled a gold stone from her belt pouch. "Do you remember this stone?"

Morna shrugged. "Trudlin asked me to toss it to Kaston. She's doing some kind of study."

"It's a stone that detects Athronians." Janin put the rock on the table. It blackened when she removed her hand. "It turns gold for an Athronian."

The Guard folded her arms. "Are you saying you're an Athronian?"

The Apprentice grinned. "No more Athronian than you are. Pick it up." Morna held the younger woman's eyes for several heartbeats before snatching up the stone.

"So this means that Kaston is also an Athronian." Morna knew that she shouldn't believe this outrageous story, but she could not deny the special skill she had held secret all her life.

Janin nodded. "Yes. That was what Trudlin was testing. Discovering that you were also Athronian was an accident."

The Guard placed the stone back on the table. "So, why am I hearing this from you and not from the Elders?"

"I'm like you. I just learned who I really am only a few weeks ago," Janin replied. "They thought it would be better for you to hear it from someone who understands how you're feeling right now."

"How did you find out?" Morna relaxed a little.

"The Elders discovered that I was the one who stopped the Ghouls," Janin said quietly, staring into the dark beyond the glowstones.

"You?" Morna started. "You stopped them?" Facing the Ghouls was one of the most horrific moments of her life. Ready to defend the villagers to the death, she had been so close to the vile creatures that she nearly retched from the repulsive stench of their bodies.

"It was not something I did consciously." Janin shook away

the memory. "Somehow, I called upon a talent that I never knew I had."

"So what about Kaston?" Morna brought herself back to the present. "What's his talent? Besides being able to fall down."

Janin wrinkled her brow. "I don't think the Elders know yet."

"Then why did they want to test him?"

Janin shrugged. "They didn't think it was possible for him to outrun the Ghouls."

"So, are you going to have one of these little chats with him?" Morna stepped back from the table to twirl her staff. She needed movement to keep her mind clear.

"Not until the Elders instruct me to," the Apprentice said. "They don't feel he should know yet."

"Why did they feel I should know?" Morna could have done very well with never knowing.

"They felt that your talent is so strong it could be developed if given proper instruction," Janin explained.

"You mean be an Apprentice?" Morna asked, incredulous. "No thank you. I'm happy being a Guard."

"I don't think they want you to stop being a Guard," Janin reassured her quickly. "Maybe something you could do on the side."

Morna casually whipped the staff around, mulling over everything she just learned. "I'll think about it. But whatever I decide will have to be on my terms."

"I'm sure the Elders will agree to anything you want." Janin watched the Guard with fascination. Her staff communicated nearly as much as her words. At that moment the movements were fluid, indicating that Morna had already accepted her Athronian background and was giving thoughtful consideration to developing her talent. The Apprentice thought it odd that the Guard was not too surprised to find out she was an Athronian. Maybe she knew more about her past than she let on. "I couldn't believe it when Gretna told me I was Athronian," Janin ventured. "I knew I was adopted but having an Athronian father—"

Morna stopped her movements. "How do you know it was your father?"

"Because the women are too old to have children by the time they come here," Janin explained.

Morna frowned. "But you look like your sister."

"It's an Athronian tradition to place a child born outside of an Attraction with the family of the Outlander—I mean, the non-Athronian."

"I'm aware of the Athronian habit of referring to us as Out-landers," Morna stated as she fingered the ring on her hand. "So, this ring may belong to my mother's family. Even if I ever find them, they may not reveal who my true mother is."

"Not if you were born in Onbersan," Janin mused. "Revealing the birth mothers of adopted children is against Onbersan law."

Morna sighed and wandered over to the heavy stone interrogating table, absently running her hand across the cold polished surface. Another dream shattered. Her heart ached for a single satisfying resolution in her life. Sometimes, she thought it would be best to just stop dreaming since every dream ended in disillusionment.

"Tell the Elders that I will think about this," the Guard finally said.

"If you need to talk about it or anything..." Janin trailed off. Who was she to offer this orphan of war an understanding ear. She could never fathom what Morna had gone through as a young child.

"I'll keep that in mind," Morna said, causing the young Apprentice to gave her a startled look. "Does Soral know?"

"She knows about me," Janin admitted. "I don't see why she shouldn't know about you."

"Let me be the one to tell her." Morna walked into the shadows to the stairs. "I'll have a better chance of catching her when she faints from shock."

❖ ❖ ❖ ❖ ❖ ❖ ❖

Panute squinted across the dimly lit tavern. The sand mark was late, and the remaining patrons were well on their way from being raucously drunk to blissfully oblivious. Spotting the small figure in the corner slumped against the comforting shoulder of Devor Locke, Panute thought that she had gotten there too late. She had taken a while to convince Jac to tell her where Dorian was and preparing the transport to the Outland was a lengthy procedure for everyone except Jac and Dorian. She'd give anything to have that special talent.

The Overseer approached the table and stood before them. Devor, who kept properly sober so he could help Dorian deal with whatever spectres were tormenting her, looked up, surprised to see an Archivist from the Tanabran Archives in a slightly disreputable tavern on the edge of nowhere in the Outland.

Dorian glanced at her when Devor shifted a little. "Panute."

"Dorian," Panute returned softly but steadily, taking the chair opposite them.

Devor stared at her. "How do you know—?"

"Panute is the new Overseer of Prophecy," Dorian mumbled as she propped her elbows on the table. "Possibly the last person I'd expect to see in a place like this."

"Just carrying on Gris' tradition of pulling you out of mud holes." Panute smiled as she took a sniff of the liquid in Dorian's glass. Grimacing, she wondered where the self-destructive tendency came from in one so intelligent.

Dorian smiled faintly. "So he's told you that little story." She was extremely fond of the old Overseer and missed him already. "One of the few that is actually true." She flashed Devor a weak grin.

"Between you and Jac, I don't think either one of you knows which are true or not." Devor smiled back, relieved to see that the liquor hadn't taken as much of a toll as it should have, given the amount and the potency. Athronians were made of tough stuff.

"I guess the Institute will be looking for a new Researcher," Panute mused.

Devor nodded. "Yes. I can have the best of all worlds in Athros." He gave Dorian's shoulders a squeeze.

"Are you going to officially resign or just fall off the face of the earth?"

Devor frowned. "I haven't really thought about it."

"I was just thinking that it may lead to years of speculation if an Archivist at Tanabran and a Researcher at the Institute fall off the face of the earth within a few weeks of each other," Panute said. "Imagine the number of treatises that would be devoted to the subject."

Devor eyed the Overseer curiously. "You didn't resign?"

"When they call you back to Athros for Overseer exams, you barely have time to pack." Panute chuckled. "Has Dorian ever told you about when she was called back to Athros for the exam?"

Devor looked at Dorian. "You weren't in Athros at the time?" The young Overseer shrugged.

Panute laughed. "She was never in Athros. Except when she was dragged back to take the truthstone every other day or so."

Devor was intrigued. "I thought your need to roam was out of your system by then."

"It's never been out of my system." Dorian took another sip of the ghastly liquor. "I just had to temper it so I could do my job."

"Do you know why she is the most respected member of the community?" Panute asked Devor. "Most respected, not most infamous. Because of what happened the day she took the Overseer exam. And it's also the reason she's having so many problems now."

"That little question got settled once and for all today," Dorian reminded her.

"Yes, but you didn't need to suffer so long if you hadn't been protecting a secret or someone with a secret." Panute eyed her pointedly.

Dorian shifted uncomfortably. "Kerit is only speculating. He doesn't know the whole truth of that particular matter."

"But he knows enough of your other truths to know what motivates you to accept blame rather than reveal the truth," Panute countered.

Dorian eyed her curiously. "Why did you go into Prophecy?"

"It was a whim when I was too young to know any better. I guess you could call it a schoolgirl crush on Gris. I never regretted it, and I think that perhaps I might be of more service to you now than if I had been an Apprentice to Knowledge," Panute replied thoughtfully.

"It's still a waste of talent where none seems to exist right now." Dorian gazed into her glass. "I don't have a successor."

Panute stared at her as the blood drained from her face. "I'd thought by now—"

"None." Dorian focused on the gloom beyond the table.

"Which leads me back to my story," Panute said slowly, not wanting to dwell on the implication of Dorian's words. She turned her attention to Devor. "The position of Overseer of Knowledge is the most important and most difficult to attain. Because of this, there is a public examination officiated by the High Overseers, three retired Overseers of Knowledge, and three retired High Overseers. Normally, one of the retired Overseers is the previous holder of the position, but since Orvid vanished rather than retired, none of the Retired Overseers knew anything about that group of Apprentices. They had all retired before Dorian was even born, so they had never heard of her either. The Retired High Overseers, on the other hand, had been in office during the rise of the Overseer Stories, so they knew Dorian all too well."

"Fortunately for me," Dorian mumbled.

"Being a public examination, the Apprentices in Athros are gathered in a special chamber in the Overseers Hall and brought out one at a time to take the exam on the Hall's green. Those Apprentices who are in the Outland are found and held there until it's their turn. Apprentices are tested in order of age, so Dorian was the last to take the exam. I know where Dorian was and what she was doing because I was one of the Apprentices assigned to find her, given my knowledge of the Outland. She wasn't drunk, and she wasn't in the middle of some trouble; she was in the care of a healer, delirious from taking a poison tipped arrow meant for a defenseless child in Icterac during the siege of Banderlin."

"A child?" Devor whispered, in shock.

"It was a terrible time, far worse than anyone could ever imagine," Dorian muttered, bitterly. Devor didn't even linger on the fact that it was also a thousand years ago.

"Dorian knew that she wouldn't be killed by the poison, so the risk to her was just a few weeks of agonizing pain," Panute continued, shaking her head at the young woman's courage and uncomplaining sacrifice. "She had just barely regained consciousness when I found her only three days after she was wounded. Jac was with her and explained to me what had happened. I sent word back that I had found Dorian with an explanation of her condition." With troubled eyes, Panute looked straight at Devor. "It was not unreasonable to expect the High Overseers to express sympathy for her plight and allow her to recover before returning to Athros to take the examination. We are a benevolent, reasonable people. We have to be, given our responsibilities to the Outlanders. But our current High Overseers are monsters, elevated unnaturally. They sent back word that Dorian had to be tested when she was called or forfeit her chance. Jac was beside himself with anger. It was as if they wanted her to fail."

"So their animosity began while Dorian was still an Apprentice." Devor frowned, adding this information to the puzzle.

"So it seems." Panute nodded, looking at the Overseer of Knowledge, who had finally slipped into an exhausted sleep. "Dorian's brilliance was anything but common knowledge. She became an Apprentice so young because it was rumored she had done too well on the Apprentice exam to be turned away. Given her subsequent history, everyone thought she was just precocious rather than outstanding. These assumptions made what happened that day all the more shocking. She was sent for in a matter of sand marks because none of the Apprentices could manage to answer the first set of questions on the examination. You can imagine the panic when the only Apprentice left was a twenty-five year old who never showed up for work, was always getting into trouble in the Outland, and on top of that, was delirious and weak from taking an arrow rather than let a child die."

"I had no idea," Devor murmured.

"Jac and I got her cleaned up and dressed, and holding her between us, we were transported directly to the green. The fresh air roused her a little, and she was able to shake some of the numbness out of her brain and could stand without being held. I'm not quite sure when she realized why she was there. I heard later that she couldn't figure out why she was being asked questions without holding the truthstone." Panute smiled weakly, giving the Overseer of Knowledge an affectionate glance. "Several Overseers, seeing how bad her condition was, protested loudly that it was not a law that she had to take the exam at that time. It was only fair she be allowed to recover. They even reminded the High Overseers that she had saved a child by taking the arrow. The High Overseers wouldn't listen and directed the Retired Overseers to begin the exam. Meanwhile, Dorian had collapsed and was lying all but unconscious on the ground. The High Overseers, still not feeling any mercy, called for Andora to revive her. Andora did the best she could, but there's just so much one can do with as much poison as Dorian had in her system. It was enough to kill many times over."

Devor looked down at Dorian. "Unbelievable."

"Dorian doesn't talk about it because she doesn't remember any of it," Panute said gently. "Anyway, once she was back on her feet, the examination began. That's when we discovered how brilliant and dangerous Dorian Riverson is. Half conscious, slumped over, using all her strength to keep from collapsing, with a voice raw from the poison, she correctly answered every question asked her. It was as simple as that. No one else has ever done that."

"She said she was the only one who passed."

Panute snorted at the understatement. "She got the highest score of anyone who ever took the exam. And it was done without obvious effort. Her powers of memorization and retention must be immense. That's how she was able to pull off what she did today, or should I say yesterday. The irony is that if she had been in control during the exam, the full extent of her powers probably would not have been recognized. When being at your worst is better than anyone else's best, it can have a sobering effect. It frightened the High Overseers, and they immediately tried to find ways of undermining Dorian's veracity. They started rumors that the poisoning was feigned and that she had used the special talent of instant transport to hear the questions put to the other Apprentices." Panute shook her head. "Both Jac and I held the truthstone for that. But they still didn't trust her. This talent of being able to jump to the Outland in a heartbeat is disconcerting to the High Overseers. That's why she had an escort to the Overseers Hall yesterday. They were afraid she would escape in a flash." Panute paused, studying Devor thoughtfully. "I personally don't think Dorian has that talent." Devor's startled look confirmed her suspicions. "She only gets into trouble when she's protecting someone," Panute explained quietly.

"That's what everyone says," Devor whispered.

"She was holding at least two very large secrets yesterday," the Overseer of Prophecy mused. "She almost got herself banished rather than let the truth be revealed. So she lied to the stone by omission and by cleverly turning a true statement false because her immense powers of retention allowed her to know the proper truth."

Dorian raised her head slowly from the table. Staring at Panute, she posed an unreadable expression, which would have been disconcerting to any one who did not know her. "What do you know of the secrets I hold?"

"Gris showed me some interesting Prophecies just before he retired." Panute held Dorian's eyes for several heartbeats.

"Prophecies he had to report to the High Overseers," Dorian said. "To the truthstone."

Panute smirked. "The High Overseers are not very thorough in their thinking. They did not have the benefit of being Overseers after all. Gris got around revealing these Prophecies by getting the High Overseers upset over one that he cleverly made up." Dorian's eyes widened as Devor leaned closer to Panute when she lowered her voice. "He used your trick of answering the questions as they were worded and was able to feed them a made up Prophecy without alerting the truthstone."

"And he was given the choice to retire or to be banished rather than let knowledge of this Prophecy be known." Dorian spat the words bitterly. Gris was her closest friend amongst the Overseers, and she valued his good sense.

Panute nodded, sadly. "Yes. He was prepared to make the sacrifice to protect the Prophecy and..." She hesitated a moment. "And by using the made up Prophecy to add fuel to the unspoken one."

"So you know what Orvid said?" Dorian ventured, knowing that this was a secret they shared equally.

"I know the missing part, and I can guess why you don't want it to be known," Panute admitted.

"Just guess? It would have led to some uncomfortable questions, don't you think?" Dorian took a sip from her glass. Panute stared at the inebriated Overseer trying to bore holes into her mind. "That answers that question." Dorian broke the tense silence casually. Panute's eyes shifted briefly to Devor as the color rose in her cheeks.

"How did you know?" Panute stammered, trying to regain control.

Dorian shrugged, irony dancing around her eyes. "I am the Overseer of Knowledge."

Panute was too flustered to think straight. "Yes, but I'm the only one who holds that bit of knowledge."

"When putting together a puzzle, one must pick up the logical pieces no matter where they lay," Dorian mused quietly. "So beware when you ask me to think of myself instead of protecting others. One of those others may be you."

Devor looked between the two women. Lengthy passages were being spoken without benefit of the voice.

Panute, remembering he was there, cast an amiable smile his way. "You must forgive us, Devor. Sometimes we speak in too many riddles."

"Panute is a fast study in the ways of the Overseer." Dorian's eyes twinkled. "I'll miss old Gris, but I'm glad he had enough sense to train a worthy successor."

"From you, that means more than it would from all the other Overseers combined." Panute's honesty caught Dorian off-guard.

The young Overseer stared into the chaotic crowds just beyond the calm of their table. Spotting the familiar hunch of her cousin over a mug of ale just two tables away, she did not betray any surprise that he was there. "Unfortunately, a blessing from this particular Overseer may be more of a curse."

"I'd rather have that curse than the respect of these particular High Overseers," Panute said seriously.

Dorian held her eyes for several thoughtful heartbeats. "I just hope you understand what kind of game you're playing."

"I have prophecy on my side," Panute finally said.

"I hope you have better luck with it than I've had with all the knowledge in the world on my side." Dorian lifted her glass and drained it.

"I have the future, and you have the past." Panute grimaced at Dorian's lack of reaction to taking in so much of the vile liquor at once. Her own stomach lurched at the thought.

"Now all we have to do is figure out who has control of the present." Dorian's eyes glazed over, and she was quickly caught in the mist of oblivion.

The bony finger deliberately pointed to the jar of white powder on the tightly packed shelves behind the apothecary shop counter. "That one if you please, young man," the ancient voice croaked followed by an ingratiating smile.

"Of course." The middle-aged apothecary shook his head at how someone so aged could still be as mobile as this one was. He couldn't even tell if he was addressing a man or woman, so wrinkled the face and indistinct the voice. The thick cloak wrapped tightly about the person and the oversized hood hid a body that trembled from frailty. "This is very good for helping to relax the muscles." He popped off the cork lid of the jar and poured some of the substance onto a flat piece of paper, which he then expertly folded. "Anything else?"

"Let me see." The aged being tapped a finger to the forehead. "There was something. Give me a moment. The memory is not what it used to be." A chortle erupted from the stringy throat, causing the face to distort until it looked like the frail creature was in pain. "Ah, that's it. I need some of that." The bony finger shot out to the end of the upper shelf.

The apothecary, following the direction of the finger,

frowned a little. "This?" He placed a hand on a small jar.

The ancient head shook impatiently. "No. The one on the end."

"Are you sure?" The apothecary knew better than to question a patron, but, as this one had conceded, the memory wasn't what it used to be. "This can be dangerous. It plays havoc with your balance."

Chortling sounded from behind the hood. "I've got a slight heart problem, young man. I know how much to take and to be sitting down when using it."

Satisfied that the withered being was a habitual user of the substance, he folded several doses into another sheet of paper.

Nodding happily, the ancient being haltingly counted out several coins and shuffled out of the shop. After turning a corner into a narrow side street and another corner into a narrower lane, the watery eyes lifted and took in a quick sweep of the surroundings. Chortling, the fragile figure vanished.

Chapter
Thirteen

Chasing Prophecy

Bary Jolner, one of the Apprentices to Knowledge who maintained the Archives, woke with a start at the muffled footsteps shuffling up the oversized central staircase to his little desk in the middle of the cavernous second floor landing. Trying to rouse himself, he rubbed his dark brown eyes and focused on the tall confident Overseer striding towards him. He quickly smoothed down his graying dark hair and beard, straightened in the well-padded chair, and put his clasped hands on the desk.

"May I help you?" The Apprentice tried to keep the puzzlement out of his voice and off his face.

"I need to find something in the Archives," Panute said blandly.

Bary stared at her before recovering himself. He nervously picked up a pen. "You want to find something? Here?" A wave of fright crashed over him. Hardly any one visited the Archives, and no one ever wanted to find anything.

"Things can be found here, can't they?" Panute raised an amused brow. She knew the Archives were rarely entered, but Gris had seemed to know his way around them.

"Certainly," Bary stammered. "We just don't get that request very often. Everything here has been cataloged and

shelved according to the instructions outlined in this manual."
He placed a hand on a formidable volume, several finger lengths
thick.

"I need to find the Hail Rangoon Prophecy and the Prophecies shelved around it," Panute stated.

Bary nervously resettled his spectacles onto the bridge of
his nose. "The exact location for the Prophecies can he ascer-
tained by following the instructions in this manual." He placed
his hand on another volume, a little less imposing than the one
containing the cataloging rules. "We are thoroughly trained when
we come to work here, but we have never had to actually use that
training." He bowed his head apologetically. "No one ever uses
the Archives."

Panute nodded. "I'm aware of that. How long do you think
it will take to locate the Prophecies?"

"Umm, I don't know," Bary stammered.

Panute pulled herself to her full height and leaned across
the little desk. "Are you telling me that there isn't anyone here
who can find these Prophecies for me?"

Bary blinked. "Dorian can."

Panute sighed. "Dorian. Thank you. It's been enlightening."
The Overseer of Prophecy turned and strode back to the staircase
muttering all the way.

Merchants were beasts of habit. If they were in Athros, they
could not think of returning to the Outland before popping into
The Golden Cloud. If nothing else, the tavern was the only place
an Outlander could get a mug of the infamous Athros Ale for the
price of an Outlander ale. The tavern was also a gathering place
for Outlanders lucky enough to be drawn into the Athronian circle. Not surprising, most of these Outlanders were merchants.
Like most cities, Athros was unable to produce many of the
things they were dependent upon to maintain their way of life.
Everything from cloth and leather to many of the fruits and vegetables for their cuisine was the result of an intricate trade system with the Outland. Certain Merchant Guilds had monopolized
trade with Athros for several millennia, keeping their knowledge
of the Overseers' home one of the secrets imparted to those who
passed through the Guilds' highest levels of initiation.

Jac settled against the back wall of the tavern, eyeing the

noisy patrons over a tall mug. This would be much simpler if he was looking for a fruit or wool trader, but how was he to find someone who handled something that wasn't sold in Athros. He couldn't go up to each merchant and ask if they sold explosives. They would know why he was asking, no matter what kind of story he gave them. According to old Marsche, the tavern owner, the explosions had been the only topic of discussion among the Outlanders for two or three weeks. He needed a different approach to get at the same information.

The Apprentice to Mischief thought he would get some ideas if he watched the merchants and overheard their conversations. Learn something of how their minds worked and their methods of interaction. He had only one chance to get to the information. If he failed, they would close ranks against him, and this part of the puzzle would be forever lost to him.

He noticed that the Outlanders didn't pay extra attention to him. Athronians were a common sight in the tavern, seeking out merchants and even conducting business there. Some Athronians visited the tavern for the novelty of being around Outlanders for an evening. Maybe that could be used to an advantage, Jac mused, leaning his back against the wall.

A pair of merchants joined him. They were curious about the Overseers' meeting and weren't going to miss a chance to get a first hand account of it. Besides business, the merchants' favorite topics of discussion were the ins and outs of the lives of some of the more prominent Athronians. Jac gladly related what he had witnessed, interested in hearing an Outlander's view on it.

"You mean she could be banished just for lying?" Granfor Likron, a leather merchant from the steppes of Outer Nagolis, shook her head in disbelief. Her heavily braided black hair swished slowly. The idea of an Athros without Dorian Riverson was unfathomable.

"If she had been caught cheating on the exam," Jac clarified.

"So they were trying to prove that she had somehow cheated because an Overseer of Knowledge can't be caught in an Attraction." Pron Tilber nodded his long thin head. Before him was a selection of rings and medallions laid out on a bright silk cloth, in case one caught the Apprentice to Mischief's eye.

"That was the idea," Jac said taking a glance at the rings.

Granfor grinned. "Then all they proved was an Overseer of

Knowledge can be caught in an Attraction. It's just never happened before."

Jac grinned back. "Exactly."

"Did they ever figure out who caused all those explosions a
few weeks back?" Pron picked up a delicate silver ring. "This
would make a wonderful joining gift." Jac took the ring and
studied it while trying to think how to turn a casual question into
something more informative.

"The explosions?" The Apprentice pulled his attention away
from the ring. "Not yet. It's been a real mystery."

"You mean, with all the mental powers of the Overseers,
you haven't been able to find out who did it or why?" Granfor
leaned forward. She was fascinated by the whole Overseer phenomenon.

Jac shrugged. "Sometimes, it's the simplest, most obvious
things that elude us. In a way, this sort of thing is much simpler
for an Outlander to solve. You can gather physical evidence of
the perpetrator. Motives are usually obvious. You may know of
individuals inclined to such behavior. It's easier to track down
where certain things such as explosives are purchased. In other
words, you can talk to a lot of people and put together something
to work with."

Both merchants were caught up in his words but with curiosity and nothing more. "What do we have?" Jac continued.
"There wasn't any physical evidence left by the perpetrator. We
can't figure out a motive or even if there was one. There has
never been anyone in Athros inclined towards that kind of
behavior, and we certainly can't acquire explosives or substances that make explosives here. There just isn't anything to
work with."

"Never thought about it that way." Pron rubbed his chin.
"Are you sure the explosions weren't made by, you know,
magic?" The merchant snapped his fingers.

Jac shook his head. Outlanders still thought that Athros was
a land of sorcerers. "The only evidence we have is the traces of
the substances that made the explosives."

"So how do you think these substances got into Athros?"
Pron asked.

Jac sighed. "Not magically. Like everything else in Athros—from the Outland. As far as we're concerned, it may as well
have been conjured by magic."

Granfor frowned. "What do you mean?"

Jac shrugged. "Anyone could have bought the explosions for an Athronian. Even an Athronian could have bought them. Most Outlanders wouldn't know one of us by sight."

Pron chuckled. "That is a big problem. What you have is the perfect crime."

"That's an understatement," Jac replied.

Pron wrinkled his brow in thought. "But still there may be a way of tracing the source of the explosive material."

"Now that would involve magic," Jac said sadly.

"Actually, it's a time honored art," Pron replied seriously. "Our political intrigue can be a little deadlier than banishments. Ages ago, some enterprising soul came upon the idea of allowing explosives and the substances that cause explosives be sold only by permit. A different filler material known only to the Explosives Guild is put into each merchant's supply. So if the substances are used for something other than a good clean fight or removing stumps and the like, it can be traced back to the merchant."

Jac blinked at him. "After it's been blown up?"

"Especially after it's been blown up," Pron said. "The filler is activated by heat and covers the residue of the explosive."

Jac rubbed his chin. "Clever." He wondered if Dorian knew about this. She had to, he realized. That thought led to him wondering how much more she knew about these incidents. "How would one have this residue tested?"

"Invite one of the Guild members to test it." Pron shrugged, resting his eyes on the ring that Jac had forgotten he held.

"Can you have this altered to fit a finger about the size of my little finger?" The Apprentice of Mischief raised an eyebrow. He didn't care how much the ring cost, the information that came with it was well worth it.

Kaston couldn't believe his good fortune: being allowed to accompany Langton as the Royal Guard visited the Retired Overseers tucked away in the hamlets and countryside of the district. He knew the area better than most because had taken an early interest in the family horse farm. Much of his youth had been spent attending auctions and races. He had even raced for a while until his limbs grew too long.

The only disappointment that Kaston experienced as they

rambled along the dusty back lanes was Langton's reluctance to talk about his adventures in the great Onbersan Wars. The older man seemed to be more interested in the bridge his troops helped build over the treacherous Drabke River or when they planted enough wheat to feed the entire village of Woht.

The Overseers were a surprise to Kaston. He had never had any interest one way or another in Athronians. Upon entering the cottage of the first Overseer they visited, he expected to be bored and took a place by the door to keep out of the way. The ancient Athronian had been the Overseer of Crime and almost immediately pulled the young Guard into the first of several accounts of some of the crimes he helped solve for the Outlanders. By the third day and the fifth Overseer, Kaston was the one doing most of the talking as they sauntered along, discussing the things that the Overseers had said and the objects that they were shown.

Langton accepted his companion's change of attitude with a smile. He was glad that the young man had temporarily forgotten his interest in war. Having been there, he was the last person to ever encourage it as a living for another. As a Royal Guard, he could never voice these thoughts out loud.

"So who's next?" Kaston paused in his theory on how the small machine that produced pure sounds worked. The Overseer of Music pulled sounds from it by simply rubbing his hands together over a series of taut wires.

"Let's see." Langton turned several pages in his battered journal. "Overseer of Machines."

"Machines?" Kaston wrinkled his nose. "What's that?"

Langton gave the young man a sidelong look. "Mechanical things, like those toys the Overseers have."

Kaston nodded. "Oh, those. I've just never heard that word before."

"What do you call them?" Langton asked curiously. He found it interesting how different parts of the same country could develop different terms or miss out completely on common vocabulary.

Kaston gave him a confused look. "We call them what they are. A yarn spinner, a butter churner, a seeder."

"Interesting," Langton mused. He looked at a well-worn map and stopped at the barely visible entrance of a lane. When he turned to enter the lane, Kaston hesitated behind him.

"Here?" Kaston frowned. The lane had been overgrown for

as long as he could remember.

"That's what the map says," Langton returned as he disappeared into the heavy overhanging trees.

Unlike most homes of retired Overseers, this one was large and rambling, like it had grown too many times without any thought to the overall architectural effect.

"If she's like the other retired Overseers of Machines," Langton said, taking in the chaotic structure, "she's always building or tinkering with something."

Kaston scratched his head as he stared at the ungainly structure. "I've passed this lane many times. And I never knew this place was here."

Langton chuckled. "Rather cleverly concealed. Athronians are nothing if not ingenuous."

Their attention was diverted by a buzzing sound coming from one of the crevices that marred the front wall of the building. Through the rough opening in the wall was a raggedly shaped courtyard that was several steps below the ground level. A tall, thin, ancient woman in a simple brown tunic stood with hands on hips in front of an unlikely looking metal and rope contraption. She glared at it as if it was its own fault for not doing what she wanted it to do. After tightening a length of rope around a roller, she stepped back and sighed.

Coming closer to the Overseer, Langton and Kaston noticed a row of impaled potatoes along the top of the machine. A long blade slanting sharply downward ran parallel to the potatoes. The Overseer gently pressed a small knob, and the potatoes unsteadily turned on their spikes as the blade shifted forward just close enough to the tubers to miss touching them by a hair width. The Overseer peered intently at the space between the blade and the spuds, muttering something about contrary vegetables.

Langton cleared his throat and was in a heartbeat on the receiving end of a curious glare. Just as quickly, the clear brown eyes were back on the machine. The Guards exchanged glances. They were used to the eccentric behavior from many of the ancient Athronians they talked to. Langton had developed a feel for when to interrupt a preoccupied Overseer and when to wait. For this particular Overseer, he motioned Kaston to several overturned wooden barrels near the entrance.

Kaston focused his attention on the collection of contraptions that cluttered the courtyard. He always had a talent for fixing the wool spinner or the cow milker. Nearly everyone had some kind of skill that contributed to the everyday life of the Trint clan. His was figuring out how to fix things. To him, it didn't take a keen eye to notice that the machines surrounding them were either broken or not quite finished. Something about them screamed incompleteness to him. His curiosity grew so much that he wished he could take a closer look at them to determine what the problem was.

"You like machines?" the Overseer croaked in a soft raspy voice.

"Yes," he stammered, wondering how she took his observation of her machines as something more than curiosity.

The ancient woman turned to Langton. "Did you bring him to me because he likes machines?"

"No. I'm here collecting relics for Queen Ketric," Langton explained. "This young man is acting as my guide for this district. I'm Langton Renor of the Royal Guards, and this is Kaston Trint of the Banish Hall Guards."

"Sending Guards to collect relics?" The old woman wrinkled her already creased face in amusement. "Peacetime makes strange bedfellows. I'm Celorus Yuhry, retired Overseer of Machines. Relics, you say. The Queen likes Overseer relics, doesn't she?"

"Yes, she has quite a collection," Langton returned, politely.

"I have no relics, only machines," Celorus grunted.

Langton looked around. "Quite an impressive collection."

"These don't work," Kaston said to him in a low voice, a little embarrassed that he didn't notice the obvious.

"How do you know that, young man?" Celorus squinted at Kaston, raising herself to her full height that topped him by a finger length. "Come closer so I can have a better look at you." When the Guards stood next to her, Kaston's eyes glanced at the potato machine, noting where some of the adjustments seemed to be a little off. "So how did you know?" His attention returned to the penetrating eyes of the Athronian.

"Um," he started, realizing that he could not put into words how he knew. "It's obvious," he finally stammered out.

The Overseer turned to Langton. "Do you think it's obvious, Royal Guard?"

The older man shrugged. "They look perfectly fine to me."

Celorus grinned. "You seem to have a bit of a gift, young man. Probably can fix things, right?"

"Yes," Kaston said with a frown. "I was always repairing things around the farms where I grew up."

"It's a useful gift," the Overseer agreed, thoughtfully. "You are a Banish Hall Guard?"

"I'm training to be one," Kaston clarified.

The Overseer picked up a dirty rag and carefully wiped the grease from her hands. "One of the disadvantages of being retired is that we sometimes miss having Apprentices to teach and nurture." She glanced wistfully around the courtyard. "It's nice to keep company with people who share the same interest. If you ever get the urge to fix things or tinker around a bit, my door's always open."

Kaston's mouth fell open at this unexpected invitation. Upon seeing the machines, he was possessed by the impulse to grab some tools and get down to work. He never realized until that moment how much he missed working with the machinery around his family farms. "Thank you. That is very kind of you."

"And I mean it." She shook a crooked finger at him. "This life can get lonely without the sounds of Apprentices tinkering away." She frowned in thought. "I don't have relics, but if you want to take back a little machine or two, I have quite a few you can select from. They just take up room."

Langton bowed. "That is very kind of you. I'm sure the Queen would be delighted with one or two of your inventions."

Devor and Dorian wandered down the long corridor towards the Archives proper. Bary turned at the second unexpected noise of the day and was relieved to see his mentor.

"You seem agitated, Bary," Dorian commented. The Archivists on desk duty were usually snoozing or reading.

"Overseer Taner was here," Bary responded. "She wanted to see something from the Archives." He held up several sheets of papers. "I can't determine whether I have to fill out these reports or not. They don't seem to have a place for when a request isn't filled."

"What did she want to see?" Dorian prompted patiently.

"The Hail Rangoon Prophecy," Bary replied. Dorian's brow wrinkled in confusion. Why would Panute want to see something on which she was considered an authority? "She wanted to browse the other prophecies around it. I explained that you're the only one who knows exactly where the prophecies are located."

"Good." Dorian nodded, still distracted by Panute's need to look at the prophecies. "You don't need to fill out a form if the request is not completed," she added smoothly, much to Bary's relief. That may not have been strictly true, but Dorian had a feeling that Panute wouldn't appreciate it if the High Overseers discovered she was trying to see the prophecies in the Archives. At least, not until Dorian had figured out what she was so interested in. "Pretend it didn't happen." She looked her Apprentice straight in the eye.

"Gladly," Bary responded.

"Now, go back to reading or something." Dorian winked at her Apprentice and then led Devor through the columned foyer into the empty reading room.

"You never told me why no one ever uses the Archives." Devor took in the neatly arranged tables and chairs perched on the edge of expectancy but where nothing ever happened.

"All the Overseers hold the information contained in these Archives," Dorian returned patiently. "They cannot be effective Overseers if they don't know everything about what they are Overseeing. So if someone wants to know about Geology, they go see the Overseer of Geology. It's a lot simpler that way."

"How do the Overseers learn all the new knowledge?"

"When we sort the knowledge, it first goes to the proper Overseer before it is buried forever in the Archives," Dorian explained, wryly. "Each Overseer has a subject stone. I feed the knowledge into each of the stones, and the Overseers memorize it by holding them."

"That's a part of your job you won't let me witness," Devor commented.

"It requires a little concentration," Dorian admitted.

Devor shook with laughter. Separating a mental stream of knowledge into fifty-six specific flows would be an impossible task for anyone except the Overseer of Knowledge.

"Panute's up to something, and if she didn't want me to find out, she should have figured out a way to sneak into the Archives." Dorian glanced at Devor. "Gris did it all the time."

"Really?"

Dorian smiled warmly, thinking of her old friend. "I'm not quite sure if he ever knew that I knew."

Devor raised an eyebrow. "Isn't that against the rules?"

Dorian laughed. "I have no use for rules that don't hurt anyone if they're broken. Come on. I'll show you how to sneak into the Archives."

A part of Dorian's mischievous nature was to think it fun to sneak into the place she was in charge of. Devor had a problem stifling a laugh every time they went to ridiculous extremes to avoid being seen by an Apprentice. Of course, once they were in the Archives proper, they didn't have to worry about being seen by anyone except the Apprentices shelving the newest additions to the collection.

Devor caught his breath at the vastness of the chambers that housed all the knowledge his world had ever produced. The means of storage was as varied as the materials stored. Endless aisles of shelves, cubby holes, and drawers spread out before them. They walked through massive chamber after massive chamber, downward to the catacombs that were carved out of the rock beneath the city streets.

"The Archives run beneath the entire University and a part of the Central Gardens," Dorian explained as they wandered through the seventh huge cavern filled to overflowing with the knowledge of the Outland world. "The prophecies are over here." Dorian threaded around long rows of shelves and cabinets, packed tight with aged books and manuscripts.

The impact of the extent of what was in Dorian's mind slammed against Devor's consciousness as he almost drowned in the sheer volume of words surrounding them. "You know where everything is in here?" he asked, trying to grasp the idea that she could point to a stack of books and rattle off the titles.

"Uh, yes," Dorian hesitated. That was one of the reasons she didn't like people actually seeing the Archives. They made the abstract impression of her mental abilities too concrete. "Don't think about it. Or think of it as magic or a trick." She met Devor's eyes.

"Please, just tell me how you were able to learn it all," he finally said. Knowing how she did it would make him feel a little better about it.

"I learned the contents through the knowledge stones. So, I didn't have to sit and read everything here. I know where things are because I simply apply our sorting and classification system to pinpoint a specific title. I know all the titles, so I can determine the order they are placed on the shelves or in drawers." The Overseer shrugged. "You see, it's not so magical. Just a lot of mental work."

"I feel a little better that I, at least, understand how you do it," Devor commented, deciding to leave it at that.

"Here's where the Hail Rangoon Prophecy is." Dorian ran a finger across a row of book spines until it rested on the volume containing the prophecy. "What's this?" She frowned at a small leather bound book squeezed against the Prophecy in question. She pulled the book from the shelf and flipped it open. Blank. A volume of blank pages.

"I take it this isn't suppose to be here," Devor ventured. Dorian raised an eyebrow at him. "Why would someone leave a blank journal here?"

"Why indeed," Dorian mused, lifting the pages to her nose. "Why, indeed." She shut the book and slipped it into her belt pouch. "Come on. It's time to pay Panute a visit."

Chapter Fourteen

Crumbling Silences

The streets in that part of Athros were much narrower than the wide central thoroughfares. The roads were forced to climb the craggy foothills of the mountains that surrounded the city. Many of the winding narrow streets were nothing more than long stretches of uneven steps, reaching tinier lanes of tightly packed residences and shops which were barely wide enough for a door and a window facing the street.

"Down here." Dorian guided Devor around the fourth corner away from the main road into a tiny lane that alternated between cobbles and stone steps. The mismatched multi-storied buildings huddled against each other as the lane abruptly ended at the high wall of the Central Gardens. Dorian led the way down several steps that took them to a door below street level. A shingle with a complicated design that represented Prophecy creaked above them.

The door stood open. Ventilation was one of the major challenges in that kind of architecture. A beige robed Apprentice to Prophecy sat on a stool behind a long counter reading a book. Aware of visitors, the young man slid off the stool to his feet.

"Overseer." He quickly put the book under the counter out of sight.

"Is Overseer Taner here?" Dorian asked.

A scraping of wood against the stone floor behind the closed door in the back of the chamber answered her question. The door swung open as Panute strolled out with a combination of curiosity and uncertainty on her face.

"Dorian. Devor," she greeted them. "What a nice surprise."

Dorian grinned. "I'm glad you think so."

"Come in," Panute beckoned them, her expression more uncertain than curious. "Sendel, please go next door for tea and sandwiches for our guests. I hope you haven't had tea yet?"

"No, we haven't," Dorian replied, as she and Devor entered the quirky parlor that doubled as the Overseer of Prophecy's office.

An odd assortment of chairs encircled a low round glass table making consultation with visitors a relaxed experience. Unless one of those visitors was the Overseer of Knowledge.

When they were settled comfortably, Panute put on a calm face and smiled at Dorian and Devor. "So, what brings you to this part of Athros?"

Dorian was waging a losing battle with a grin. "It's my duty to show Devor all of Athros, and while we were in the area, I thought we'd drop in to see how you're adjusting to Overseer life and being back in Athros after such a long absence."

"It hasn't been as traumatic as I anticipated." Panute chuckled, letting a little of her tension flow out. Dorian may be up to something, but she didn't seem to be too concerned about it.

"I had a terrible time adjusting," Dorian confessed. "Regimented discipline has never been my strong point."

"I admit I miss my friends in the Outland," Panute said thoughtfully. "The Tanabran Archives was actually a pleasant place to work. And I enjoyed interacting with the students from the University."

"You were always the most helpful of the Archivists when I was one of those students," Devor observed.

Panute gave him a thoughtful look. "I could never understand that standoffish attitude of some of my colleagues. They acted like it was beneath them to serve the students even though that was a part of their job."

"They weren't raised on the Athronian creed to always be of service to others," Dorian mused. "So what was Devor like as a student?"

"Hey," Devor protested good-naturedly.

The young Overseer wagged a finger at him. "You know all

about my youth from second hand sources; it's only fair that I seek the same."

"It just so happens," Panute stepped in smoothly, "that Devor was not only studious, as one would expect from a future Researcher, but he knew how to relax and have fun."

"Oh, really?" Dorian eyed Devor before returning her attention to Panute. "Of course, you only know this because you know how to relax and have fun, too." Panute colored a little. She kept forgetting that Dorian knew a lot more about her than anyone in Athros.

A soft rap on the door told them that tea had arrived. Sendel entered and quickly laid out the tea service and sandwiches on the low table, then slipped back out. Panute deftly poured the tea and milk and passed the sandwiches.

"I still can't get over the flavors of the food here," Devor commented after savoring a bite.

"I rather like Outlander food," Panute admitted as Dorian grimaced.

They spent a cheerful sand mark chatting about inconsequential things until Dorian determined that Jac would be escaping his obligations at work and be in search of them.

"Oh, I almost forgot." Dorian snapped her fingers, catching the others' expressions. They both knew that Dorian was incapable of forgetting anything. "I think this is yours." She pulled the journal from her belt pouch and handed it to a bewildered Panute.

The Overseer of Prophecy looked questioningly at the volume before opening it and flipping through the blank pages. Catching a unique scent, she shot her eyes back to Dorian, who watched her closely.

"Thank you," the stunned Overseer stammered.

"I thought you might want to know, our paperwork at the Archives only covers filled requests. So I'm afraid there won't be any record of your visit today." Dorian smiled at Panute's expression of gratitude. "Have a pleasant afternoon." The Overseer turned and strode out of the chamber followed by a bewildered Devor.

Panute dropped down onto the nearest chair, shock being the least of what she felt. Dorian had obviously figured out that Panute didn't need to see the Hail Rangoon Prophecy, and her curiosity led her to investigate further. The most stunning thing was that Dorian had not tried to recover the hidden text in the visibly blank volume. She was truly a creature of honor.

Janin sat on one of the heavy stone chairs around the inter-rogation table on the prison floor as Morna paced, absently swirling her staff in intricate moves. Gretna had found out Kaston's special skill. The Retired Overseer of Machines contacted her old friend about the remarkable young man and his aptitude for—what was the Athronian word? Machines. Once Gretna had explained that machines were all those little contraptions for things like spinning yarn and cutting wood, they understood at once. "Useful skill" was Morna's practical reaction.

"I wonder how many more of us there are out there," Janin said as she absently traced her finger along the marbled design of the table.

"Must be more than we think," Morna mused. "Look at us. Three in one place without any effort of looking."

Janin frowned in thought. "But we were all brought here because of special talents."

"I wasn't," Morna reminded her.

"But you stayed because you were good with the staff," Janin reasoned. "And you are good with the staff because you can read bodies."

Morna tapped the table top with the end of her staff. "I wonder what knowing about machines has to do with being able to run like crazy."

"Huh?"

The Guard did a lazy set of complicated whips of the staff before resting her restless hands. "Kaston's running ability was what got the Elders curious about him in the first place."

Something tickled the back of Janin's mind. Something she read. No. She was remembering something she had absorbed through one of the knowledge stones. "Athronians have talents that don't necessarily have anything to do with what they Apprentice to. Like Dorian's instant transport talent."

Morna grinned and leaned on her staff. "I thought her talent was mischief."

Janin laughed. "That, too. My talent of making things hap-pen by just concentrating on them has nothing to do with knowl-edge."

Morna chuckled. "I guess my talent for upsetting the weapons keeper doesn't count."

"What's so amusing?" Kaston's head appeared in the stair-well followed by the rest of his long lean body.

"We were just discussing Athronian talents," Janin replied.

"You and your Athronians," Kaston scoffed as Janin and Morna exchanged looks. "What?"

Morna arched an eyebrow. "What do you have against Ath-ronians?"

Kaston shrugged. "Nothing. I just don't understand what you find so fascinating about them."

"You've met a lot more of them than we have." Morna casu-ally flipped her staff. "You didn't find them interesting?"

"They were interesting," the young man hesitated. "But they were so old."

"So, what about young Athronians?" Janin asked.

"What about them?" Kaston was getting dizzy from their silly questions. "They're all in Athros."

"Not all of them."

"Are you trying to tell me there are young Athronians here in Onbersan?" He flipped his staff in disgust. Why did they love to tease him like this?

"Yes," Janin said simply.

"Just walking around." Kaston had to admit they were good at the tease. Not even a hint of a smile.

Morna nodded. "Just walking around."

"Do we know any?" He smirked as he casually peeked into the prison cell.

"Oh yeah." Morna smirked back, following him with her eyes. A defensive chill run up his spine when he saw her specu-lative look.

"What?"

"We invited you here to join our little society of young Ath-ronians," Janin said matter-of-factly. "Now, if you don't want to join—"

"You're pretending to be Athronians now?" Kaston gave Janin a pained look.

Morna casually leaned on her staff as she pinned him with her eyes. "Not pretending."

"You're saying, you're Athronians?"

"Yes, we are," Janin replied. "And so are you."

Kaston stared at them a heartbeat and then laughed. "And how do you know that?"

Morna shrugged. "You passed the test."

"Test," he repeated warily.

Janin held up the gold stone. "Recognize this?"

Kaston looked at Morna. "Sure. You tossed it to me, and I tossed it back."

"What color was it when you held it?" Morna asked.

"Gold. Same color as it is now." He looked at them as if they were crazy.

Janin placed the stone on the table, and it turned black. "It only turns gold if an Athronian holds it."

"It's some kind of magical trick," the young Guard protested but less certain about his convictions than before.

"Soral." Janin raised her voice a bit. The Elders Assistant poked her head out of Gretna's office door. "Would you be kind enough to pick up this stone." Soral, who had been waiting to make this demonstration, grinned as she approached the table and picked up the stone. It remained black in her hand.

"Here." Soral held the stone out to Kaston. The young Guard stared at it before stepping forward and taking it. The stone blazed gold in his hand. "What they are telling you is true. You are an Athronian and so are they. I'm just an honorary member of the society."

Morna grinned. "Talented Outlander." They had quickly adopted the Athros terminology for those not fortunate enough to be Athronian.

"Have you been testing everyone?" Kaston scratched his head. The idea that he was an Athronian did explain some things that tickled at the back of his mind.

"Only the four of us have been tested," Janin explained before going into the whole story, interrupted by many questions from Kaston.

"That explains how I was able to see why something didn't work when others couldn't." Kaston sank down onto one of the stone chairs. "I could never figure out why they couldn't see what was so obvious to me."

"It took me a long time to realize that others couldn't read a sparring partner like I could," Morna confessed. "You'd have to be blind not to see it. Even Rane and Fent didn't understand what I'd be talking about. They just said some people have the gift."

Kaston's mind drifted back to the rambling house full of interesting contraptions only two villages away. "What happens now?"

"We explore our talents on our own until the Elders have worked out a curriculum for us," Janin explained. "They want to teach us everything about Athros and what it means to be an Athronian."

"School." Kaston's enthusiasm sagged noticeably.

"With no homework or tests," Janin reminded him. "Just learning about who we are and what we can do. In the meantime, I don't see any harm in doing some research on our own. I've learned a lot about Athros and Athronians, reading these journals and, of course, the definitive compendium on Athronian life."

Kaston stared at the brooding stone wall. Why was being a Banish Hall Guard suddenly not as important to him as it had been just a few heartbeats before?

"I can't believe that after all these years they're still trying to prove you cheated on that exam." Jac couldn't let go of his anger at the most recent trial that Dorian had endured. "You were barely conscious. How could you possibly cheat?"

Dorian glanced at him before kneeling in front of the craggy face of Windfound Mount. Gently tapping the rock with a small hammer and chisel, she exposed a thin purple thread of ore. "Found it." Devor, on her other side, held a small metal box against the rock. Dorian carefully chipped and scraped out the ore into the box. "All the other stuff will burn off when we melt down the ore."

"You are avoiding me." Jac stood with arms crossed and legs parted in a defiant stance.

"Don't push it, Jac. You may hear things you don't want to know." Dorian's voice had a dangerous edge to it. Devor looked at her a little startled.

"If you're going to tell me that you somehow cheated on that exam, I'm not going to believe you." Jac knew it was impossible under any circumstances.

"All right, then. Why are we having this discussion?" Dorian tried to keep the testiness out of her voice, but Jac caught it.

"We're having this discussion because—I can't believe it—it's true!" Jac stared at his cousin, aghast. "If it wasn't true, you'd say so."

"It wasn't intentional." Dorian sighed, moving the contents

of the box around with the handle of the hammer, estimating how much ore she needed.

"How can you unintentionally cheat?" Jac threw up his hands. Life was just too complicated around Dorian.

Dorian scraped out a little more ore. "That should do it," she said to Devor, who absently put the lid onto the box. He was in as much shock as Jac. As she stood up and brushed off her leather clad legs, Dorian sighed with the resignation that she was going to have to explain this paradox. "All right. I'll tell you the story, over dinner. I know a nice restaurant in Klindan. One of the few Outlander inns that specialize in Athronian cuisine." She raised an eyebrow at her staring companions.

Taking a deep breath, Jac relaxed a little. "Klindan. Fine. Hold tight."

The best word to describe the establishment was cozy. And all the patrons were thankful because Klindan was in the middle of a vicious thunderstorm. The deluge complemented the mood of the party from Athros nicely.

"What to order." Dorian pretended to study the rather extensive menu.

Jac, who let his stomach dictate his life, put his distress at his cousin's revelation aside while he pondered the selections. When a slim young woman with curious eyes approached them, he took the serious matter of ordering into his capable hands and rattled off a number of dishes, including how they were to be prepared. The Outlander, impressed by his knowledge of Athronian cuisine, carefully jotted down the orders. Devor was captivated by Jac's ability to pull together a feast for them.

"Do you want to add anything?" Jac finally addressed his table companions.

"As always, you've covered everything with your superior skill," Dorian acquiesced. Devor, not knowing half the things that Jac ordered, simply shook his head "no."

Jac then gave the young woman an irresistible smile. "I think that will be it except for three large mugs of Athronian Ale, Special Brew."

The young Outlander grinned back. "Three large mugs coming right up."

"You're incorrigible." Dorian shook her head when the

young woman was out of earshot.

Jac shrugged. "She probably has to put up with a lot of snooty Outlanders who think they are being trendy by eating here. Just giving her a little taste of true Athronian manners."

Jac gave his cousin a smug look when the Outlander quickly returned with the ale.

"Now," Jac said after he took a satisfying sip of the deep red liquid. "To the matter at hand."

"All right." Dorian took a long sip of ale herself. "Not long after I became an Apprentice, Orvid was curious about whether I had any special skills besides getting into mischief. He was intrigued by how I did so well on the Apprentice exam at such a young age and without any apparent scholarly aptitude."

Jac shrugged. "You always could soak up things and retain them."

Dorian stared out into the room. The young woman was heading their way with the first course. After she delivered the delicacies and they filled their plates, Devor and Jac returned their attention to Dorian.

"After I became an Apprentice, I was a little too good at soaking up the daily knowledge. That wasn't all." Dorian scooped a delicate herb sauce onto a piece of tender asparagus and munched thoughtfully for a heartbeat. "When I touched the stone to deliver the knowledge, it fed knowledge back. That's not supposed to happen." Dorian anticipated Devor's question. "Orvid suspected something was going on because I knew things that I couldn't possibly have picked up any other way. I was getting the knowledge in little chunks, so it wasn't as if I suddenly knew everything in the Archives." She took another long sip of ale. "Orvid wanted to test the strength of this talent. You have to have the skill a little bit or else you can never become an Overseer of Knowledge. But it usually doesn't show itself until after many years of practice. Instead of using one of the Overseer stones, he decided, for reasons he kept to himself, to test me with the Great Stone. The one that holds all the knowledge. The one that is kept in a vault in the Archives that only the Overseer of Knowledge knows how to get into."

"So, that's why you have to go into the Archives every day." Devor looked up from munching his way through the tidbits on his plate.

"Yeah. Just one of my exciting duties. The Great Knowledge Stone has to be always up to date." Dorian sopped up a puddle of green gravy with a thick slice of grainy bread. "This food is really good."

Jac nodded in agreement. He had been eating steadily all through Dorian's narrative. "I was entertaining the idea that they have some wayward Apprentices of Culinary Delights in the kitchen."

"It wouldn't be the first time," Dorian mused. "Anyway, Orvid took me on the tour of the Archives that all the Apprentices have to suffer through. When we came to the vault, he opened it and without a word picked up the Stone and tossed it to me."

Jac stopped in mid chew. "He tossed the Great Knowledge Stone?"

"He tossed it and fortunately, I caught it," Dorian said dryly. "To make a long story short, I held it long enough to absorb everything."

Devor's fork stopped in mid air. "Everything?"

"Everything," Dorian repeated.

"And how did you know that?" Devor wasn't quite sure if he wanted to hear the answer.

"Because after it gave me all the knowledge, it was quiet," Dorian returned steadily.

Jac swallowed quickly. "How did Orvid take this?"

Dorian pushed an assortment of vegetables around with her fork. "I never told him."

"What did you tell him?" Jac's attention was riveted on his cousin.

Dorian shook her head. "I told him what he wanted to hear. I said that the knowledge was coming to me but sorting it out was difficult."

"So you gave the impression that the talent was reasonably strong and that you would learn to use the stones much faster than the other Apprentices," Jac surmised.

"Yes."

"Out of curiosity, how long did you hold the Stone?" Devor asked.

Dorian shrugged. "A few heartbeats."

"So that's why your cheating was an accident," Jac said thoughtfully. "Your little brain held as much knowledge as Orvid's. Knowing you, I'm sure you found some way to keep up with the new knowledge."

Dorian gave him a sheepish look. "I tried to keep up as best

I could."

"Why was it cheating then?" Devor looked at them confused.

Dorian sighed. "Because no one except the Overseer of Knowledge is allowed to touch the Great Knowledge Stone. Orvid knew this, but I guess he didn't think any harm would be done, and he never liked to do things halfway. A true test for him could not be made with any stone except the one that really counted. Besides, who would know he let someone else touch the Great Stone? It wasn't possible to absorb more than a fraction, if that, of what was in the Stone. Certainly no more than what an Apprentice was expected to acquire anyway."

"Except you did absorb it," Jac said. "And that is why you couldn't tell Orvid. Because he broke Athronian law by letting you handle the Stone."

Devor frowned. "So how did you not lie to the truthstone about cheating on the exam?"

"I took advantage of how the question was worded," Dorian admitted. "It implied intent to cheat. My cheating was accidental not intentional. I got lucky. I was very close to getting caught."

"Whether you cheated or not, you were the right choice as Overseer. How could you be condemned for having the skill to absorb all the knowledge from a stone in a few heartbeats? No one else can come close to your abilities."

"It's not completely about skill," Dorian said quietly. "It's about trust. Overseers have to live by a high code of standards because of what we are entrusted to do. I was an untrustworthy Apprentice, and I'm an untrustworthy Overseer, because I chose to protect my mentor and not turn him in for breaking Athronian law. I am haunted by the idea that his own inability to cope with what he had done may have led to his disappearance."

"Why would you think that?" Devor asked.

"Because I think he eventually realized that I had absorbed a lot more than I had let on," Dorian explained. "There just didn't seem to be anything that he needed to teach me. That's why I spent so much time in the Outland. I was bored, and I think he was uncomfortable with having me doing things that the other Apprentices required years of instruction and intensive practice to achieve. The less I was around, the less he would have to explain, so I stayed away. Disappearing would have been a way of allowing him to deal with his conscience."

"I knew you were bored." Jac stared at the rain cascading

down the glass of the window next to their table. "And I knew that you learned a lot faster than the others. I just never thought to wonder why."

"I don't think you should suffer for Orvid's rash actions," Devor said, resolutely. "You would have become Overseer whether it happened or not."

Jac nodded. "I agree. Now, are there any more of these little secrets that the High Overseers can pounce on?"

Dorian laughed, a little relieved for letting out this heavy secret she had held in for so many years. "No, Jac. I think I'm safe now."

With that happy admission, the little party held up their mugs to salute the delicious food.

Chapter
Fifteen

Against the Will

"An Overseers Corps? Has Ketric lost her mind?" Gretna muttered as she pulled her hand from the communications stone. "Employing Overseers for public works projects. Insane."

Soral looked up from her little table near the large window in the corner of the office. The afternoon sunlight streamed in, filling the chamber with comfortable warmth. "Why?" she asked curiously. Gretna squinted at her. "Why is it an insane idea?"

Gretna nodded her understanding. "Because Overseers are used to being in charge. Our position is to be the supreme expert in a particular field of knowledge. We expect to be looked to for the answers and not have our expertise questioned. When was the last time a government let the experts do a public works project their way instead of the way the government wanted it done? Overseers don't like to be told how to do what they consider their job. There's also the problem of having more than one Overseer of a single discipline here in Onbersan. There could be monumental conflicts of ego."

"I hadn't thought about it that way."

"That's one of the reasons Overseers leave Athros when they retire," Gretna explained.

"I've always wondered about that."

Gretna shook her head. "The Queen thinks she can order Overseers around like she does the Guards."

"But if none of the Overseers join this Corps—"

"I don't think the Queen is used to being refused, especially for her pet projects." The Elder pulled up from the chair and stepped across the floor to gaze out the window. The Guards were bashing away at each other in the practice yards, the clashing and yelling a distant echo on the warm breeze. Baniston was so peaceful. Far enough off the main roads to be overlooked by the Crown. The isolation was one of the reasons why Gretna had settled in Baniston. She was not going to let her peace be shattered by a meddlesome Queen without wars or political intrigue to keep her occupied. "Unfortunately, Overseers also aren't used to being forced into things they don't want to do. Not a real good situation."

Soral grinned at Gretna's tendency towards understatement. "She wouldn't try to force you, would she?"

Gretna raised an eyebrow. "She is skilled in the art of forcing without making it look like force. On the other hand, we are equally skilled at delaying without appearing like we're delaying. Years of dealing with impatient Athronians has turned that talent into an art form."

"Sounds like too many games to me," her assistant commented.

Gretna sighed. "And games get you nowhere in the end. They're just a waste of time."

"Surely the Queen won't bother you or the other Elders. You are already working for the Crown."

"That's true. But that won't keep her from wanting to use the other Overseers in this district for these so-called improvement projects." The Elder scowled. "We don't have any of her pet problems like unemployment or lack of food here."

"Maybe she'll leave us alone."

Gretna shook her head. "Unfortunately, we have more Overseers than in any other district."

Soral's eyes grew wide in amazement. "Really?"

"It's a quiet, out of the way place, and they can keep to themselves," the Elder explained. "There are more of us around here than people suspect."

"Then," Soral hesitated as the thought formed. "Then it isn't such an odd coincidence that Janin and Kaston are Athronian."

Gretna lifted her eyes to her assistant as an amused expression blossomed. "Talented Outlander. Most Athronians keep track of their Outlander children. Sometimes, they're the only children they have if they don't get caught in an Attraction."

"That's sad." Soral only half understood what an Attraction was.

"Sometimes it is," Gretna agreed, staring out onto the green and seeing the Athros of her youth. Some of her friends, when they were young Apprentices reveling in the freedom of being able to roam the Outland, had found themselves in that position. She quickly let those memories fall away. The worse part about retirement was not being in Athros. Sometimes she'd give anything to be able to wander the crooked back lanes or sample the delicacies of the street vendors, "So how does it feel to suddenly discover that your best friend is an Athronian?"

Soral easily went with the change of subject. She had been around Gretna long enough to recognize that distant look she always got when reminded of her home. "Finding out about Janin first kind of softened the blow. But it does explain a lot. There was always something different about her."

"Besides being tall, beautiful, and deadly with a long stick?" Gretna responded amused.

Soral laughed. "That, too. But there was always something different on the inside. Something that didn't let being tall and beautiful get in the way of who she really was."

Gretna nodded thoughtfully. "And that is as good a definition of an Athronian as I've ever heard. Our young Athronians are another reason why I don't want the Queen's attention on our district. If it ever got out we were starting the equivalent to an Apprentice School, who knows what would happen."

"Fortunately, we have the Elders School to act as a cover," Soral said.

"Hopefully, it will be enough." Gretna sighed, and turned away from the window. Her weather sense told her that they were in for a bout of storms.

Fenchan grinned as he rechecked the ledger. The day had been profitable. Nothing compared to a small war to make life interesting. The lamplight flickered in the gloomy back office of the House of Fenchan. He glanced up, barely distracted by a slight change in the air. The front door to the shop was locked and his assistants were long gone. Not hearing anything, he returned to the sheet. The appearance of a man in the curtained doorway gave him a heart-stopping jolt.

The merchant's hand flew to the hilt of his dagger before recognizing the shaggy black hair and sharp gray eyes. Still not relaxing, he eyed the newcomer warily.

"Sorry to have startled you." Jac grinned amiably and sauntered into the chamber. Behind him was a tall thin young man with tousled blonde hair and weak blue eyes. He was dressed in a simple but well tailored linen tunic. The style alone marked him as another Athronian. "I'm Jac Riverson and this is my friend, Enoc Robt."

Fenchan, having regained his composure, sat back in the chair, steepling his fingers together. "And what can I do for you?"

Jac sat on the corner of the desk facing the merchant. "Help us solve a little mystery."

Fenchan smiled, desperately trying to keep it from looking like a nervous twitch. "That's not exactly my line of work."

"Perhaps not. But I think you may be surprised at how much help you might be with this particular mystery," Jac returned smoothly.

"Now you have me intrigued." The merchant placed his hands on the desk to prevent them from trembling.

"Good, good." Jac rose and walked casually behind the merchant, laying a hand on each shoulder. "My friend here is an Apprentice to Truth. I brought him along to help me uncover the facts that I need to solve this mystery."

"Apprentice to Truth?" Fenchan did everything in his power to keep his shoulder muscles from tensing under the Athronian's hands. Relax, he repeated to himself.

"I've been put in charge of investigating the explosions that happened in Athros a few weeks back," Jac began conversationally. "We had the residue of the explosives tested and much to our surprise, we traced them to your stock."

"That's not surprising." The merchant tried to shrug against the deceptively casual grip on his shoulders. "My House probably sells more explosives than any other. Especially in times like these when there is a war going on."

"And you keep careful records of everything you sell," Jac clarified.

"I'd be thrown out of the Guild if my books were not in order."

The Apprentice to Mischief bent down close to the merchant's ear. "So you have an account of my cousin, Dorian, buying explosives from you?"

"That's correct." Fenchan tried to straighten. "She came here several weeks back and bought a selection of highly explosive substances." Jac straightened and looked at Enoc, who was leaning against the far wall with his arms folded. The Apprentice to Truth's eyebrow flicked up almost imperceptibly.

Jac released Fenchan's shoulders and plopped down on the desk to the side of the merchant. "Do you know how they go about selecting Apprentices to the Overseer of Truth?" Jac picked up a glass paperweight to study it. "They test for the ability to sense the truth." Enoc was glad the merchant's eyes were riveted on Jac because his eyebrow shot all the way up at this. "Enoc got a very high score on that test." Fenchan's eyes quickly shifted to the Apprentice of Truth. "And I don't think he's detecting the truth from you." The Apprentice to Mischief twisted around to catch Enoc raising both eyebrows at him.

"Of course, it's the truth," Fenchan sputtered. "I sold the explosives to her myself. I have the paperwork right here in this cabinet." He fumbled through a cluster of keys hanging from his belt.

Jac reached out and stayed his hands. "That's all right. I have no doubt the records are in your cabinet. You sold the explosives to someone because they caused the explosions in Athros. I just have the feeling that you grossly misspelled the buyer's name."

"Why would I sell the explosives to someone else then pretend I sold them to Dorian Riverson?" Fenchan spluttered, trying to make it appear as if he were indignant.

Jac carefully put down the paperweight. "Because someone paid you a good sum to do it."

"I am an honorable merchant," Fenchan protested, catching Enoc's expressive eyebrows.

"And I'm sure it was an honorable sum of money," Jac replied. "And I'm sure there isn't anything in the Guild's bylaws about using pseudonyms for client names or about feeding lies to a High Overseer."

The merchant straightened. "Pseudonyms are necessary sometimes when dealing with explosives. We cannot afford to take sides in a conflict."

"Of course."

"As for feeding lies to a High Overseer, foolhardy would be a mild word for it." The merchant laughed nervously.

Jac rubbed his chin. "Only if you thought you'd get caught. Fortunately for you, the High Overseers mistrust Dorian more than they mistrust you. Even after Dorian swore to the stone that she had nothing to do with the explosions."

Fenchan looked Jac in the eye. "I think my word is worth more than the hunch of an Apprentice."

"That's true." Jac nodded. "That's why we brought along a pair of truthstones."

The merchant wrinkled his brow. "Truthstones only work on Athronians."

"Athronian truthstones only work on Athronians," Jac clarified. "Outlander truthstones work on Outlanders. It's funny how these things go."

"Outlander truthstones?" Fenchan blinked up at Jac. "I've never heard of such a thing."

Jac shrugged. "They aren't used very often."

"I don't believe you," Fenchan said resolutely. "This is a trick an Apprentice to Mischief would play."

"Possibly," Jac mused. "But only an Apprentice without much imagination. If I were playing with you, this would be a lot more entertaining. However, this is an official investigation on behalf of the Overseer of Mischief."

Fenchan jumped at a noise coming from the main shop. A young woman peeked through the curtain. "Am I late?" she asked cheerily.

"Just in time." Jac grinned broadly as he beckoned her in before turning back to Fenchan. The merchant stared wide-eyed at the rather plumpish young woman in a bright, color-splashed cape. "Our third witness. Shotle Gracht, Apprentice to Magic."

"Witness?" The additional person in the small chamber made Fenchan feel trapped.

Jac smiled graciously. "We can't have one of these little discussions without witnesses, now can we? The Overseers are such sticklers for protocol."

"The Overseers," Fenchan repeated. "But they know my word to be true."

Jac held up a finger. "They want to believe your word is true. At the moment, they think that my cousin has figured out a way to lie to the truthstone. The Overseers want to prove whether this is true or not. And you, my friend, are the only one who knows the truth. The stones, Enoc."

The Apprentice of Truth pulled a pair of gray stones from his belt pouch and put them on the desk. "Place your fingers on each stone and speak a lie."

Fenchan, his mouth falling open, stared at the thin young man, unable, at first, to find the right words for a response. "You can't make me do this," he finally stammered out.

"That's true," Jac agreed, thoughtfully. "Of course, we don't have anything else to do this evening or even tomorrow. And our Overseers really frown on it if we don't put an effort into performing these assignments. If you take too long, I have permission to call upon my good friend, Caplot Graud. She's an amazingly adept Apprentice to Sorcery. Her specialty is persuasion spells."

"You expect me to believe everything that flows off that smooth tongue of yours?" Fenchan responded, praying for anything to help him out of this mess.

"Of course I do," Jac responded. "I'd tell it to the stones, but they only work on Outlanders."

The incredulous merchant fell back into the chair. "You expect me to meekly do as you ask?"

"Yes, actually," Jac replied. "If you told the truth about selling the explosives to Dorian, you have nothing to worry about. If you didn't tell the truth, there's still the question of why you did it."

"What do you mean?" the merchant asked warily.

"A part of the mystery is what would motivate a sane, successful merchant to lie to the High Overseers," Jac explained. "As you've already stated, it's a foolhardy thing to do. But what motivates a merchant? The desire to make money. More importantly, making money in a risk free manner. Whoever paid you to pass the lie to the High Overseers convinced you that you would not get into trouble."

"Someone more powerful than the High Overseers?" Fenchan laughed. "Someone who could protect me from the High Overseers' wrath?"

Jac shrugged. "My job is just to determine whether you lied."

"Just for the sake of argument, how could you keep me out of trouble with the High Overseers if I did accept money to pass a lie to them?" Fenchan, ever the merchant, was ready to deal with the Apprentice to Mischief.

"Because the person who paid you to pass the lie was a High Overseer." Jac focused on Fenchan's tightening expression. He inwardly thanked the heavens that he had stumbled onto the truth. "Which means that if the Overseers don't want to face a sudden rash of retirements, the High Overseers will not ever be privy to the results of this investigation. On the other hand, if you don't clear Dorian's name for the Overseers, they could make life very difficult for you. You enjoy a healthy trading relationship with many of them. I'd hate to see something happen to that."

Fenchan glared at the Apprentice to Mischief. "Is that a threat?"

"No. Just a realistic view of your current position," Jac posed thoughtfully. "All you have to do is speak the truth to the stones, and life will go on as if nothing has happened."

Fenchan eyed Jac warily. "You expect me to trust you?"

"You can trust me." Jac captured the merchant in his steady gaze. "I'll even put it in writing for you in front of these witnesses."

Fenchan looked at the seemingly sincere Apprentice for several heartbeats. "Put it in writing," he responded, pulling a blank parchment sheet from a small drawer. He knew that a document was the highest form of currency in Athronian society. The written word was also the best form of protection that Jac could offer and that Jac would be liable, not him, if the document was disputed.

Jac grinned and signaled for Fenchan to vacate his chair. After dipping the pen into the bottle of ink, Jac scribbled out several lines in a neat, official-looking script, then added his signature with a flourish. The Apprentice allowed Fenchan back into his chair, and the merchant read through the document. He had to admit that it was concise and covered both the situation and his concerns very well.

"I will put my signature to your document and say my piece to your stones," the merchant agreed.

"You'll also have to sign one more document that summarizes what you said to the stone." Jac rubbed his chin. "Just a formality for the Overseer of Justice. Shotle will jot down what you say to the stone, and everyone here will sign it. We always have to have a backup for the stones."

Fenchan nodded, just wanting to end the interview at that point. He put his fingers on each stone. "I say a falsehood?" He looked up at Enoc.

Enoc nodded. "Yes. That is to set the stones to your touch."

"I am not a merchant." Fenchan blinked, startled, as the stones blazed a bright deep blue. Jac grinned at Sortle and Enoc, who had a resigned expression on his face as he picked up one of the stones.

"State your name and your position and why you told the High Overseers you sold explosives to Dorian Riverson," Enoc instructed.

"I am Fenchan Parack, merchant and owner of the House of Fenchan. Late one night, about four weeks ago, when I was checking the books, I was alarmed by the sudden appearance of an ancient being. This person was shrouded in a cloak, and the voice was so raspy I couldn't even tell if it was a man or a woman. This ancient one showed the ring as proof of being a High Overseer but would not give a name. Placing a heavy metal box on my desk just before it was dropped, this ancient one told me that the contents of the box were mine if I did as instructed. I said that I was open to hearing anything this being had to say."

Enoc gave Jac an impressed look. The Apprentice to Mischief had indeed figured out the puzzle.

"This person said, all I had to do was have an order of explosives ready to be picked up the next day by a courier. Then I would go to High Overseer Huask, with whom I've had extensive dealings, and tell him that Dorian Riverson came to my shop and bought these explosives. I was ready to refuse when this person reminded me that I could not get into trouble because it wanted the other High Overseers to believe this story. Being familiar with court intrigue, I've seen more than my share of these games of deception. But I wasn't aware that this sort of thing went on in Athros. Anyway, this person's reassurances and the contents of the box eventually convinced me that I was just a small player in whatever game the High Overseer was playing and that the risk was minimum. So, the order of explosives was picked up by a young man the next day, and I visited Huask and, following the High Overseer's instructions, sold him the story that Dorian Riverson had come to my shop and bought explosives."

Jac smiled amiably. "Now that wasn't so difficult, was it?" Shotle carefully tore a sheet from her journal as Fenchan gratefully released the stone. She handed it to Jac, who extended it to the merchant. "Please read this. Make sure we have the facts correct." Fenchan scanned through the neat summary of his confession.

"It's fine," he mumbled, apprehension creeping up on him once more. "Are you sure that I won't get into trouble with the High Overseers?"

"Believe me, none of the Overseers will want this to fall into the hands of the High Overseers," Jac replied. "In fact, they will do everything to protect you because they now have something on one of the High Overseers."

"But you don't know which one," Fenchan responded.

"That is something that we will be able to quickly figure out. There's only four of them after all," Jac replied as he dipped the pen into the jar of ink. "Sign." Fenchan took the pen and, after only a little hesitation, put his signature to the confession. The Athronians each signed the document. "I thank you for your cooperation. Don't be surprised if some more Overseer business comes your way."

With that, the trio disappeared.

When Langton took on "relics duty," he never imagined that he would be reporting his finds in person to the Queen. But she was just that kind of monarch. Her skill lay in the one-on-one encounter. She could make the other person feel like she wanted nothing more than to be friends. This gained her deeper loyalty than any speeches made from balconies and from horseback. Individuals couldn't wait to tell their friends how good and kind their Queen was and how she was so down-to-earth and genuinely concerned about the welfare of her subjects.

Langton had only seen the Queen twice since the end of the Onbersan Wars, both times as a part of a parade of the Royal Guards for a foreign dignitary. Several years had passed since he had been back in Praen, and he couldn't help but gawk at all the new construction. How on earth did they get this much done so quickly? "They must be working day and night," he commented to the young Guard who skillfully led him to the Queen's audience chamber.

"Every day and every night," the young man sighed. "Making so much noise that no one can sleep, even the Queen. But she doesn't make them stop."

"Some people will stop at nothing to get what they want,

and I hear she wants the new palace completed by her ten year anniversary."

The young guard chuckled. "The rate she's going at, she'll have two new palaces done by that time."

They cleared the last of the construction and entered the rather intimate audience chamber. The Queen was seated at a delicate table, looking over an odd assortment of objects. Her expression was as pleased as any child's on their birthday. Langton was relieved to see that the relics had been delivered.

"Captain." The Queen looked up, her enthusiasm hard to resist. She jumped to her feet and rushed to the Royal Guard, who remembered that this bubbling woman was his Queen and bowed. "I am so delighted to meet you. You have a gift for collecting things. These little machines are just wonderful."

"Thank you, Your Majesty," Langton managed to get in before the Queen grabbed his arm and led him to the little table.

"Now, you must tell me who gave you each of these," the Queen bubbled.

Langton explained each relic and answered many questions regarding the character and disposition of the Overseers. As he talked, he noticed that, despite her efforts to keep the discussion light and conversational, there was an intense concentration with which the Queen absorbed his words and followed up on little details.

"There was something interesting in your report about the village of Baniston." The Queen held up one of the little machines that Celorus had built, marveling at the ever-changing, multicolored patterns that were created as a little engine rotated the center of the machine. "I had forgotten that they have an Athronian Banish Hall. Talk about relics. And they keep it in good repair and maintain a Guard for it. It's more than a relic; it's a national treasure. You mentioned that the Guards live in a warren of buildings behind the Hall."

Langton smiled fondly, remembering the peaceful village. "Yes, Your Majesty."

"Do you realize that we haven't had one public works project in that district. Not a one." Ketric said this as if it were the worst possible tragedy. "Wouldn't it be wonderful to build a living quarters for these dedicated Guards? A structure that complements the architectural wonder of the Hall itself?"

Langton managed a half-enthusiastic smile, but something in him sank. The Banish Hall Guards lived in a comfortable

quaintness that made his heart ache. The simplicity of their
existence reminded him of the things he liked about being a soldier. The sparse lifestyle that emphasized camaraderie and skill.
Their dedication to the Hall was almost a spiritual reverence and
changing their living quarters wasn't going to enhance that.

"It could be the first in my efforts to save and preserve
things created for Athronians. Things too big to put in my
museum. A Banish Hall reflects such a different aspect of Athronian life that it would draw people to it out of curiosity. The village would benefit greatly from having it as a part of an
Athronian pilgrimage." At this the Queen's imagination took off.
"Now, there's an idea. Having a pilgrimage route between Athronian artifacts and monuments that are scattered through the
countryside and have living monuments such as the Baniston
Banish Hall as highlights on the route."

"That would be quite an interesting undertaking," Langton
responded, wondering how people like Morna, who enjoyed the
isolation in her part of the world, would react to it. Not well, he
readily guessed.

"First things first. New quarters for our brave Banish Hall
Guards. They were the ones who stood up against the Ghouls?"
The Queen barely waited for Langton's nod. "Such brave souls.
How would you like to be in charge of it?"

"You are very kind," Langton stammered. On the one hand,
he would love to go back to Baniston. On the other hand, these
weren't the best of circumstances for a return visit.

Ketric waved her hand. "You seem to have developed a rap-
port with these people. The Elders seem to be amiable enough.
Consider the project yours."

"Thank you, my Queen." Langton, knowing that he was in
no position to protest, bowed. Maybe it wouldn't be as bad as his
gut instinct told him it was going to be.

Chapter
Sixteen

Nothing Is As It Appears

Jac maintained his innocent look as the Overseers of Truth and Justice stood crossed arm in front of him. Only Lincim had an amused expression. "I don't see why you're upset. I got the confession."

Tigren threw up his hands. "By setting up a ruse."

Lincim grinned. "But you have to admit, it was a pretty clever ruse."

"Truthstones for Outlanders?" Kerit's sensibilities were beyond outraged.

"All it took was for Shotle to do a little magic—" Jac began.

"How'd you ever get Enoc to agree to it?" Kerit asked.

"I told him he wouldn't have to lie, and he didn't," Jac answered.

"How did you know that it was a High Overseer who tried to frame Dorian?" Tigren frowned. Perhaps he had underestimated Jac's abilities.

"I didn't until he admitted to it," Jac conceded.

"It was a logical deduction," Tigren agreed. "So obvious, yet so improbable, that none of the rest of us even thought of it."

Except Dorian. The unexpected thought came to Jac's mind. Of course, Dorian had figured it out, but why did she keep quiet about it?

"Now, will you quit being indignant at my Apprentice's tactics and congratulate him for solving a part of the mystery of the explosions. You forget he is an Apprentice to Mischief. We are not required to do things by the canon as long as the results are by the canon," Lincim reminded his colleagues.

"We also remember that he is the cousin and genetic brother to the Overseer of Knowledge," Tigren said. "The mixture of intelligence and mischief is strong in both of them."

"Except I'm the responsible one," Jac interjected.

Lincim gave his top Apprentice an affectionate smile. "That's because you're the eldest. Now, are you ready to tackle the next part of the puzzle?" Jac blinked at him, confused. "The script and the Rock of Teyerbom."

Jac looked at the Overseers of Justice and Truth. "You want me to continue the investigation?"

Kerit shrugged. "Since we can't use the best person for the job, we have to use the next best."

"You think I could come anywhere near Dorian's abilities?" Jac asked incredulously.

"Closer than the rest of us," Lincim replied. "Your minds work the same. That's no secret."

"I hope you realize that she probably has the explosions figured out." Jac kept his amusement hidden at their surprised expressions. "I didn't find out anything that wasn't already known to her, and her deductive skills are much quicker than mine."

"Then why hasn't she said anything?" Kerit tried to keep his frustration down.

Jac sighed. "I think she's convinced that it doesn't matter what she says, because it will all be taken as a lie. The High Overseers don't know it, but they have succeeded in beating her down a little, despite her outward bravura."

"All the more reason to keep up these investigations," Tigren stated resolutely. "We can't have an Overseer of Knowledge suffering from a loss of confidence."

Jac leveled a grateful gaze at the three Overseers. "I will continue to do this for my cousin. I've spent my life rescuing her from outrageous situations. Sometimes I think it's my special talent."

Tigren studied the young man for a few heartbeats. "Why haven't you sought her help, if you think she's already figured out much of it?"

"If there is to be complete credibility in my investigation, I have to do it all myself. Even the most casual discussion on the subject with her could cast doubt on the veracity of my findings," Jac replied. "She doesn't even know I'm doing this, and I don't want her to find out until it has been solved."

Tigren bowed his head. "I owe you an apology. I've never thought to go beyond the Stories in my assessment of you. You truly do have the steady good sense that Dorian has to struggle to maintain."

Jac bowed back. "Thank you, Overseer. That means a lot coming from you."

Tigren grinned. "At least I got the chance to understand why you're the top Apprentice to Mischief, which is something I never understood while Dorian was an Apprentice. Fortunately, Orvid could see her formidable abilities."

"You are much too kind," Jac responded. "I'll let Dorian be the Overseer in the family. I am content to be an Apprentice."

Tigren raised an eyebrow to Lincim, who just shrugged.

"Now go out and enjoy the evening," Lincim said to his Apprentice. "The Labyrinth will be laid down soon."

Jac laughed. "The Labyrinth. Every year I spend it looking for Dorian, and when I find her, she's already passed out in a gutter."

"She'll have Devor with her this year," Kerit reminded him.

Jac winked. "That makes it easier. All I have to do is find a gutter big enough for two."

A gathering of so many Athronians in The Land Out of Time at once was rare, if indeed it had ever happened before. The ancient souls gathered at the rough tables in the Banish Hall mess chatted and greeted each other like it was a typical day in the Overseers Hall. Although they kept in contact through their communications stones and occasional visits, their being together in one place brought back memories of Athros. The majority of the Athronians in the Banish Hall district had been Overseers at around the same time. Whether that was coincidence or not was something that none of them felt the need to discuss.

Gretna looked out at the gathering of ancient beings and sighed. Many of them had been Overseers when she was young.

Like many young Athronians, she had been inspired by their dignity and command of talents to become an Apprentice herself and perhaps in time, if she excelled, to become an Overseer. That time was known as The Golden Age even before she left Athros. In those distant days, Athros had sparkled as a city, and Athronians had shone as truly wondrous beings to the Outlanders they oversaw. The first wave of Overseers Stories came from that period. The perfection of the Athronians in those stories led a new generation of Chroniclers to latch onto the antics of a pair of less-than-perfect youthful Athronians to give new life to the then old-fashioned Overseer Stories.

Janin, standing with Soral behind the head table occupied by the Elders, realized that she was trembling. The idea of being surrounded by Athronians invaded her senses like a sweet, yet fortified, wine. Not just Athronians but Overseers. "Look at all of them. Can you believe it?" she kept murmuring.

Soral simply grinned at her friend and looked at the entryway. Morna and Kaston stood guard on either side of the closed door. Gretna wanted to include the young Athronians and the talented Outlander in the meeting without causing suspicion. Kaston, having met many of the Athronians on his travels with Langton, was the center of an amiable sea of wrinkles and white hair. Celorus had to be dragged away from the bemused Guard by the Overseer of Animals when it looked like she was ready to spend the entire evening talking with the young man.

Gretna rose and it took only a short time for the Overseers to give her their attention. "In a gathering of Outlanders, the Elders Council is the ruling body. In a gathering of Overseers, that honor goes to the Overseers of Justice, Prophecy and Knowledge. We are fortunate enough to have two of the three here. You all know Otlic Rigtu, Overseer of Justice." Gretna nodded to a striking man with long, flowing white hair and pale blue eyes shining from a thin, roughly wrinkled face. "But you haven't had a chance to meet the latest retiree from Athros, Gris Twaene, Overseer of Prophecy. He had just become Overseer when I retired." The other Overseers looked at Gris and smiled and waved.

The newly retired Overseer had headed for the sleepy district as soon as he found out about it. Fortunately, he was transported to a village in Onbersan that was accustomed to having Overseers appear out of nowhere. After an orientation of sorts conducted by a very aged group of Athronians, the newly retired

Overseers were free to go wherever they wanted in The Land Out of Time. The moment that Gris learned about Baniston, he knew that was where he had to be. Even though it was generally believed that there were once several places where banished Athronians were transported to, Baniston was the only one that remained. That much he had learned before leaving Athros, making one less worry about what he perceived as his personal mission in The Land Out of Time.

Gretna had to wait several heartbeats before the Overseers returned their attention to her. "In the absence of an Overseer of Knowledge, I recommend that we vote on a third member of the Council. The members of the Elders Council will now take their proper place in the regular body of Overseers." With that, the Baniston Elders Council vacated the little table at the head of the hall.

Otlic and Gris, used to being in charge, rose and took their place behind the table. Gris, having spent much time teaching young Outlanders while he masqueraded as a Professor of Prophecy, smiled pleasantly at Janin and Soral, who remained standing against the wall. The young women couldn't help but grin back at this charming man who seemed incredibly young compared to the rest of the group.

"To get this formality out of the way, I recommend Overseer Alcot to be a part of the Council," Otlic began, raking his striking pale eyes across the group. "Do I need to take a vote?" The response was a rustle of the old-fashioned robes that many of them wore. "Overseer Alcot, would you please take your place with the Council."

Gretna, surprised by this honor, exchanged glances with the other Elders, who smiled at her encouragingly, and returned to the main table. Janin and Soral beamed as she took her seat.

Gretna bowed her head. "Thank you for the honor."

Otlic smiled at her. "You have had much experience as a leader and you're also in practice. Of course, Gris is also very much in practice." The Overseer of Justice winked at the newcomer before turning his attention to the reason they were there. "There has rarely been a reason for us to come together like this, besides just wanting to visit and reminisce. Unfortunately, we are here for a very serious reason. Overseer Alcot, would you be so kind as to relate the particulars of the problem."

Gretna stood. "As you know, a member of the Royal Guards recently made a tour of the district looking for Overseer relics. It wasn't the first time, and none of us had any reason to give it a second thought. Unfortunately, our Queen can't seem to satisfy her curiosity about us. I think the difference this time was that the collector of the relics was a member of the Royal Guards, and he showed a natural curiosity about our Banish Hall Guards. He also was very familiar with the talents of one of our Guards. They, too, were interested in him and he spent time socializing with them. He mentioned to the Queen that our Guards had saved the village from the Ghouls and how dedicated they are to the preservation of the Hall. The Queen realized that she never had a public works project in this district and got it into her head that building new living quarters for the Guards would make a good project. Langton Renor, whom you all met, sent me a letter of apology concerning this. He has, at least, enough insight to understand why we don't need such a project here and that it would probably do more harm than good to the district." Gretna sighed. "Ordinarily, this would be the problem of the Elders Council, but our good Queen is on a mission to put Overseers to work."

"It's not her place to order us around," Celorus's voice rang out, starting a chorus of grumbling. Gretna made a soothing motion with her hands.

"This may be inconvenient, but as long as we live in her country, we have to abide by her wishes," Gretna reminded them. "Until now, Onbersan has always been a good country for us to settle in."

"That's because we're left alone," Hergin Wokem, the Overseer of Gardens, piped up.

Yern Yebotin, the Overseer of Animals, scowled. "We were left alone. Onbersan's no better or worse than any other country now."

"I don't think we should be packing up and moving just yet." Otlic eyed the group. "Remember that this is only a temporary situation. When this Queen is gone, hopefully her obsession will go with her."

"What about in the meantime?" Celorus demanded. "Rubnic says that if a project doesn't use an Overseer's particular skill, she creates something in the project that will. It's not only a waste of skills, but also it's a waste of everyone's time. Doing things just for the sake of doing them. Besides, I don't trust her motives. She calls them public works projects, but look at what she's been doing. Strengthening bridges, reinforcing walls, cultivating more fields, and now she wants to improve the living quarters of our Guards." She turned to a straight-backed Overseer garbed in black. "I ask Tersius. What does that sound like to you?"

Tersius Sentin, the Overseer of War, turned to the Overseer of Machines with a cold glint in her eyes. "Sounds like preparations for war." A feral expression spread across her face.

Otlic raised an eyebrow. "Maybe she'll put a little war into the project to make sure you don't feel neglected."

The Overseer of War's expression drooped a little. "These Outlanders don't know how to have a proper war."

"They just haven't had the benefit of your skills, I'm sure," Gweder Asron, Overseer of Geology, sympathetically patted the Overseer of War on the back.

"What are we to do about this problem?" Otlic studied the aged faces before him, almost picturing them when they sat in the Overseers Hall in another place and time. "We can't each have excuses to delay this project. I think this particular Outlander would catch on to our tactics very quickly."

"Perhaps something that would delay work in a more natural way," Gretna mused. "A few torrential rains, for instance."

Hergin shook his head. "The Queen would only ask you to change the weather."

"She doesn't know enough about how we control the weather. I think I can pull the old trick of convincing her that a change of weather in one place influences the weather somewhere else, so it takes time to do it just right without dire consequences." Gretna flashed a mischievous grin at her compatriots.

Gweder chuckled. "That was one of Dorian's tricks. If the Queen knows the Overseer Stories, it may work."

"I have no doubt she knows all the Stories by heart," Gretna responded.

"So, are we all agreed to let the weather be unpredictable for a while?" Otlic swept a judicial eye over his former colleagues. The only response was some shifting of weight on the hard benches and quite a few grins. "Be prepared for a soggier than usual summer then. Thank you for coming. The Banish Hall kitchen staff has been kind enough to prepare some tidbits for us. I think that's as good of a reason as any to visit for a while."

The Overseers relaxed and felt better than they had since the news of the Queen's meddling trickled to them. Maybe the unpredictable weather would give them time to think of a more permanent solution. Meantime, they took advantage of the gathering to do some socializing. They grilled poor Gris so hard on how things were back in dear old Athros that he almost regretted attending the meeting. The longtime retirees expected him to know every obscure friend and relative living in Athros. He guessed this happened to every newly retired Overseer.

The Overseer of Prophecy sighed. Retired. Forcibly retired. These Athronians would never understand High Overseers who did not respect the position of Overseer. Thinking a little more on it, maybe retiring hadn't been such a bad choice to make after all.

"There's an Overseer Story about the Labyrinth." Devor stared out the large front window of Dorian's house. The street was bathed in the intense orange that happened just before the sun dropped below the horizon. "I only heard it once when I was very young. Something about children getting caught in a part of the Labyrinth where the entrances and exits keep changing."

Dorian nodded. "A Sorcerer's Maze."

"Right. That's it," Devor replied. "Anyway, you and Jac somehow figure out that they're stuck in this maze and go in and rescue them."

Yanos walked up behind them to watch the citizens of Athros gather in the street. "I don't remember that story."

"I saw it when it came through the sorting chamber," Dorian mused. "An intriguing piece of fiction. Whoever created the story knew nothing about how the Labyrinth works."

"The irony is, that's the impression most Outlanders have of the Athronian Labyrinth," Devor said, and then, as the last rays of the sun pulled away from the earth, he caught his breath. The people gathered in the street and the houses across the way floated in a pale gold light. Blinking, Devor realized the buildings were changing shape. Doused in soft pastel lights, they sprouted fantastical towers and turrets, spilling into each other and into the street. The laughing, cheering people chased the movements like a wave on the beach. The street itself writhed like a serpent until it changed where it had come from and where it was going to.

Dorian laughed at Devor's dropped jaw. "Ready to go play in the streets?"

The Outlander took several deep breaths. The scene beyond the safety of the house was both fascinating and frightening. "How could I possibly be in Athros and not experience the Athronian Labyrinth?" he asked resolutely.

Yanos laughed and waved a plump hand. "You run along and have fun."

"Come on, we don't want to miss anything." Dorian grabbed Devor's hand and pulled him to the door. "Have fun yourself, Father," she called back to Yanos before dragging Devor into the street.

"Whoa," Devor reacted, grabbing Dorian's arms to maintain his balance.

"It takes a few heartbeats to adjust." Dorian chuckled, as she glanced around to gauge if the Labyrinth had settled down yet. "The transformation is almost complete." As if on cue, the street and the buildings stilled into a dazzling jumble of impossible architectural delights. "It's a different design every year. All the Apprentices to Sorcery contribute something to it. The results can be pretty bizarre at times."

"It's incredible." Devor wandered into to the newly created street and turned completely around. Even the sky was filled with patterned fluffy clouds, floating in and out of fat rainbows and crystallized stars. "How do you ever figure out where you're going?" Devor laughed as they sauntered through a twisted, distorted Athros of the imagination.

"You don't, and you're not supposed to care," Dorian instructed. "Once you set foot outside your door, you don't know where you are until the Labyrinth is lifted at dawn."

"There seems to be a lot of people willing to take that chance." The little lane they were in opened up onto a square packed with grinning, giddy Athronians. A bubbling music rolled out from a corner of the square. As Dorian and Devor pushed closer to the source of the music, they beheld a whirling contraption with wide benches on ropes of metal hanging from a round canopy. Screaming Athronians on the benches hung on for their lives as they whirled around and around.

Devor stopped and stared at the spectacle. "You have a dangerous sense of fun."

"That's one of the more sedate rides." Dorian cast the Outlander an amused look. "Don't worry. Being a part of the Labyrinth, no one can get hurt." Meeting Devor's skeptical eyes, she shrugged. "It's a part of the magic."

"So, if someone is thrown off?"

Dorian had a distant expression of fondness in her eyes. "They find themselves bouncing on a cushion of air."

Devor gave her a knowing look. "Why is it I get the feeling that you let go on purpose?" The Overseer answered with an impish grin and a mischievous tug on his arm. "Now what are you up to?"

The contraption slowed until the benches hung limp and the giddy riders slid off in relief. Devor allowed himself to be pulled onto a bench.

"I guess I don't have to tell you to hang on." Dorian grinned as Devor inspected the apparatus. He didn't see any mechanism to propel it, much less someone controlling it. "Until I tell you to let go, that is."

The Outlander's attention was immediately on the innocent looking Overseer as the canopy jerked a few times to set it into motion. The sensation was heart-stopping until Devor got used to the motion. Then it was actually enjoyable in a scary sort of way.

"Knew it," Dorian whispered in his ear.

"Knew what?"

She grinned. "That you would enjoy this."

"Knowing that it won't kill me helps." Devor laughed as they whirled almost parallel to the canopy. "We're not really going to jump off this thing, are we?"

"Not until the time is right," Dorian solemnly assured him.

"And when is that?"

"The point at which we'll be thrown the farthest." Dorian couldn't keep the grin off her face. "Maybe crash into a few Athronians before we hit that cushion of air." Devor gave her an alarmed look. He knew she was kidding, but there was always that hint of doubt. It didn't help that she was laughing at his expression. "Relax. Enjoy the ride."

They whirled around, watching the lights of the imaginary square run together in continuous streaks, the tops of heads bobbing in a dizzying, color-filled sea. The magic did not just create the Labyrinth but also the atmosphere within it. The cacophony of music and soft kaleidoscope of lights pressed the air of festive abandonment straight into the soul. The whirling of the ride lost its frightening aspect and took on a trance-like quality. Devor had completely given himself over to it when they spun closer to the ground in a gentle descent. About half way between being parallel to the ground and at a dead standstill, Dorian gave Devor's arm a squeeze.

"Get ready," she whispered. "And don't hesitate or you really will crash into a bunch of Athronians."

Devor sighed. "How do I get myself into these things."

Dorian scanned the area around them for one rotation, then tensed. "Let go," she shouted, and much to Devor's surprise, he let go of the chain.

Dorian had calculated that they would land in a cleared space between a juice vendor and a trinkets booth. They bounced on air before it deflated, then they stood on solid ground. A splattering of applause from those who were paying attention accompanied the performance.

Devor laughed. "That was amazing."

"Many, many years of concentrated practice." Dorian eyed the juice vendor. "I think it's time for something to drink."

Several heartbeats passed before Devor realized he couldn't figure out what kinds of juices he was looking at. He finally turned to Dorian's impish grin. "Don't tell me. It's all magic."

The Overseer nodded with a twinkle in her eye. "I think you're catching on. The fruit that made these juices has never existed and never will again."

"So what would you recommend then?" Devor glanced over the glass jars.

"I always go with colors I like," Dorian replied. "I'm usually not disappointed."

The grinning juice vendor looked on amiably. "First Labyrinth?"

"Yes," Devor admitted. "I've never seen anything quite like it."

The pleasant faced young woman laughed. "The night's still young. Wait till the Labyrinth starts to dance."

"Dance?" Devor arched an eyebrow at Dorian.

"Don't worry. I'm going to have you good and drunk by then so you won't know the difference," the Overseer assured him.

"Drunk?"

"Oh," Dorian tapped her temple with two fingertips. "Did I forget to tell you that the imaginary fruit produces toxic juice?"

"Toxic?" The grin tugged too hard at Devor's mouth for him to keep up a serious expression.

"Extremely toxic." Dorian gazed into his eyes.

Devor fell into those gray eyes. "Do you think some colors are more toxic than others?"

"We could test them all and find out." Dorian tore herself away from his gaze. That was too intoxicating in itself. "What should we start out with?"

Chapter
Seventeen

The Calm

The people of Baniston were generous in providing Gris with everything he needed to be comfortably settled. Roge, the green grocer, had a spare set of rooms roughed out in the attic above his family's second floor residence. Unlike many of the retired Overseers, Gris did not seek a place on the village outskirts. He had spent much of his life with Outlanders and enjoyed their company. Besides, the Elders School offered an assortment of intelligent young people for him to engage in interesting discussions, and the Elders were delightful in their enthusiasm for the tidy village. If he was to be retired, he couldn't think of a more pleasant place.

The Overseer of Prophecy took a stroll each evening through the grounds of the Elders and Banish Hall. Villagers and Elders Apprentices and Guards all mingled and relaxed on the grassy expanses. The peacefulness of it reminded Gris of Athros.

The four Outlanders present at the Overseers meeting were familiar to him, and he didn't put it together until he took a walk the following evening. Those four were always lounging together on the unusual step-like wall surrounding the Banish Hall. When he had ventured close enough on previous evenings, he had overheard the young blue robed Elders Apprentice reciting an Overseer Story. He thought it a strange coincidence that they spent their spare time together and were also at a meeting exclusively for Athronians. What really made him notice them in the first place was the tall, striking Guard. When he first saw her, he literally blinked and shook his head. She looked enough like Panute to make him muse about how friendly some of the Overseers had gotten with the Outlanders.

Gris sauntered close enough to the small group to hear which story was being told, quite well, he noted. Both the speaker and the listeners were so engrossed in the tale that they did not see him nearby. The Overseer had to back out of earshot. Another Dorian story. Just hearing her name filled him with a wave of longing for a place he had chosen to spend very little time in. He had had a choice then and that was the difference. Athros was home, and Dorian was a personification of the place. Not only for Outlanders but for many Athronians as well. That was what made the recent Inquiry of Impeachment so shocking for the common Athronian. No one could envision an Athros without Dorian. She had been a public figure longer than most Athronians ever achieve, despite her young age. Her well-deserved status as a true legend placed her beside the ancient noble Athronians whose lives and deeds were little more than myth.

"Do you know Dorian?"

Gris blinked back to the present to see the little group coming his way. "Yes, I do," he replied with a fond smile.

"Really?" Janin did not even try to hold in her enthusiasm. "You really know her?" Her mind filled with dozens of questions she desperately wanted answered. What a wonderful coincidence that someone who actually knew Dorian moved to Baniston of all places.

"Yes. Very well in fact." Gris's eyes shown in amusement at this obvious hero worship. "We served on the Overseers' Council together."

"Overseers' Council?" Janin responded surprised.

"Dorian is the Overseer of Knowledge," Gris clarified.

"What?" asked a low voice. The old man turned his attention to the tall Guard. "There hasn't been a retired Overseer of Knowledge for several hundred years." Morna eyed the Overseer curiously.

"That's true." Gris nodded, taken back by how much this young woman reminded him of Panute. "The previous Overseer of Knowledge disappeared."

"Disappeared?" Janin whispered in shock.

Gris frowned a little at her reaction. "Yes. About seven Athronian years ago. Dorian passed the Overseer's exam and succeeded him. She's a very good Overseer and as brilliant as you can get." The Overseer smiled with pride that Dorian was able to get past the notoriety and go into the next phase of her life with a diligence that had shocked just about everyone. "Now, how is it you know when an Overseer has retired?" He turned his attention back to Morna, who leaned casually on her staff.

"I read about it in the Archives." Morna shrugged, without glancing at Kaston or Janin. The trio had actually been devouring everything they could on Athronians. "Because this is a Banish Hall, it is a custom to keep an account of such things."

Gris cocked a curious head. "I wasn't aware that the Guards were into more academic study."

"Only if we want to be," Morna returned, leveling a gaze at him. A muscular, younger Panute, Gris mused.

"You remind me of one of my Apprentices, who is probably the Overseer of Prophecy now," Gris ventured. "Just a bit of a resemblance. Same body type and all."

"Are Athronian women taller than the women here?" Morna, whose mind raced at the idea that she resembled an Athronian, kept her expression carefully neutral.

"Not particularly," Gris replied. "A mixed bag. Dorian, for instance, is about the height of your young storyteller. Maybe a little shorter."

Janin scratched her ear. "Somehow I pictured her as being taller."

Gris smiled. "She's muscular and agile. That has come in handy for her on more than one occasion."

"The Overseer of Knowledge." That fact was sinking in for Janin.

"It was a surprise for all of us when she passed the exam," Gris confessed. "But she was the best Apprentice." Janin nodded her head as if this wasn't news for her. Gris felt the undercurrents of a mystery surrounding these young people. And he had thought he would be bored in his retirement. "I enjoyed her company and she will be one of things that I regret having to leave behind."

Kaston squinted at him. "The person you're describing does not sound like the Dorian of the Stories."

"There are many layers to Dorian Riverson," Gris returned thoughtfully. "The Dorian of the Stories is very much alive and well, but the Dorian who was the Apprentice to Knowledge is also there. It's the combination of the two that makes her the unique individual she is."

Janin let out a breath of relief. "I was ready for you to say that she's nothing like the person in the Stories. That that person is just a figment of the Chroniclers' imagination."

Gris laughed. "No one, not even the Chroniclers, has enough imagination to create a Dorian Riverson."

Devor shook his head. "I know we haven't had that color yet."

"I'm the Overseer of Knowledge. It's my job to keep track of these things." Dorian concentrated on the differences between the two jars in front of her. She could barely stay focused on which color they were talking about, much less which they've sampled.

"We can go over every color we've had so far at each vendor," Devor suggested. "Or we could take a chance and go with this color, just in case the blue one or the green one temporarily impaired your flawless memory."

"I like the way you think," Dorian agreed, solemnly signaling the patient vendor and pointing to the deep brown concoction.

"I'm glad to hear that." Devor chuckled as he reached for the two mugs and handed one to Dorian. "Here's to—what haven't we toasted yet?"

"Here's to this muddy-colored stuff we're about to drink." They lifted their mugs and took a long sip. Both simultaneously wrinkled their noses. "Not only have we had this before, we didn't like it." They almost lost their balance in a giggling fit.

"The Labyrinth dances." An inebriated voice drifted down the lane to them. They saw several younger people prancing around the lights that replaced the cobblestones in the road. Laughing and crashing into each other, the group was oblivious to the world.

"I'm not quite sure I want to get to the point where I see the Labyrinth dance," Devor commented.

"Believe me, if you get to that point, you'll be beyond caring." Dorian took another long swig of the juice. "It's not too bad once you get over how awful it tastes." Devor, taking the challenge, also swallowed another gulp. It wasn't so bad because their taste buds were numb from all the alcohol.

"I'm glad you're still relatively sober." A very sober voice came from the food booth next to them. The pair squinted into the little crowd waiting to order the Labyrinth enhanced delicacies.

"I can't believe you're completely sober," Dorian commented as she focused on her cousin pointing out a half dozen items off the trays in front of him to the vendor, who obligingly wrapped each one in delicate paper.

Jac shrugged. "I've been working."

His cousin giggled. "You take your job much too seriously for an Apprentice to Mischief."

Jac straightened in mock indignation. "Mischief can happen at any time. We must always be prepared to encourage it. And tonight of all nights is nothing but mischief."

"But it's innocent mischief," Devor responded. "And I don't think it needs much encouragement."

Dorian chuckled at the indignant expression on her cousin's face. "Well spoken, Outlander."

Jac sighed as he picked out a couple of wrapped delicacies from the bag he held and placed them into Devor and Dorian's hands. "I guess the subtleties of mischief will never be truly appreciated."

Dorian looked at Devor. "I didn't know you could use the words 'subtleties' and 'mischief' in the same sentence."

"I revise my initial appraisal of your condition," Jac said. "You're both roaring drunk."

"Disgustingly so," Dorian agreed gravely. "We can't even remember what colors we've had."

Jac was actually surprised by this. "That is drunk."

"It's Devor's first time. I think we got a little carried away," Dorian admitted.

"A little?" Devor raised an eyebrow at her. "I have one question. Does this fermented liquid of imaginary fruit produce real hangovers?"

Jac turned to Dorian. "Now he thinks to ask." Catching Devor's widening eyes, the cousins laughed. "No hangovers," Jac assured him. "That's why nobody's worried about how drunk they're getting."

"Good," Devor said in relief.

Jac laughed. "If you're worried about hangovers, you

picked the wrong person to bond with."

"I don't remember being given any choice," Devor mumbled around a mouthful of a fruit pastry. "This is good. Different. Don't tell me. Labyrinth food."

Dorian grinned as they continued down the street. "You're catching on."

A commotion at the far end of the broad boulevard was more serious sounding than the usual Labyrinth noise. A growing crowd was focused on something in a side lane as a trio of Apprentices to Medicine pushed through them, carrying a folded stretcher.

Devor gave Dorian an accusing look. "I thought you said no one can get hurt in the Labyrinth."

Dorian frowned. "No one can. Not unless there is a flaw in the execution of the Labyrinth. But the structure is constantly monitored for weaknesses. It's a part of the exercise."

The number of curious revelers quickly spread to where they stood. The rumor of what had happened drifting to them nearly as fast.

"Usaf took a fall," Jac heard as he leaned into a group huddled next to him.

"What do you mean, 'took a fall'?" he asked. The others shrugged.

Someone scowled. "Doddering old man shouldn't be allowed into the Labyrinth."

"Is he really hurt?" Dorian asked.

"Just his pride if you ask me," a young woman answered. "No one can get hurt in the Labyrinth."

"I hope he doesn't take it out on the Apprentices to Sorcery for not being able to walk without tripping over imaginary scenery." Jac shook his head in disgust. Usaf had a reputation for clumsiness.

"If anyone can hurt himself in the Labyrinth, it's Usaf." A voice wafted to them amidst drunken giggles.

"Come on, paying attention just makes it worse." Dorian pulled her two companions away from the scene. "Jac has to catch up on his colors, remember." Usaf was immediately forgotten as they returned to the more important business of the night.

Greenar and Rubnic didn't travel much anymore. Habit had

gradually taken over the need for change of scenery. Trooping down the road with packs on their backs and sturdy walking sticks in their hands vividly reminded them of how much they enjoyed the feeling of being vagabonds.

"Why did we ever stop doing this?" Greenar asked as she took in the earthy aromas wafting off a small stand of trees.

"Sometimes we don't miss things until we're doing them again," Rubnic replied.

"Let's not forget this one." His bondmate reached out to rub the forehead of a black and white splotched cow. The animal, contentedly chewing, raised lazy brown eyes to the Overseer.

"I wish the reasons for this trek were just for relaxation." The Overseer of Sorcery fought back the strange apprehension that clung to him since his meeting with the Queen.

They topped a small hill. The fields stretching before them were covered with half grown grains. In the distance, they could just see the tops of the stone Halls of Baniston lifting out of the Kittle River valley.

Greenar gazed across the valley. "What a peaceful place. Hard to believe that Ghouls came through here not long ago."

"Unfortunately, Ghouls can show up anywhere," Rubnic returned, as they unconsciously increased their pace. Curiosity about the Banish Hall drew them to the valley as much as the more serious reason they were there. The Hall stood as a fascinating relic to the Athronian sense of justice.

The large stones of the main road changed into impacted cobblestones on the edge of the village.

"I suppose we ought to find the Elders Hall." Rubnic couldn't hide his reluctance to get on with the reason they were there, but two ancient Athronians sauntering into town did not go unnoticed for very long. They might as well make themselves and the purpose of their visit known as soon as possible.

With only one main road, finding the Banish Hall grounds was not difficult. A question to a black-garbed Guard strolling across the green brought them quickly to the steps of the Elders Hall.

Greenar looked up at the imposing building. "I've never seen an Elders Hall this large."

"There is an Elders School here," Rubnic said. The building seemed too large for even that.

Upon entering, they recognized the traditional Elders Bench from which the district affairs were conducted. "I suppose the

Elders are on the second floor." Greenar sighed, eyeing the staircase. She could walk all day over the countryside but found
stairs unexplainably uncomfortable.

"You could stay down here," her bondmate offered.

"Nonsense." Greenar scoffed. "A stair has never hurt me
yet."

Step by step, the ancient couple climbed to the second floor.
The sight of blue-robed students hunched over haphazardly
placed desks caused the Overseers to stop and stare for several
heartbeats. The scene was eerily reminiscent of an Apprentice
alcove in Athros. Maybe there was more to the joking reference
of the Baniston district being a little Athros than they thought.

Rubnic approached the nearest Apprentice. "Excuse me.
Could you tell us where we can find Elder Alcot."

The young man blinked up from his studies. "She's in the
big office on the prison floor. Up one more floor."

"Thank you." Rubnic turned back to Greenar, who sighed
and looked up the steps.

If the second floor was familiar, the third floor was shockingly alien. The Apprentice had called it the "prison floor." Banished prisoners. The Overseers exchanged slow glances.

In the far corner, a young woman was intently scribbling.
Closer to them was an opened door to what looked like an office.
As they peeked through the door, Gretna looked up and eagerly
beckoned them in. "Greenar. Rubnic. Come in. Come in. What a
pleasant surprise." Gretna came around her desk and led them to
her little parlor. "Soral, would you please bring us some tea?"
the Elder requested over her shoulder.

"What an interesting place," Rubnic commented after they
were settled around a low table. "Was this floor really created to
be a prison?"

Gretna nodded. "Yes, it was. As far as I know, it has never
been used."

"But to maintain it all these years," Greenar mused.

"Traditions are strong here," Gretna explained. "They are
always prepared for a banishment. Only the need for more room
for the school forced me to move up here. Since there probably
won't be a banishment, we may as well make use of the space."

"Banishments are certainly a thing of the long past," Rubnic
agreed. "But the Banish Hall is quite impressive."

"Unfortunately, it caught the attention of the Queen."
Gretna scowled. Soral entered with a tray. "This is my assistant,

Soral. Greenar Siderling, Overseer of Justice. Rubnic Siderling, Overseer of Sorcery and High Overseer."

Soral smiled at the visitors. "How do you do."

Greenar smiled back. "It's a pleasure, Soral."

"Are you a student here?" Rubnic asked, noting the blue robe.

"Soral is one of our top students," Gretna answered before Soral had a chance to open her mouth. "She'll make a fine Elder someday."

"You are too kind." The young Apprentice blushed at the praise.

"Now, could you ask Janin to join us?" Gretna asked her assistant before turning to her guests. "Janin has a special interest in Athros and the Athronian people. You will be surprised at how astute she is."

Gretna barely had four cups of tea poured out when Janin paused in the doorway. The Elder beckoned her in with a wave of a hand.

"This is Janin, a very promising student at the school. Greenar, Overseer of Justice. Rubnic, Overseer of Sorcery and High Overseer. They are bondmates, Janin." Janin's eyes widened as Gretna pointed to the seat next to her before distributing the tea and plates of small sandwiches. "Janin has just been studying the Attraction and bonding."

Janin gazed at the ancient couple. "I read it was rare for both bondmates to become Overseers."

"It is rare because the opportunities to become Overseer are relatively rare," Rubnic explained. "Greenar was Overseer a good twenty years before I had the chance to become one. It is unusual for an Apprentice to get a second chance. They usually retire long before that."

"I hope you'll join us for the evening meal," Gretna invited. "To give Janin a chance to pick your brain on the subject."

"We would be delighted," Rubnic graciously replied. "To the point, though, we must speak of the reason we are here." His gaze briefly shifted to Janin.

"Janin has been following the Overseer problem quite closely," Gretna said smoothly. "If that is what this visit is about, I would like her to be present."

Rubnic bowed his head in acceptance. "As you already know, I've been made the Queen's liaison to the Overseers. I'm not quite sure if it was because I was the headmaster at her daughter's school or because I'm both a High Overseer and former Overseer of Sorcery. Since I couldn't gracefully refuse, I decided to take advantage of the fact that I will be privy to what the Queen has in mind for the Overseers and give fair warning as needed."

"If it's about the Banish Hall living quarters, we've already been informed," Gretna stated.

"That's only the half of it." Rubnic sighed as Gretna and Janin exchanged looks. "The Queen plans to put Baniston on a pilgrimage route."

Gretna frowned. "Pilgrimage route?"

"She's connecting all the Overseer relics that can't be moved to her museum with roads, bridges, whatever it takes and then plans to encourage the people to travel these routes to view the relics," Greenar explained with a sour expression. "Since the Banish Hall is so impressive and unique, she wants it to be one of the highlights of this route."

Gretna's mouth hung open. Her peaceful, sleepy Baniston was going to be lost forever to the mad ideas of a Queen with too much time on her hands.

"Do you think people will really journey these routes just for the sake of doing it?" Janin asked as she turned the strange idea over in her mind.

"In peacetime, there is always a need for diversion and challenge," Rubnic replied thoughtfully. "The people will get caught up in the challenge of making this pilgrimage. The Queen talked about having a booklet stamped at each stop and some kind of reward for completing it."

"How does she expect us to run a school if people are tramping around all the time?" Gretna's distant look came back into focus with a vengeance. "And this village can't accommodate an influx of visitors. We'll be forced to build inns and clear land for camps. We'll have to add more Guards to keep the peace. We'll have to increase trade to bring in supplies to keep them fed and provide the proper comforts."

"The Queen sees all these things as a part of the general project for the area," Rubnic said dryly.

"She will destroy the town," Gretna responded in dismay. "She will remove the uniqueness that captured her attention in the first place. More importantly, Baniston will lose its purpose for being here. There are rules attached to maintaining a Banish Hall. Not the least of which is the fact that no one is allowed to enter the Hall except those who inhabit these grounds. The only exception is by special invitation and accompanied by a Guard. We wouldn't want just anyone stumbling upon a banished prisoner from Athros for who-knows-what terrible crime. That is why the prison is here. The prisoner can be taken through a tunnel that connects the two Halls without even seeing the light of day."

"Isn't it dangerous to have the school below?" Greenar asked.

"The school wasn't here when these Halls were built," Gretna explained. "This building was originally just for the village government and the prison. When the idea of establishing an Elders School was proposed, it seemed logical to use this Hall since there was an abundance of empty space. A banishment hasn't happened in ages, so it seemed like a good use for the Hall."

"So, you have a Banish Hall and an Elders School to protect from the whims of our Queen," Rubnic said.

"Not to mention a delightful sleepy village in a district overrun by Overseers looking for a little peace," Gretna added.

"We will spend a few days here," Rubnic stated. "Maybe we can think of some way to stop our misguided Queen."

Chapter
Eighteen

Confusion Before the Storm

The Banish Hall Guards were engaged in morning sparring with an enthusiasm that impressed Gris as he and Greenar paused on the edge of the dusty practice yards. An older woman barking commands saw the pair and strolled over to them, revealing an easy grace that came from a sinewy muscular strength.

The Guard saluted the Athronians. "Lieutenant Rane Inderson-Lintan."

"Gris Twaene and this is Greenar Siderling," Gris graciously introduced.

"It is my pleasure to show you around." Rane worked best with formal statements when dealing with civilians.

"The pleasure is ours." The Overseer of Prophecy bowed. "You are the one who raised the talented staff wielder, Morna?"

"Yes," Rane responded keeping surprise and curiosity off her face. She and Fent had always taken Morna's penchant for prowling the Elders School Archives in stride. They thought it was good that she had other interests than just being a soldier. The longtime friendship with Soral only surprised those who could not see beyond the tough fighter. The Athronian obsession, they figured, was just the latest in a line of things that captured the fleeting attention of young people. The fact that the Elders not only indulged them in this obsession but also allowed them to socialize with Athronians puzzled them only a little. The

Elders were, after all, Athronians and neither Lieutenant pretended to understand their customs or attitudes towards such
things. As far as Morna's guardians were concerned, anything to
promote camaraderie amongst the inhabitants of the Elders and
Banish Hall grounds was good for the whole community in a
time of crisis.

Gris nodded. "Very fine young woman. You must be proud."

Rane allowed a rare smile. "We are."

"I understand she's adopted." Gris rubbed his chin.

"We rescued her from a battlefield when she was five,"
Rane explained. "I was told there would be three of you."

"My bondmate was unexpectedly called away on Athronian
business," Greenar explained. "He wanted so much to see where
you live and work. He was hoping you could give him a tour
when he returns." The reminder of Rubnic's absence clouded
Gris' thoughts. There were only two reasons for a retired High
Overseer to be called back to Athros, and he knew it wasn't for
the more desirable one.

"It would be my pleasure." Rane bowed her head before
turning to the activity in front of them. "We spend much of our
time keeping both our mental and physical skills sharp. Guarding
the Hall is a solitary activity, so many of us use it as an opportunity to practice meditation drills."

"Meditation drills?" Gris repeated curiously as they sauntered past the sparring pairs.

"Working with the sword or staff to focus the mind rather
than to do injury to someone," Rane clarified, dryly.

"Interesting," Greenar said thoughtfully.

Rane led them through the living quarters and the mess hall,
which Gris had already seen. Unlike the tour given to a new
Guard, Rane led her visitors into the Banish Hall through the
front double doors, which were wide open to catch some of the
summer breeze. The first thing that caught their breaths was not
the brooding round chamber but the figure engaged in graceful
intricate movements of body and staff following a precise inner
rhythm.

"We will not disturb her," Rane assured her spellbound visitors. "She has mastered the art of meditation to the degree that
she is aware of every movement and sound we make without
breaking her concentration."

"Extraordinary," Gris murmured, having to pull his eyes
from the Guard who looked so much like Panute. A part of him

ached for his Apprentice's always treasured company. Panute was his daughter in every way except by blood.

"This Hall was built many centuries ago after a banishment occurred on this spot," Rane explained. "There was a small settlement on the bank of the river at the time. When the people realized that this was where banished Athronians were sent, they decided to build a Hall around the spot where the banished Athronian was found. The prison room was originally in here, but for some reason, it was moved to the Elders Hall after that was built. Of course, the school wasn't housed there until many years later. By that time, it was realized that banishments were rare, and the need of the Elders Hall as a court and district jail diminished as Baniston settled into a peaceful, sleepy village."

Gris looked at the hard stone floor and shuddered at the thought of dropping, hooded and gloved, onto it. "What happened to the banished Athronian?" he asked curiously. The last banishment he knew of was for stealing a stone from another Overseer.

Rane shrugged. "He was put to work, helping to build the Banish Hall for no pay other than room and board. A fitting punishment for a first time offense of a nonviolent crime." The Overseer of Prophecy was relieved at this. These people had a sensible streak in them, and it was also lucky that the Elders were Athronian. Noting Gris' relieved expression, Rane eyed him curiously. "You are not aware in Athros of our Banish Hall?"

Both Greenar and Gris chuckled at this. "Athronians know nothing of this land. They only know that it exists," Greenar replied. "That is by choice of the Athronians who come here. We don't want to do anything to spoil it for the retirees, and we don't want the High Overseers to decide that this is no longer a suitable place for the punishment of an Athronian. Our crimes are based more on breaches of honor than on violence or damage to property and such. Being the upholders of exemplary behavior for the Outlanders, we have to live up to the highest standards of honor and trustworthiness. To be banished is enough of a punishment for not living up to these standards. We are very attached to our city and our families. When we retire, we willingly make the choice to leave Athros. When banished, the choice is made for us, and we are not allowed to prepare our families or bring along our bondmates."

Gris refrained from stating the relatively new concept of

forced retirements. Although the bondmate was allowed to accompany the retiree, there was no time given to prepare the rest of the family. Best let the old timers remember their Athros.

As the three stepped into the bright morning sun, Morna wound down her exercises and stood staring after them for many heartbeats. Hearing about how Athronians were separated from the place and family they love touched something deeply buried within her. So deep, she didn't even know it was there. Tears soaked her cheek before she realized she was crying. Where did that come from? She shook her head not so much disturbed but surprised that she was capable of such depth of feeling. She never knew that there was such emptiness in her soul.

Lifting her staff, she stepped into a world in which she felt the most at ease. The world that melded her mind with her body so that it worked in a single flawless unity.

The parchment in the Overseer of Crime's hand shook uncontrollably. Tyml had to get a solid grip on his wrist to finish reading it. The color fled from his face as he glanced at the six High Overseer Guards in his outer office. He would rather be banished than do what was asked of him by the High Overseers, but that would only leave his successor with the hapless task. After rising from behind his desk, he neatly refolded the parchment and slipped it into his belt pouch, took several deep breaths to settle his trembling body, and set his mind to do the most distasteful task he had ever been ordered to perform.

Dorian was diligently scribbling her name on each sheet of paper in the pile in front of her, and Devor was hunched over a book. The Apprentices steadily shifted through the day's knowledge. The Overseer of Crime took in the peaceful scene, regretfully realizing that it was about to change forever. Signaling the Guards to remain on the green, Tyml strode into the open walled chamber to stand before the table occupied by Dorian and Devor.

The Overseer of Knowledge raised puzzled eyes to him. Tyml, unable to find a voice, laid the parchment before Dorian. Her eyes rested on it for long moments before picking it up and unfolding it. The look of confusion and disbelief on her face told him what he already knew in his heart. A terrible injustice was about to be committed.

Her shocked eyes captured his. "How could they possibly

think I had anything to do with this?"

"Usaf said you did it," Tyml replied bitterly.

"So, they don't need the truth then." Dorian went very still and lowered her eyes. Her whole world crashed noiselessly around her as her brain numbed. Feeling Devor's eyes burning into her, she passed him the parchment without turning.

"But I was with her the whole time we were in the Labyrinth," Devor protested.

"It's a High Overseer's word against everyone else's," Dorian replied, wearily.

"I can take the truthstone." Devor became lost in desperation.

"The truthstone doesn't work on Outlanders," Tyml said miserably. "Besides, as Dorian said, they aren't interested in the truth."

Dorian jerked imperceptibly before slamming her mind with curses. She turned to Devor and wrapped her hands around his, a desperate urgency on her face. "I'm sorry you have to be dragged into this. What I'm about to say won't make sense right now, but it will later. When I'm separated from you, there will be questions you'll want the answers to. The only person who will be able to answer those questions is Panute. I am not going to put on an optimistic face for you. Tyml is here to take me before a banishment hearing. As far as they're concerned, I've been tried and found guilty of this crime because the word of a High Overseer cannot be argued or contested."

"But it's a lie!" Devor faltered, unable to believe that Dorian was about to be separated from him forever.

Dorian glanced at Tyml. "Could we have a few moments alone. I promise I won't disappear."

"Of course," Tyml murmured and strode back onto the green.

"They couldn't get me with the truth, so they will settle for getting me with a lie," Dorian said steadily, looking Devor in the eyes. "I'll be in the Land Out of Time. There are ways of getting there." Devor's eyes took on a look of understanding. "Sometimes retired Overseers pop back to visit their families. It's done very quietly. Very quietly. But it's done. So don't give up hope. We will see each other again."

"How will you survive the pain?" Devor's voice was ragged.

"Since no one has ever been banished before a bond has

been completed, the Overseers will probably lobby either to allow us to complete the bond or to have it broken. It's in the code of law, so the High Overseers will have to consider it."

"Broken?"

"Don't worry. That will not change how we feel about each other." Dorian grasped his hands tighter. "If we had met as two Outlanders, we would have felt the same." Devor breathed a sigh of relief. He hadn't been sure how that worked. Glancing at Tyml and noting some agitation in his body language, Dorian sighed. "We don't have much more time." She stood, bringing Devor up with her, and wrapped her arms around him, holding him like she was memorizing everything about the experience. They gently kissed, knowing how far the bond could be pushed and stared long and searching into each other's eyes. "I won't say good-bye." Dorian's voice faltered as she kept her tears unshed. "We will see each other again."

"If you believe it, I won't give up hope," Devor responded hoarsely.

Dorian finally turned to her Apprentices, who had stopped their work and alternately watched the Guards and their Overseer. Not letting go of Devor's hand, the Overseer of Knowledge approached the group.

"It looks like I've got the interesting piece of knowledge for the day." Dorian tried to swallow down the lump forming in her throat. "I've been summoned to the High Overseers Hall to face banishment procedures." Several of the Apprentices opened their mouths in shocked response, but Dorian held up a hand. "For what it's worth, I'm innocent of what I'm accused of doing. But innocence doesn't count for much anymore. Take that as the best words of wisdom I can give you. I will miss all of you, and I will miss all of this. Good luck to you."

Dorian turned and, pulling Devor with her, walked swiftly to the Overseer of Crime. He saw the raw emotion on her face that she didn't want her Apprentices to see. She didn't see the stricken reactions of her Apprentices. His mind burned with anger at the thought that she was being ripped out of their lives. Despite everything, they were known for their almost militant devotion to their Overseer. To a person, the Apprentices dropped whatever they held and gathered to follow Dorian to the High Overseers Hall.

"I'm ready," Dorian said to Tyml. "I hope you don't mind if Devor accompanies me. I don't think you want me doubling over with pain on the way there."

"It's only right that he should be with you," Tyml said softly, not able to stop from feeling anything but pity for this tragic young woman. "I've sent messengers to your family."

"Thank you," Dorian breathed in grateful relief.

A large crowd followed this small convoy as they trooped through the winding streets of Athros. People, in shock, stopped whatever they were doing at the realization that the Overseer of Knowledge was being led somewhere by the Overseer of Crime and six High Overseer Guards. Six was the significant number. Six was the number required for a prisoner being taken to a banishment hearing. This hadn't happened in so long that it was only recited in fireside tales. The crowds rumbled with mutterings of disbelief. No one could even speculate on what she could have done to deserve banishment. All the attempts of the High Overseers to trip her up had ended in failure, proving to the people of Athros that these power brokers were just bullying her. A banishment hearing meant that she had finally been convicted of something, but there hadn't been an Impeachment Inquiry. Uneasiness spread through the ghostly crowds as they shadowed the solemn group.

Dorian was oblivious to the growing crowds. She was trying to wrap her mind around the unfathomable idea that she would never see her family again, never see Devor again, despite her efforts to reassure him that there was a way they could be together. Squeezing Devor's hand, she never wanted to let it go. Letting go meant never holding it again. Choking back tears, she shook her head to clear all these thoughts away. She could give in to them later. Later. When she was no longer in Athros.

"They're there," Devor whispered, squinting at a small group huddled miserably in front the High Overseers Hall door. Dorian shuddered with relief.

"You'll allow me to say goodbye to my family?" Her soft voice was saturated with emotion.

"Of course," Tyml replied. The High Overseers could do what they wanted with him afterwards; he was going to make this ordeal as humane as possible for Dorian.

"Thank you," came the soft response. They were close enough for Dorian to see her family's stricken expressions. "If I can survive this, I'll be able to survive anything." Devor turned to her, realizing she meant saying goodbye to her family.

The Guards parted to let Dorian and Devor step onto the

green alone. Dordan closed the distance between them and had her daughter in a tight sobbing embrace before Dorian had a chance to collect her thoughts.

"I'm sorry," was all that Dorian could stammer out.

"Why?" Her mother's tear-filled voice wrenched at Dorian's soul. "Why are they doing this to you?"

"I don't know." Dorian's voice cracked. "I'll probably never know." Dordan reluctantly released her daughter as Yanos took her place. "Father." The intense emotional strain tore Dorian into little pieces.

Her aunt and uncle each pulled her into a tear stained embrace. She had always felt as if she had two sets of parents, and she had broken the hearts of them all. Finally, she wrapped her arms around Jac, who was so miserable that he was almost in shock.

"Looks like you can't rescue me this time, cousin," Dorian whispered. Jac nodded, unable to speak. Dorian put him at arm's length and shook him a bit. "Jac, I'm relying on you right now." Jac focused on her. "Take care of my parents."

"You know I will," he whispered, unable to push air through his speech.

"And Devor." She pulled herself closer and whispered into his ear, "He's going to be in pain when I go in there."

"What?" Jac tried to pull back to look at her but she held on.

"Listen," Dorian whispered urgently. "Just get him out of here as fast as possible. It won't do him any good for everyone to see him react to a bond separation."

"But—" Jac was truly confused.

"Panute knows the answer," Dorian said.

Quickly embracing her family and Devor one last time, Dorian resolutely returned to her place between the Guards and entered the High Overseers Hall.

Jac, ever the creature of duty, left his family at the doors of the High Overseers Hall to fulfill Dorian's last request to him. Saying he would explain later, he pulled a confused Devor away from the curious crowd gathering on the green.

"Dorian told me to get you away and out of sight as quickly as possible," Jac tried to explain as he hurried Devor into a deserted narrow lane.

Devor frowned. "Why? Does she have a reason to fear for my safety?"

"I don't see why they would bother with you..." Jac's voice trailed off as Devor doubled over, his face twisted in agony. "It's really true." The Apprentice to Mischief grabbed Devor and pulled him up.

"What's happening?" Devor felt as though he was falling into a vat of burning anguish.

"I think this is starting to make sense." Jac seized Devor and hurried him along. "We've got to get some bondroot into you."

"Bondroot?" Devor rasped. "I'm not supposed to be having a reaction."

"First things first." Jac dragged the miserable Outlander down several lanes until he pushed him into a whitewashed, sunny building fronted by a neatly hedged garden. The high ceiling chamber was dominated by a scattering of cushy chairs and sofas with low-lying tables. A white robed Apprentice to Attractions helped Devor into a chair as another Apprentice pulled a steaming kettle off a warming shelf in the fireplace. She poured hot water over a bundle of herbs already in one of the mugs lining the mantelpiece.

"The tea needs a couple of moments to steep," Kanar, the Apprentice by Devor's side, explained softly. "I thought he was an Outlander," he added with mild curiosity.

"So did I," Jac replied.

"How'd they get separated?" Kanar and Jac held Devor down during another spasm of pain. "They must be close to completing the bond." The Apprentice gauged the intensity of the attack.

"They were three days away." Jac tried to swallow the bitterness of the words, but the image of his cousin being led into the High Overseers Hall pressed hard against his soul.

Kanar's eyes shot up at him. "Were?" The young man's chest clutched at the thought that something serious had happened to Dorian Riverson.

"Let's get Devor comfortable first." Jac had to focus on something before the blackness of despair wiped out all the light in his world.

Laner, the other Apprentice, shuffled over, holding the mug in both hands, taking care not to spill the precious contents. Between the three of them, they managed to get all the vile tasting liquid into Devor. Carefully leaning Devor back into the chair, they noted that the tea's effect was already working as his face and body relaxed. Bondroot was cultivated for the specific purpose of relieving the pain of a bond separation. The unfortunate side effects of the herb were the awful taste and that it wore off after only a few sand marks.

Devor sat back staring at Jac. "Now, will you please tell me what's going on?"

"You, my friend, are an Athronian," Jac said bluntly.

"How is that possible?"

"It's more possible that you might think," Laner mused. "There are children of Athronians who grow up in the Outland without ever knowing their true parentage."

"All right, all right." Devor put up a hand. "It's obvious that I'm an Athronian. How did Dorian know?"

"I don't know."

Devor blinked at him. "Why would she keep this a secret?"

"You must believe me, she had a very good reason," Jac responded, needing to reassure himself as much as Devor. Dorian's drunken conversation with Panute popped into his head. As was his habit, he had placed himself within easy rescue distance of his cousin in the disreputable tavern she and Devor had sought refuge in and overheard the curious exchange of words between the two Overseers. What was that they said about a part of Orvid's quote being left unsaid?

Devor frowned. "She told me to ask Panute." Jac glanced up, startled that Devor mentioned the very person he was just thinking about. "She said Panute would be able to answer my questions."

"But where is Dorian now?" Kanar pressed rather anxiously. "Shouldn't someone be out looking for her? She needs the tea, too."

Jac and Devor exchanged horrified looks as they had the same thought. "Kanar, what happens when a bonded person is banished?" Jac asked steadily.

"Banished?" both Apprentices to Attractions responded in alarm.

"It has never happened," Kanar clarified. "It's rare for an Overseer to be bonded while Overseer, much less get banished at the same time."

"Why do you ask?" Laner drew the words out slowly, dreading the answer.

"Dorian is being banished." Jac's voice cracked on the words. The reality of it seared into his consciousness.

"What?" the Apprentices reacted in shock.

Devor stared wide-eyed at the stricken Apprentices. "She said the bond can be broken."

Laner, taking deep breaths, sank into a chair. She had to push away her own troubled feelings and do her duty. The Apprentice was a close friend of Dordan and Deidan. She had been present the day Dorian was born and had participated in her naming ceremony. Pushing all this out of her mind, she focused on Jac and Devor. "Even though a bonded person has never been banished, a law was devised to cover the possibility."

Jac and Devor released their breaths.

"Bless those lawmakers," Jac muttered.

"The High Overseers have the power to break the bond before a banishment," Laner continued.

Jac clenched his teeth. "The High Overseers."

"Surely the banishment is punishment enough." Kanar frowned, realizing what he had just said. "What could she have possibly done to merit this?"

"She's been accused of pushing Usaf down some steps on Labyrinth night." Jac's anger was barely controlled.

The Apprentices looked as if Jac had slapped them. "Dorian would never do anything like that. Everyone knows that." Laner couldn't stop the tears.

"It's a High Overseer's word against hers and Devor's and mine," Jac replied miserably. "We were with her when the alleged incident happened. They betray their own deception by not putting us on trial as accomplices. We aren't even important enough to help their little lie. They want Dorian banished, and they obviously are beyond caring if anyone believes their accusations or not."

Chapter Nineteen

Where Dorian Goes So Does Truth

Dorian was barely conscious when the High Overseer Guards let her crumble to the unforgiving stone floor. Pain from the bond separation, mingled with the realization that she would never see her family or Devor or Athros again made her wish she could die like an Outlander. Gasps from the Overseers gallery on one side of her brushed her hearing before she sank into the pit of agony that had enveloped her mind and body.

From the retired High Overseers bench opposite the Overseers, Rubnic was on his feet before he realized that it was inappropriate to react. Much to his relief, the other three retired High Overseers had followed their instincts and were also on their feet in outrage, gesturing at the young woman sprawled on the floor.

"Is this any way to treat an Overseer?" Lasco, the eldest of the retired High Overseers, leveled a furious glare at Huask.

Huask straightened. "She has been found guilty of an unforgivable crime."

"She is an Overseer and must be shown respect." Lasco couldn't believe that common courtesy had been forgotten in Athros. "What is she suffering from?"

"She's bonded." Huask nearly spat the word.

"Then have some bondroot brought to her." Lasco stared at

Huask, unable to comprehend how he could have become a High Overseer.

Huask scowled. "Why waste time coddling her when she's to be banished?"

The Overseers erupted in protest, not caring if they would be the next to be forced from Athros. The retired High Overseers exchanged incredulous glances. This lack of compassion stung like a winter-time sleet. Much had changed in Athros since they resided in that Hall.

Huask, not pleased with the demonstration from the retired High Overseers in front of the Overseers, beat his walking stick against the stone table to get their attention. When the angry and upset group members finally resumed their seats, he rose to his feet. "You have been gathered here to witness the banishment of Dorian Riverson, Overseer of Knowledge. She has been found guilty of pushing, with the intent to cause injury, High Overseer Usaf on Labyrinth night—"

"That's ridiculous," Rubnic interrupted. Huask turned an angry eye to him before he realized that he couldn't lash back at the retired man. "No one can be hurt in the Labyrinth, so no action within the Labyrinth can be made 'with the intent to cause injury.'"

Huask glared at the former High Overseer. "The intention can be there."

"That's only assuming that the person doing the pushing is not aware of this fact," Rubnic clarified. "Yet, every single Athronian old enough to talk knows that no harm can come to them within the Labyrinth. The Overseer of Knowledge knows it for certain."

"The maliciousness of the act is enough to merit an intention to cause injury. Whether an injury can be caused under the particular circumstances or not is irrelevant." Huask held his temper in check. "Dorian Riverson pushed High Overseer Usaf, causing him to fall. That is enough to merit banishment."

Rubnic realized he could argue the point forever and not get Huask to see reason. This was not about reason. A chill shot up his spine. This was about getting rid of Dorian Riverson. A formal trial wasn't necessary. Witnesses weren't necessary. Only a High Overseer's word against everyone else's, and the High Overseer was above reproach. He looked at the stricken faces of the Overseers, helpless to do anything.

"The punishment is immediate transport to The Land Out of

Time. Guards, prepare the prisoner for transport." Three guards, stationed behind the High Overseers table, picked up the heavy hood and gloves that lay in a heap on the floor.

"Wait." Tigren rose to his feet. I dare you to retire me, he screamed at them with his mind, but I can't have her condemned to die a terrible death. "At least break the bond first."

Huask rubbed his chin, gazing thoughtfully at the suffering Overseer doubled over her knees, face contorted in agony. "We feel that the bond should remain as a part of the punishment."

The Overseers and the retired High Overseers were on their feet with angry shouts. "What kind of monsters do we have overseeing Athros?" Lasco demanded, his fury shaking his thin ancient frame. "What about her bondmate?"

Huask shrugged. "He's an Outlander."

A strangled noise came from the hunched figure before them. With incredible effort, Dorian raised up so she could face the High Overseers. "He's an Athronian," she gasped.

Panute, who had been stilled as if stricken by a spell, let out a ragged breath.

Huask grinned wickedly at Dorian. "You told us yourself that he's an Outlander. Now you lie to save yourself a little pain."

Panute choked back words as miserable tears rolled down her face. She had to tell herself that the High Overseers wouldn't believe her any more than they believed Dorian, and she had to stay out of trouble with them. She was the only one who knew the true meaning behind this terrible nightmare.

"I told you he was from the Outland." Dorian's voice was strained but steady as she concentrated on each word. "You drew your own conclusion that he was an Outlander."

Huask glared at her, furious that she could still argue soundly even in her present state. "That's of little concern." He waved his hand. "We have made the decision not to break the bond, and that decision will stand." He cast a penetrating glance around the chamber, challenging anyone to say more. The group settled into a miserable silence of acceptance that the High Overseers were not going to show any mercy to Dorian. "Guards, prepare the prisoner."

"Wait," Dorian gasped, pulling to her feet and straightening, using nothing more than her strength of will. The pain ripped through her abdomen leaving her short of breath and light-headed. Everyone, including the High Overseers, were transfixed by this feat of determination. "I wish to take the High Overseer's exam," she announced in a hoarse whisper before sinking onto the stone floor.

"Are you ready for your new duties?" Morna arched an eyebrow at her sparring partner.

Kaston didn't know whether to be enthusiastic or wary. "What new duties?"

"The proper response to the question is a 'yes' or 'no.'" Morna leveled steady eyes at him. "Are you ready for your new duties?"

"Yes," Kaston returned, still wary.

"Follow me." Morna turned as a confused Kaston dogged her heels. Her behavior was gruffer than usual, and he wondered if he had done something to offend her. So deep he was in his thoughts that he wasn't aware of entering the Banish Hall until they ducked into the small back door. Leaning against the opposite wall was a Guard reading a small book. Kaston blinked in the dimness and cast curious eyes at Morna.

Morna held out a strong elegant hand. "Give me your staff." Kaston obeyed her request. "Now, go pick up that staff." She pointed to the middle of the Hall. On the floor was a dark polished staff.

The muffled echoes from Kaston's soft boots against the stone floor was the only sound for the several heartbeats it took for the young man to go to the staff and pick it up. Feeling the polished dark wood beneath his hands, he fingered the mark of the Banish Hall Guards carved near the tip of the staff.

"Is this mine?" he asked, turning to Morna.

Morna nodded. "It's yours. When a Guard receives his or her weapon, it is time for them to take their turn standing guard duty in the Hall. I will show you everything now. Your first watch will be tonight at the tenth bell."

"Tonight?" Kaston reacted with excitement. "So soon?"

Morna laughed good-naturedly. "Guarding the Hall may be our greatest privilege, but it is also the least exciting thing we do. It's a good way to practice how not to get bored." She led him to the front vestibule. "Do you see the hole in the beam up there?" She pointed directly above them at the low ceiling with a beam that jutted out even lower. "In that hole is the mechanism that rings the Banish Hall bell."

Kaston stared wide-eyed. "Have you ever heard the bell ring?"

Morna shook her head. "It only rings for one purpose. A banishment. It has never been rung."

"Then how do you know it still works, after all these centuries?" In spite of himself, Kaston's mechanical mind asserted itself.

Morna shrugged. "Faith." As far as she knew, no one had ever questioned whether the bell would be able to perform its special duty after sitting dormant for so long. "If there is a banishment, you take your staff and push it into the hole until the bell rings, then pull the staff back out. The prisoner will be hooded and gloved and disoriented. Do not approach the prisoner; just watch carefully and wait for Captain Janvil and the Elders. It's as simple as that. Keep away from the middle of the floor at all times. We wouldn't want an Athronian plopping down on you."

"That's how it happens? They just come shooting out of the air?" Kaston asked.

"That's what they say," Morna returned.

"There must be some kind of machine that does that," Kaston mused, almost to himself.

Morna chuckled. "You can wrap your mind around that while you are going crazy from boredom tonight. Maybe figure out some way of checking to see if the bell is in working order without actually ringing it. Now, there's a good puzzle."

"We'll never use it anyway."

"Never doubt that the bell will be used." Morna gave him a warning glance. "It is our duty to believe in this and to be ready for it."

"Aye, ma'am." Kaston saluted without the least bit of sarcasm. Morna narrowed her eyes at him briefly before smirking and giving him a soft slap on the shoulder.

"You'll do just fine," she commented before leading the way out the front door of the Hall.

"Good for you," Rubnic whispered in admiration as the shock wore off from Dorian's request.

"She's just trying to postpone the inevitable." Huask

scoffed. "Guards."

"Wait." This time the word came from Lasco. "She has the right to take the exam."

"She's been banished. She has no rights." Huask's frustration boiled over.

"The banishment is not official until she is no longer in Athros," Lasco said steadily.

"She's in no condition to take an exam." The words were out before Huask had time to think. The cold silence from the Overseers told him that he couldn't use that argument since he forced Dorian to take the Overseers exam under similar circumstances. Glancing at the unreadable expressions of the High Overseers at the table with him, he knew he couldn't fight this one. It was law. "We will honor her request. The Overseers may leave." When no one in the Hall moved, his expression went from puzzlement to anger. "Leave. You'll be called back in for the banishment."

Lasco rose, shaking his head at Huask's lack of knowledge of Athronian law. "According to the law, a person cannot take an exam before witnesses that have brought charges or made accusations against that person. Will the Overseers of Crime, War, Sorcery, Justice and Prophecy please escort the High Overseers to the holding chamber and see that they are securely locked in. Sorcery can be responsible for the key." The five Overseers rose to their feet, secretly delighted to participate in this little victory over the High Overseers.

As Panute passed the crumpled heap of the Overseer of Knowledge, she fought the need to apologize for not being able to fight for Devor's birthright and freeing him from a life of misery that came with a bond that was not completed.

Huask avoided the accusatory looks of the other High Overseers as they followed the formidable Overseer of War through a small doorway behind the stone table. The other four Overseers loosely flanked the ancient group with the Overseer of Sorcery bringing up the rear.

Granwin was on her feet and rushing to Dorian as soon as the group was out of sight. The Overseer of Attractions stuffed the bitter dried leaves of the bondroot into Dorian's mouth. "Water." Granwin looked up as a half dozen Overseers sprinted to the High Overseers table.

Rubnic walked over to Dorian. "A bonded, banished Overseer of Knowledge. She's extremely young." Dorian, still shaking from the pain, looked up at him with curiosity. "What do you think to accomplish by taking the exam?" he asked gently.

"When I prove that the High Overseers have falsely banished an Athronian citizen, Athros will have at least one High Overseer left," Dorian replied steadily after swallowing the bondroot leaves.

"You know Athronian law very well," Rubnic returned.

Dorian arched an eyebrow. "I am the Overseer of Knowledge." Someone handed her a pitcher of water from which she drank deeply.

"You must have a remarkable mind indeed," Rubnic murmured. He had heard from Gris about the disappearance of Orvid and that the legendary Dorian Riverson had replaced him. "I left Athros long before you were born, but stories about your adventures are well known in The Land Out of Time."

Dorian blinked at him. "Really?" With Granwin's help, she climbed to her feet. The pain subsided slowly since chewing the root did not bring on the immediate results as drinking the tea. "Thank you, Granwin."

"Here." The distraught Overseer of Attractions pulled a rounded pouch from her bag. "This will help for a while, at least."

"Thank you," Dorian mumbled hoarsely, taking the pouch and tying it to her belt. She then turned to Lasco. "While you are preparing for the exam, may I write a few words to my family."

"Of course." Lasco bowed his head, amazed at the composure of this young woman, who just moments before was not only in agonizing pain but also banished from Athros. He could tell from the actions of the other Overseers that they not only believed that she had not committed this alleged offense, but they had a great respect, even fondness, for her. Why were the High Overseers so determined to get rid of her?

Armed with a flask of bondroot, Devor and Jac returned to the High Overseers Hall.

"It should be all over by now." Jac looked around puzzled as they pushed through seemingly half the population of Athros to get to the Riverson clan.

Zore ran to them, not trying to stop the tears flowing down her cheeks. She just couldn't stop crying since she heard the terrible news.

"Oh, Jac. What are we going to do?" She cried miserably as she fell into Jac's arms. "Tell me it's not really happening."

"I can't save her this time," Jac mumbled. That realization was going to hurt for a long time. Rescuing his cousin was his special talent, and not being able to do it crushed parts of his soul he hadn't known existed.

"I'm so sorry, Devor." Zore reached out a hand to the grim Outlander. "I never saw her so happy and as comfortable with herself before she met you. Now it is the worse kind of misery for both of you."

Devor straightened. "Jac may have given up on rescuing her, but I haven't." Jac looked at him, surprised at the determination from the quiet Outlander. "She told me there may be a way."

"If she told you that, then there must be." Jac's mind, so dark just a bare moment before, raced at the possibility. A sliver of light penetrated the dark place he was in. "Why is it taking so long?"

"No one knows." Zore shook her head as they walked to the rest of the family. "They've sent out for food. Lots of food. Enough to feed all the Overseers."

Jac emitted a humorless laugh. "Leave it to Dorian to think of a way to complicate even the banishment process."

"Do you think she can beat it?" Zore's expression was so hopeful that Jac would have done anything not to change it, but he couldn't give her a false hope.

Unhappily, he shook his head. "Not this time. But it's been several sand marks. What are they doing in there?"

The long High Overseers exam was finally completed a sand mark before dawn. As Lasco placed the High Overseer ring on Dorian's finger snug against the Overseer of Knowledge ring, the Hall echoed with shouts and cheers that at least one victory had been won that day.

"I truly wish you could take your place here where you belong." Lasco held her hand in his for a long moment. "When we are together in The Land Out of Time, I want you to tell me your story."

"I would be honored, High Overseer." Dorian graciously bowed her head. "I have one more request before the High Overseers are brought back. I would like to swear my innocence to the truthstone, so it will be on record for when I return to Athros to plead my case against the High Overseers."

Lasco bowed back. "That would be most prudent of you."

Dorian turned to Kerit and beckoned him to them.

"I swear, Dorian, I'm ready to do injury to the High Overseers myself for what they are doing to you," Kerit muttered as he approached her.

"When I have my honor back, you will be a hero." Dorian clasped her friend's shoulder and looked him in the eye. "I want to swear my innocence to the stone. The High Overseers have gone too far this time, and what little trust the people had in them will be completely gone. Then the people will turn to the only place where they know the truth will always be. The truthstone. It will happen. It has to happen or Athros is doomed."

"She speaks the truth," Lasco agreed and walked to the High Overseers table. "Attention please. Dorian Riverson, High Overseer and Overseer of Knowledge, wishes to profess her innocence to the truthstone. Are there any here who object to this request?"

The silence of approval answered that question, and Lasco signaled to Kerit to make the formal inquiry.

The Overseer of Truth handed Dorian both truthstones; their eyes met with the realization that their long, strange association was about to come to an end. This tore at Kerit's insides in a way it would take him a long time to understand. "Say a falsehood to the stones," he directed in a husky voice.

Dorian had to swallow down her own surge of emotion before answering. "I will walk out of this Hall a free person." Tears rolled down her cheeks as the stones burned a bright blue.

At that, no one in the Hall felt any need to hold in their own over-stretched emotions. It almost felt intimate as exhaustion and the realization that Dorian's time in Athros was almost over penetrated their collective consciousness.

Kerit took one of the stones, and they stood side by side holding the stones so everyone in the Hall could see. "Did you push High Overseer Usaf on Labyrinth night?" Dorian turned and captured his eyes. He wore a look of defiance that startled her. Perhaps her banishment would be the catalyst to set the Athronians against the High Overseers, she mused. She hoped some good would come of it. Leaving out the part about the intention to do injury took away all discussion on the subject. She either pushed Usaf or she didn't.

"I, Dorian Riverson, Overseer of Knowledge and High Overseer, did not push High Overseer Usaf on Labyrinth night." Her voice, thick with the grief that she could no longer hold back, echoed through the still Hall. The unchanged truthstone brought home the injustice that was about to be committed. Wiping the moisture off her cheeks with her sleeve, Dorian straightened and turned to Lasco. "Let's get this over with."

As the five Overseers crossed the Hall to retrieve the High Overseers, Dorian stopped Panute with a hand to her arm. The Overseer of Prophecy forced herself to meet Dorian's eyes, startled to see regret and sympathy there.

"Take care of Devor," Dorian whispered.

Any answering words caught in Panute's throat as she nodded her head. Dorian released her arm, and Panute rushed out of the Hall after her colleagues.

The High Overseers, not in the best of humor, entered the Hall scowling at their escorts. Relieved to be done with that chore, they hurriedly returned to their places on the Overseers bench.

Huask sneered. "I see you have succeeded in making a travesty of these proceedings by elevating this criminal. It doesn't matter. She'll be out of all of our lives soon enough." The sneer turned into a vicious grin. His moment had come. Nothing was going to take away the joy at seeing Dorian Riverson banished. The Athronian people will finally have the proper respect for the power that they, the High Overseers, held. This one act would finally bring the people to their knees in fear. Then he and the other High Overseers would be able to rule over Athros in the way that they had dreamed about so many years before when they were ambitious young Apprentices. "Guards! Prepare the prisoner!"

The onlookers voiced no more shouts of protest. No more delays this time. Dorian passively allowed the Guards to fit the hood and gloves onto her head and hands, accepting the request from each to be forgiven for their part in this travesty of justice. They were, after all, Athronian citizens and they treated all Overseers and High Overseers with respect. After turning Dorian so she faced the High Overseers, the Guards backed quickly away from her.

"It is our pleasure to banish Dorian Riverson from Athros forever." Huask casually waved his hand, and Dorian was gone.

End of Book 1 of The Athronian Chronicles.

To be continued in

Book 2: The Bond Paradox.

Coming Soon from
Silver Dragon Books

Well of Souls
By Sheri Young

Freak lightning storms. Large warrior women. Evil dark gods. Fabled cities. Magic... Coming from modern day Earth, Alex doesn't believe in any of these things. Until unexplainable things happen to her on her twenty-fifth birthday.

Her car breaks down in the middle of a forest highway and strands Alex in the woods during a torrential rainstorm, Alex is not having a very good birthday at all. Fate realigns all that was wrong with her life and sends her back to a world far from Earth in the hands of a disgruntled, large woman warrior to a time when technology is a sword and the will of one's own mind.

Strange destiny put the two different women together on a journey toward a fabled city to restore balance and order, with a small group of people determined to change Alex's life, whether she likes it or not. Alex finds that she, an average, ordinary woman from Earth is destined to save the world she must call home until she can find the god that sent her to it in the first place. Why her? Alex doesn't know anything about swords or magic or of this new world in which she finds herself struggling for her life and her true identity. She is disheartened to find that she bears a small silver tinted mark about her right eye due to an accident from the storm which brought her to this new world. Only she finds out it is the mark of the Chosen One—her birthright.

Other titles to look for from
Silver Dragon Books

The Athronian Chronicles By C. A. Casey
> **The Bond Paradox**
> **In the Land of Time**
> **The Athronian Tunnel Dance**

When the Wave Breaks By Ciarán Llachlan Leavitt

The Elflore Trilogy By Christine Morgan
> **Silversilk**
> **Knight of the Basilisk**
> **Truegold**

Twilight of the Gods By Ronald L. Donaghe
> **Cinátis I**
> **Cinátis II**
> **Gwi's War**
> **War Among the Gods**

The Claiming of Ford By T. Novan

Tales of Emoria: Present Paths By Mindancer

The Peacekeepers By Jeanne Foguth

Forest of Eyulf: Instincts of Blue By Tammy Pell

Originally from the Midwest, C.A. Casey is currently a librarian at a university in the northwestern United States. Although she gets a greater enjoyment out of writing fantasy novels, she has written several sleep-inducing articles published in library and education journals. For some baffling reason these articles have earned her a biographical entry in Who's Who in the World.

Her interests range from outdoor activities such as hiking and bird watching to collecting Celtic music and, of course, reading fantasy fiction. Her three cats fuss at her about the lack of felines in her stories, but never right before mealtime.